Winning my Wife

MOST IMPRUDENT MATCHES
BOOK THREE

ALLY HUDSON

Busy
Nothings

Winning My Wife Copyright © 2024 by Ally Hudson

Digital ISBN: 979-8-9882181-3-5

Print ISBN: 979-8-9882181-5-9

Cover design by Holly Perret, The Swoonies Romance Art

First edition

To Martha,
Thank you for listening to me complain about all manner of
things. Also, thank you for imparting your love of all the period
dramas. We will never agree on the best Mr. Darcy.
I will die on that hill.
Love,
Your Favorite Niece

What is wedlock forced but a hell, an age of discord
and continual strife? Whereas the contrary bringeth
bliss and is a pattern of celestial peace.

— WILLIAM SHAKESPEARE, HENRY VI

Winning my Wife

One

HUGH

THE RHYTHMIC ROCKING of the carriage lulled me to the first rest I found in three days; the three cold, miserable days since I learned of my father's death.

It was a stilted respite, interrupted by frequent fits and starts. Each time I startled awake with agonizing hope only to be met with crushing despair when memory set in.

Father was gone. It was not a nightmare; it was my life.

Never again would he and I race across the fields of Kent. Never again would he correct my form with a foil. He would never see me grow to become the man he was raising. Never would he hold any grandchildren. And that knowledge was an ache too deep and too crushing to bear.

Michael's letter reached me at school. It was cold, with scant details, written in his usual reserved tone. My father's ward was typically aloof and frigid, at least toward the family. Apparently, informing me of my father's passing warranted no change in tone.

If I had been there, I could have saved my father. Michael

wouldn't have put forth the effort, I was certain of it. If I could not have prevented his death, at least I would have given comfort and assurances. Or, I could have received them.

Michael always haunted the estate, lurking around corners —rarely seen or heard. Surely, he would have been as distant at my father's end as he was in the man's life. The bile and choked back tears warred for purchase in my throat. Images of my father's last gasps met with Michael's ungrateful apathy, refusing to leave me to sleep.

A peek behind the carriage curtain indicated that we were approaching Thornton Hall. It was time to abandon my hopes of further rest in favor of righting my appearance. It would not do to worry Mother. She would be distraught enough; and she had my brother, Tom, to comfort.

I brushed the tears that had escaped with the back of my hand and checked my pockets for a handkerchief to see to the rest. Though I could have sworn I had it when we set off, a thorough search produced nothing, and I was forced to use the back of my sleeve.

The carriage jolted to a halt outside the familiar hall. A footman opened the door and all I could see was Mother, with little Tom clinging to her skirts. Not for any force on earth could I have stopped myself from running to her arms, and burying my face in her shoulder. My tears returned in a flood, sobs ripping through me. Tom wriggled himself between us, joining in my sobs. Only Mother retained composure.

When I was finally able to bear pulling free, it was to the sight of Michael, standing unaffected off to the side. My anger at him pricked beneath the surface but the exhaustion of the past few days and release of the last few moments kept it pressed down.

The redheaded maid and the tall gangly servant he always had hanging about were lurking a few feet behind him, trying and failing to look occupied. With an uncomfortable cough

Michael nodded. "Welcome home, Hugh. When you've rested, perhaps tomorrow, you and I can go over a few things."

I could not imagine what I could possibly have to discuss with him but nodded rather than argue the point. Mother ushered Tom and me inside to the drawing room where tea and biscuits waited. At home, in her presence, I finally felt the hunger that had been missing for the last few days. Mrs. Hudson's raspberry biscuits proved to be a comfort even in the darkest of all times.

"I've made the funeral arrangements. I'd like you to look over them to see if they meet with your approval. I've consulted your mother on certain matters, but I would like your input as well."

Michael had made himself comfortable in father's study. The desk was strewn with pages and half the china cabinet's worth of tepid cups of tea and coffee. More disheveled than I had ever seen him, Michael's eyes were heavy with dark circles and his clothing was wrinkled beyond measure. His hair, too, stuck up in every direction as though he spent more time with his hands in it than without.

I took the proffered pages warily, reviewing them without truly seeing. If Mother had considered the arrangements, I was certain they were satisfactory. All that besides, what did I know about funerals? I had never seen a dead body before. Now my father lay at rest in his bedroom. Last night and this morning, I stared at the closed door, unable to force myself to enter.

While I was pretending to read the documents, the redheaded maid returned with yet more tea, this time a cup for me as well. "Here you are, my lord, cream and two sugars."

For one blissful second, I actually forgot. At those two

words, *"my lord,"* my head shot up, eyes darting around for Father's imposing presence. For all the joy that blissful second brought me, the realization afterward was more devastating for it.

She meant me. I was *"my lord."* No longer "sir," I was now Lord Grayson.

The sick feeling that had finally dissipated in my mother's calming presence returned in full force. Michael handed me a bin while the maid made a quick escape. I brushed him aside, just managing to hold back last night's biscuits.

My entire life, I had been raised with the understanding that someday I would be the Right Honorable Viscount Grayson. It was an abstract, flimsy idea, imbuing me with a sense of pride and a vague, amorphous purpose. Somehow, I never connected the idea to Father's death. It was a concrete understanding now.

For the first time, I wished my title away. I would forsake it, give anything, without a second's hesitation, for my father's strong arms wrapped around me.

I shoved the pages back to Michael haphazardly. "They're fine."

He merely nodded, clearly not convinced that I read them.

"Hugh, there are a great deal more documents to review. Accounts need to be transferred over. Settlements must be arranged. Would you like to wait for another day? Would you prefer I get your mother?"

The thought was already exhausting. "How long do you suppose it will take?"

That only earned me a bitter chuckle that had me grinding my teeth. "I've been at it for four days, and I haven't found the bottom of the pile. Why don't you go check on your mother? I'll try to condense them further."

Michael acted as though arranging my father's estate was a burden. The man who had raised him out of the kindness of his heart was a burden to him. I bit back more indignation and bile, and escaped the study, managing to only shut the door slightly harder than was proper.

I DID NOT SEE Michael again for two more days. He still failed to join the family for mealtimes and greeted few of the visitors who came to mourn such a great man.

Finally, he sent his favorite gangly footman for both Mother and myself when the solicitor arrived. The study was in an even worse state than the last time I had entered. Every cup and plate that we had was strewn about every horizontal surface.

The footman tried to remove a few of the cups and plates but Michael, head still buried in documents, stopped him. "I'm not finished with that."

The footman plucked one of Mrs. Hudson's wonderful biscuits off the plate and tapped it against Michael's forehead with a hollow *thunk*. "Yes, you are. It has been here for three days. It's harder than your head."

Mother's mouth fell open at the impertinent display—about to reprimand the man—when Michael replied. "Really, Augie? Was that necessary?"

"Obviously," he answered with a gesture to the rest of the plates and cups.

"Fine, I think those are even older." Michael gestured to the pile on the bookshelf to his left.

"I don't care how old they are. They're all going."

That comment was followed by a silent argument, full of furrowed brows and pointed glares, before Michael gave way. While "Augie" cleared up the dishes, the redheaded maid returned with a fresh plate of biscuits and tea before helping gather the remaining dirty dishes. It seemed as though the interruption shook Michael from his reading, and he finally made to introduce Father's solicitor, Mr. Smithson.

Mother, still unrecovered from the shocking display with the staff, merely nodded.

"Lord Grayson, Lady Grayson, words cannot express my sorrow at your loss. Please accept my humblest condolences." The title was still foreign to my ears. Five days of being addressed as such was hardly enough to render the words familiar. I merely nodded, picking at a biscuit, while Mother accepted his words graciously.

"My lord, have you considered whether you plan to return to school? Or whether you intend to take on your duties full time? You are fortunate that your brother is finished with his schooling and would be able to run the estate in your absence within whatever authority you wish to give him."

For the second time in a week, the world crashed down around me.

Brother?

He could not possibly be referring to Tom who had not yet left the school room.

Mother's startled gasp and Michael's sheepish wince answered the question I had not fully managed to piece together.

The man in question cleared his throat awkwardly, with a glare at the solicitor. "Sorry Hugh, I should have considered how best to tell you. Grayson—your father—I wasn't just his ward. He was my father too."

"But?" It was the only word that I could manage, and I gestured toward where Mother was making a choked, angry clucking noise, like a disgruntled chicken.

"Lady Grayson is not my mother. I don't know my mother," he spoke clearly, unaffected by the slight against Mother implied in his existence.

"But? Wouldn't that make you—"

"No, your father never married my mother. You're still the viscount, Hugh."

A thousand tiny pieces were falling into a thousand tiny places. For once in my life, a complete picture formed. I felt sick once more. I was beginning to suspect that feeling might never leave me. In fact, I was certain I would spend every day of the rest of my life nauseated, one wrong word away from being sick on my own shoes.

"Apologies, my lord," the solicitor said. Adding, "I thought you were aware. As it stands, with a few signatures, Mr. Wayland can take over the bulk of the estate management on your behalf until you come of age. That way you could continue your education with relatively little interruption."

Mother had moved to gaping like a fish. If the afternoon continued in this manner, she might be presented with the opportunity to display an entire barnyard's worth of impressions. In spite of her performance of shock and outrage, it was plain that she was well aware of the situation.

The realization that I had been lied to my entire life was turning the few biscuit crumbs I had managed to eat, instead of crumble on my plate, to ash. Without a word I took the papers from the solicitor's hands and signed without reading.

At the moment, I did not particularly care what Michael did with the estate. It should have been his anyway. Apparently, I wasn't Father's first born. I wasn't entirely certain what I was, now. I threw the quill down on the parchment, ink splotching the document. The chair scraped away from the desk with a loud scratch over the mahogany floors when I stood, stomping out, with Mother calling after me down the hall.

Two

KATE

I WAS FAIRLY certain this wasn't what Aunt Prudence intended when she suggested ingratiating myself to my host. She spent three months teaching me to curtsy gracefully, dance elegantly, and smile enticingly. In less than an hour, I'd managed to slop an entire glass of lemonade down the front of a gentleman. If the number of eligible ladies fawning over him was an indication, a titled gentleman at that.

My first ball was going swimmingly.

It started with such promise. I looked more beautiful than ever before. My gown was a pale, almost-white lavender silk that hinted at my ample curves rather than displaying them outright. Pearl pins adorned my hair with matching flowers rather than the enormous feather my aunt had favored. I even managed a passable curtsy to Her Grace upon entry.

And better still, I refrained from gawking at the ostentatious nature of the Hasket House and the ballroom. Every surface that could be carved from marble seemed to be. The entirety of the home was styled in some variation of black and white with accents of gray.

But I had been so close to success, even in the face of such an odd setting. Not one, but two gentlemen had asked for sets on my dance card.

The first set had been with a duke no less—Alexander Hasket, Duke of Rosehill and the son of the evening's hostess. He was equal parts handsome and charming and so light on his feet. When we danced, I felt as though I was flying as he whisked me around the room. He was all dark hair and dark eyes and impossibly thick brows. I even managed the full set without trodding on his feet once.

All I wanted was a glass of lemonade between the sets. Such a simple desire.

I had stepped up to the bowl when another lady appeared at my side, brushing against me. I backed merely half a step out of her way. That single step was all it took.

I hit a wall.

Except the wall hadn't been there before. I was certain of it. Also, walls didn't grunt. Or spill down my back.

Turning, I discovered that the wall was, in fact, a chest.

A broad, decidedly male, lemonade covered chest.

I tipped my head back, then a bit farther, and farther still before I found a stern brow and an angry slash of a mouth.

Apologies spilled from me as I whipped around to find a napkin. Without conscious decision, I pressed said napkin against the hard, flat planes of his chest, dabbing and rubbing hysterically.

He ripped the napkin from my grasp, and I was left with an empty hand fluttering uselessly over his, still damp, torso.

In my periphery, I heard snickering from the lady who bumped me, but I was too distracted by the sight of the gentleman.

He was tall. Everyone was tall compared to me, but he had several inches on most of the gentlemen here. Thick, chocolate, close-cropped, tousled waves sat overtop a furrowed brow. His nose was straight and proud and his lips, pulled into a frown, were full and soft looking. His wide, square jaw featured a prominent dimpled chin.

But it was his eyes that were most captivating, a haunting brushed steel framed by long, charcoal lashes. He was the most beautiful man I had ever seen. Steely and disgruntled to be sure, but beautiful none-the-less.

"Stop that." His voice was musical, even in irritation. It took a moment to comprehend his meaning, and I dropped my, still jittery, hands.

"I'm sorry," I said. It was the latest in a long line of apologies that had been spewing forth from the moment I'd turned to face him.

"Stop apologizing."

I would never, for the rest of my life, be able to explain the next word out of my mouth. "Sorry."

Immediately after it escaped, I wished it unsaid. I shut my eyes against the shame, but it was an ineffective barrier. His answering glare awaited when I braved a glance.

I bit back yet another apology. Without permission to continue my expression of regret, I began to notice the eyes on us. The entirety of the ballroom, in fact, was staring with keen interest. There were even a few titters here and there, mostly from the lady who had caused the upset.

No longer filling the silence with excessive reparations, I could feel the disquiet, palpable in its unease. Words bubbled inside me, filling me to bursting, ready to spill over at the slightest provocation.

Unable to stand it a second longer, they escaped. "I'm Kate. Summers. Miss Kate Summers."

As soon as they were liberated, I regretted it. The impertinence of it—Aunt Prudence would have a fit of apoplexy.

I hadn't thought the disdain on his face could strengthen but it quickly transformed into scorn accompanied by a derisive huff of breath.

It was that display of blatant contempt that sparked my own ire. I was just as covered with lemonade as he was. I had been just as jostled. I wasn't glaring at the lady who nudged me—even though she was finding the entire situation far too amusing. Before I could unleash my fury, I felt a small hand on my sodden shoulder.

It proved to be Lady Davina, His Grace's sister, gently tugging me away from the table, preventing a further scene. Another lady I had never met joined her in ushering me away from the ballroom, wrapping me in a shawl as we rounded a corner.

They pressed me silently, hurrying me along, before we reached the ladies' retiring room. There, the stranger burst into a flurry of French that I didn't understand. Though the words were foreign, the tone was less than kind. Her words were directed at Lady Davina, and she gestured repeatedly toward the door.

Lady Davina replied in English. "You're right, we shouldn't have invited her. We just felt there would be more scandal if we snubbed her."

The stranger switched to English though her accent remained. "Clearly, inviting her prevented *all* the scandal." She tossed the words with casual sarcasm. I was in awe that such a tone could be directed toward the sister of a duke. "At least she would not be terrorizing your guests were she not present."

Finally, I could take no more. "What is happening?"

Lady Davina put her arm around me consolingly. "I am so

sorry. Lady James bump had nothing to do with you. She is unhappy that you danced with my brother."

"Who? Why would anyone be unhappy about that?"

"Charlotte, Lady James, the woman who knocked into you."

"That was an accident. Surely you don't think otherwise?"

The mysterious Frenchwoman interjected. "That was no accident. That was a punishment for dancing with His Grace."

"She and Xander—Rosehill, the one you were dancing with, were courting. He ended it before she could drag him to the altar. She hasn't taken it well," Lady Davina added. At what must have been a confused expression on my face, she continued, "She has since married a baron. But obviously, she is less than pleased with that outcome. She shoved you on purpose because you danced with my brother."

"But... it was just a dance. Not even a waltz."

"Xander was the wealthiest eligible gentleman in the room, with the highest title to accompany it. And she failed to secure him. You've been in society for mere weeks, and at your first ball, you're asked to dance by him for the first set. I believe she meant to set you down."

"*Oui*, it was masterfully done as well. Almost no one saw her efforts, only the aftermath. Except perhaps Mr. Parker, for she loves to impress him by being wretched."

"I'm sorry, we haven't been introduced?"

"Oh, I'm so sorry." Lady Davina said. "This is the Marchioness of Rycliffe. She is my eldest brother's widow. Cee, this is Miss Kate Summers, she is the niece of the Dowager Duchess of Sutton."

"A pleasure to meet you formally, *mon amie*."

"You as well, Lady Rycliffe."

"Celine, please."

I was certain my aunt would not approve, but I agreed to the informality. If she could rescue me from a ballroom, I could refer to her as she wished.

Lady Davina continued, "We will need to call for your carriage, Kate. Do you want me to find your aunt? Or do you wish to send your carriage back for her?"

"My carriage?"

"Your dress…"

"Yes, it's quite sticky, but that's hardly the end of the world."

"It's transparent, Kate."

My blood ran cold.

How could I not have considered that? Oh lord, the entire ballroom… The entire ballroom had seen me.

"How bad?"

"Oh, I'm sure no one noticed." Her tone and uncharacteristically small hand gestures told another story. When I lifted a brow in disbelief she continued. "At least it's only your back?"

My hand met my face as I pinched my brow against the rising headache.

"I'll send the carriage back for Aunt Prudence. Would you mind calling for it?"

She scurried off to do just that, and I was left alone with Celine. She dampened a cloth from the nearby basin and attempted to remove the sticky residue of the lemonade.

She moved with an indefinable grace, each action used sparingly to elegant effect.

Her gown was a deep aubergine color with little in the way of embellishment. It displayed more than a little décolleté while managing to remain on the correct side of modest. Her gold curls were clearly natural but styled effortlessly in the latest fashion. I couldn't help but feel that such a woman, the very definition of poise, would never slop lemonade all down the back of her gown or the front of a gentleman—oh lord, the gentleman.

"May I ask if you're familiar with the gentleman I accosted?"

"I am... acquainted with his brother. He is Lord Grayson. He's a bit... young."

"Young?"

"He's only one and twenty, I believe. He could have used a few more years before he came into the title."

"I'm not certain I understand."

"You will when you're older. I would not set my sights on him if I were you. I expect it will be some years before he joins the marriage fray."

"Oh, I wasn't. I wouldn't—not after that display. He is quite handsome though."

That drew a lyrical laugh from her. "More so, even than his brother. I still prefer the brother though."

Lady Davina rushed back into the room just then. "The carriage is readied. I let your aunt know you've had to return home due to a wardrobe mishap. She seems to have missed the display—or is feigning ignorance—regardless, she has no issue with your absence."

"I very much doubt that, but thank you nonetheless."

She winced. Confirming my suspicion that Aunt Prudence hadn't been as effective in hiding her displeasure as she intended.

"We will have to sneak you out through the servants' quarters. I hope you don't mind terribly?"

"Oh no, I think I'd much rather go out through the ballroom."

"Really? Because I don't think—"

"She was joking, Dav. She is a funny one. I quite like her."

"Oh, all right then. Shall we?"

Lady Davina held out an arm for me to take. Lady Rycliffe

covered my back with her shawl once more before taking my other arm. Together they led me out to the waiting carriage. Lady Rycliffe refused the wrap when we reached the carriage, instead encouraging me to keep it. As the carriage pulled away, I released a long-trapped sigh. At least I couldn't possibly humiliate myself worse in the future.

Three

HUGH

I AWOKE WITH THE SUN. The previous evening ended earlier than anticipated and I hoped to use the additional time to review correspondence from my solicitor and steward. Unfortunately, the increase in hours of sleep did not result in an increased sensation of rest. The words swam across the page, nonsensical and blurred.

A sharp rap startled me, and I sloshed fresh coffee over my thumb with a pained curse. My youngest brother's knock was a deliberate performance, delivered to the desk instead of the door. Pointedly.

I was, in point of fact, aware that I was staring out the window instead of at the letters. It was hardly necessary for him to make a show of it. Three cups of coffee had left me an uncomfortable combination of bored, exhausted, and jittery. It was not worth the energy necessary to check him.

"Afternoon. Anna gave me these for you," Tom said. He handed over a plate of sandwiches, grabbing several for himself before settling them into a pile directly on the desk in front of him.

"Why did she not deliver them herself?" The maids should not hand off duties to family members.

"It's no matter. I offered when I saw where she was headed."

"Still—"

"Hugh..." he sighed.

My brother was easygoing and generous to a fault. Once he finished his studies and let a bachelor dwelling, his staff would rob him blind.

"Should you not be in school?"

"Break," he mumbled in between enormous bites of sandwich.

I took a nibble off one. Delightful as always. Mrs. Hudson was a truly exceptional cook.

"I thought to come visit with you and Mother. Then perhaps dine with Michael."

My half-brother's mention earned only a grunt. It was more than he deserved. I had not spoken to him in nearly three years. Not since he insisted on opening that degenerate gaming hell of his.

It was a sore spot between Tom and me, his insistence on acknowledging the man. Our father never legitimized him, I did not see why Tom felt the need to.

"Yes, yes, I know. Michael is the devil himself. He is determined to ruin the entire family for all time and leave us all destitute." Tom mocked me with a mouth half-full of sandwich.

"Chew your food. Were you raised in a barn?"

"Same table as you. Anyway, do you have some older ledgers I can review? I need them for one of my courses."

I nodded my head toward the shelves under the window.

My mouth was too full to answer, and unlike my brother, I had manners. Swallowing, I directed him toward the earliest books. "I shouldn't need anything before 1807."

"Thank you," he said, sliding four or five of them from their dusty home. "What do you have planned for today?" He flipped them open distractedly, confirming the dates.

"Staring at letters from my solicitor until my eyes bleed."

"Have you considered reading them?"

"Certainly not."

We both chuckled, and he returned to the desk with a hefty stack of books. He grabbed another sandwich, chomping into it. I understood the inclination. If my access to Mrs. Hudson's cooking were limited, I would stuff them down as well. Still, I had no idea where the boy put it all. He was a string bean, taller than me and rail thin.

"I intended to go to White's this afternoon, but I'm exhausted. It was an... eventful evening last night."

"How so?" he asked.

"Rosehill Ball."

"Ah, fell desperately in love with some stunningly beautiful debutante, did you? Hopefully not the daughter, you're not nearly fashionable enough for that family."

"I am fashionable enough for any family. And quite the opposite. Some chit backed into me, spilling my lemonade all down my front and her back. I was forced to leave early."

"Poor girl. I hope she managed to clean herself up."

"Poor girl? My shirt, waistcoat, and cravat are all beyond repair. I am quite certain of it."

"Stevens can't clean them?"

"He says he will be able to. But I do not see how. Worse still, she insisted on attempting to dry me with a napkin. The entire ballroom got an eyeful of her caressing my chest."

Tom's snort of laughter was clearly at my expense. The

lord punished him in short order when he inhaled a crumb and choked on it. He was left coughing between chuckles for nearly a minute.

"Am I to understand that you're complaining about a lady rubbing your chest? You should have leaned back and enjoyed it."

The look I shot him would have had a lesser man cradling his bollocks. Unfortunately, my brother has never respected my authority as head of the household.

"I assume she was homely, then? Since it was such a burden to have her hands all over you," he asked.

"She was no great beauty, certainly."

"What does that mean?"

"I do not know. Short, dark hair, big mouth, spilling out of her dress a bit..."

"I'm given to understand that you're supposed to appreciate that part." I could only roll my eyes.

"I suppose. She was a disaster though. Completely devoid of propriety and decorum."

"She sounds delightful. I look forward to the wedding." His accompanying grin was cheeky and unfazed by yet another withering stare.

"There will be no wedding."

"Of course not, Brother," he said in a tone that was all sarcasm.

"I mean it. I am far too young to wed."

"I'll agree there. Far too immature to marry."

"That is not what I said."

"I know. But I'm also right. Shall I ring for more sandwiches?"

Lord, he was irritating. And the plate was empty but for a few crumbs.

"... yes."

He rose, wandering over to the pull before returning and settling on the desk, rather than the chair.

"How is Mother? Will she approve of your new bride?"

I ignored his assessment of the mess of a woman who accosted me last night. It was, perhaps, the only thing that would convince Tom to let the subject lie.

"Mother has another megrim. The doctor came by yesterday and prescribed a tonic. It's had no effect thus far. Perhaps your presence will revive her."

A pained expression crossed his face. It was one I knew well. Mother in a fit of megrims was to be avoided at all costs. His presence did tend to bolster her though. Even if she relapsed after his departure.

"How long has she been abed with this attack?"

"Nearly a week."

Of course, she did manage to recover well enough to berate one of the servants because the broth was only lukewarm. And, when her friend Lady Parker called the other morning, she recovered enough to dress and sit for several hours. The fit mysteriously returned shortly after her friend's departure.

The tonic was likely a particularly expensive peppermint tea. Neither Tom nor I were willing to say as much. Mother's belief was often enough for efficacy.

The redheaded maid knocked on the doorframe with her elbow. In one hand was a second plate, piled high with more sandwiches. The other hand managed the tea tray.

Tom took the opportunity to relieve her of the sandwich plate burden, grabbing four or five sandwiches in the process before setting the plate on the desk.

He crammed the sandwiches into his mouth, one after another, before pointing at the ceiling. Apparently, he intended to visit Mother.

I waved him off, feeling slightly improved for the sustenance and company. I set the London solicitor's letter aside in favor of the country estate's steward. His letters rarely contained anything other than tenant complaints to solve. This one was more of the same.

Four

SUTTON MANOR, LONDON - OCTOBER 3, 1812

KATE

BREAKFAST WAS sure to be an unpleasant affair. Aunt Prudence would not be pleased with my showing last night.

I fought every instinct to dawdle before heading to the breakfast room, knowing it would only add to her complaints. The worst was the understanding that last evening had started with such promise. A dance with a duke, my aunt could have no cause for complaint in that respect.

If only it hadn't been immediately followed by such a humiliating incident. I still cringed every time I closed my eyes. The images of the night before refusing to leave my eyelids. They were permanently burned there, and I was to spend every moment of the rest of my life reliving the shame.

I made my way to the breakfast room, a few minutes early as Aunt Prudence insisted. At least, she would not have that failing to add onto the list.

Of course, she was already waiting for me. Not for the first time, I cursed her refusal to take a tray in her room like other ladies of her station.

"Good morning, Aunt. I trust you slept well?"

"Good morning, Katherine. I slept well enough, indeed."

Indeed—that means she slept poorly. It's how she offers complaints since it's "unladylike to express displeasure or ill-health."

"I understand you had quite the eventful evening," she added, pursing her lips around the last words as though she ate something sour. It was the only physical manifestation of her irritation. She was unaware of it, I was certain, or she would have stopped that, too. In fact, I suspected the few wrinkles around her mouth that managed to defy her have deepened with my visit.

Even in her distaste, my aunt was every bit the elegant dowager duchess. Having raised her own children to much acclaim and superior matches, she set her sights on her most unfortunate brother's even more unfortunate daughter. Me.

As the second son of an earl, my father found the life of a clergyman suited him well. He married the daughter of a wealthy but untitled gentleman for love.

In the Lincolnshire Wolds of Alford, he raised two daughters and a son to have modest expectations for life. My sister married a farmer and was raising my four beautiful nieces and nephews. My brother was studying to be a solicitor in town. And I had the misfortune to be unmarried and unoccupied when Aunt Prudence discovered that the season was most uninteresting without matchmaking prospects. Apparently, doting on a grandson of only two years and cooing at a newborn babe occupied very little of one's day.

What my aunt failed to grasp was that I was not raised for a society match. No amount of dancing lessons and propriety lectures could counteract twenty years of tussling with parish children and racing across the countryside astride a horse.

Still, I appreciated her efforts, and I did try to heed her lessons.

"Yes, Aunt. Unfortunately, there was an incident with some lemonade."

"So I heard. With Lord Grayson as well. You could not have chosen an untitled gentleman to spill all over?"

"It was a mistake, Aunt Prudence. I apologized."

"Yes, I heard about that as well. A lady does not fall all over herself apologizing, once is sufficient."

"Yes, Aunt Prudence."

"In the future, should you commit such a foible, allow the gentleman to blot his own chest. Yes?"

"Yes, Aunt Prudence."

"Good. I don't expect you will have many callers today given your showing last evening. Nonetheless, we must be at home to receive any who dare to brave your potential mishaps. That dress does nothing for your coloring. Go change into the yellow one after breakfast."

The robin's-egg blue gown I was wearing did more for my complexion than the yellow one she mentioned. None of the pastels favored by debutantes did much for my pale coloring. I much preferred richer jewel tones. Even the earthen tones I favored in the countryside for their practicality were preferable. Especially after last evening's betrayal by the lavender, I abhorred the pastels.

Still, it was not worth an argument with her. Especially since I received rather less scolding than I deserved after last night's poor showing.

~

MY AUNT WAS PROVEN CORRECT.

It was two days without a single caller before she allowed me a respite. Finally, I was given leave to call on Jules and Aunt Sophie at Dalton Place.

My mother's sister, Sophie, married the Earl of Westfield

who had an infant daughter from his first marriage, Juliet. She and I were close friends and confidantes. She wrote to me regularly from the time we both learned our letters.

Unfortunately, Aunt Sophie had a difficult pregnancy and birth nearly a year ago. She had been unwell since. The babe died shortly after birth, and Aunt Sophie scarcely left her room in the months since.

Jules delayed her entrance into society to care for her stepmother. Though I was glad that Aunt Sophie was being so well looked after, I couldn't help but wish Jules had been by my side the other night. I could not imagine I would have made such a poor showing with her to assist me.

Unlike me, Lady Juliet Dalton was the picture of a debutante. Lovely in both form and person, she mastered all the expected accomplishments and a few more besides. Were she less kindhearted, I should hate her a bit for her perfection.

The single greatest advantage that London has to offer was proximity to both Jules and Aunt Sophie. I had spent as much time at Dalton place as I was able in the weeks since my arrival to town.

As a regular visitor with a standing invitation to the sickroom, a footman ushered me straight there. I wasn't familiar with the man, but they did seem to go through staff at an alarming rate here.

I was pleased that today appeared to be a good one. Aunt Sophie was upright in bed and the drapes were open to allow light into the room while Jules read to her.

"Kate! Darling, how was your debut?" Aunt Sophie urged me closer.

I perched at her side on the bed. Even though she was much improved today compared to recent days, she was still a shadow of the woman I remembered from my youth, and it saddened me.

I gave her a half smile. "I danced with a duke."

She pushed herself more upright against the pillows. "Oh, tell me everything!"

"He was very charming and handsome. We danced a quadrille. He was everything a young man ought to be."

"Which duke?"

"Rosehill, his mother was the hostess."

Juliet fussed with the bedding while we chatted.

"I thought he was already married?"

"Oh, no. Unfortunately, his elder brother passed away a few years ago, and his father died a year or two after that. I had the good fortune to meet his widow. The younger brother is now the duke."

"Oh, dear, how sad for the family. You say he was charming and handsome?"

"Yes, and so kind."

"Oh, I'm so happy for you, dearest! Now, I think I would like to rest a bit, why don't you and Jules go and giggle over all the romantic details. The ones you don't wish to share with your ancient auntie."

"Aunt Sophie!"

"Go." With that dismissal, she slid down on the pillows, turning off to one side.

"Do you want me to close the drapes?" Juliet asked.

"Yes please."

Following her instructions, Jules followed me out, closing the door softly behind us. She dragged me down the hall to her room. She flopped on the settee beside me in an uncharacteristic display of pique.

"I was so hoping she would make it to luncheon today," she whispered.

"She's not improving, is she?"

Jules shook her head sadly in response. "I do not know how to help her."

She lolled her head onto my shoulder, and I wrapped my

arm around to rub her back soothingly. It was surely an uncomfortable maneuver; she was more than half a foot taller than me. But she seemed unbothered.

"What does your father say?"

"Nothing."

I did not fully understand Juliet's relationship with her father, but it was somewhat strained. I didn't press any further. With a deep sigh, she sat back up and turned to face me, one leg curled under the other.

"Tell me what really happened at the ball."

"I have no idea what you mean. I danced with a duke."

"And?"

I couldn't hide the wince. "I spilled lemonade down the front of a viscount."

She tried in vain for a moment to hold back the laugh. It escaped her in a half-splutter, half-snort.

With that noise I felt my own embarrassment turning to laughter as well.

"How on earth did you manage that?"

"A lady bumped into me at the punch table. I backed out of her way. Straight into him. It spilled down my back as well. My gown was completely translucent."

"Oh, Kate..."

"It gets worse. I tried to help clean him up."

"You...?"

"Rubbed at his chest with a napkin or five. Yes."

"Oh, Kate..." Her sigh of my name was full of shared humiliation.

"I know."

"I am so sorry. It would be funny if it had happened to anyone else."

"I know. I had to leave the ball after. There was nothing to be done for my gown."

"Have you had any callers since?"

"Not a one."

She considered me thoughtfully for a moment. "Was his chest nice at least?"

"Juliet!"

"I have not left the house in nearly a month. I need something to sustain me. If you are to die alone, you should at least have enjoyed yourself in the process."

I flushed considering that chest. I did enjoy myself. "It was lovely, all right? Very... firm."

"And the attached viscount?"

"Unbearably handsome, even more so than His Grace. Tall, gray eyes, dark hair, impossibly cross mouth."

"He was rude to you?"

"I had just spilled on him."

"He spilled on himself," she snapped. "And it was clearly an accident."

"He told me to stop apologizing."

"How many times did you apologize?"

"I lost count. I haven't told you the worst of it. When he told me to stop apologizing? I apologized again."

"Oh, Kate..."

"I know."

"I love you. You know that, right?"

"But I'm a disaster?"

"A little bit."

"What am I going to do, Jules? How am I to make it through the entire season? I couldn't even manage a single hour."

She merely shrugged with a laugh, wrapping her arms around me.

Five

HYDE PARK, LONDON – OCTOBER 28, 1812

HUGH

IT WAS UNSEASONABLY WARM, perhaps the last stand of summer before it surrendered completely to fall. Hyde Park was full of members of the *ton* there to see and be seen. Everyone who remained at the end of the Season could be found promenading today.

Even my mother rallied in the face of her ever-present megrims. She coerced Tom and I to escort her.

She was somewhat overdressed for the occasion, but I could hardly begrudge her excitement. She had been bedbound for the last several days, after all. Still, I thought her turban could have done with one or two fewer feathers. And her signature perfume seemed to attract more than a few wasps, but they were always more active at the end of their lifespan. It was a struggle to refrain from swatting at the insects and batting at the feathers, though.

Not everyone felt the same need to maintain propriety.

There was a couple ahead of us on the path. They were silhouetted in the evening light. The breeze whipped her bonnet strings across her face, and he tugged playfully at the ends. Her head was tossed back in laughter before she jerked at his cravat with equal tease. Then she grabbed his top hat from his head before sidling away from him. With a jovial chuckle, he chased after her.

Mother gave a disapproving tut at their indecorous display. "So shameful, to behave in such a manner in public. We should not have to be subjected to such antics."

"They're just teasing, Mother," Tom replied.

Personally, I agreed with Mother.

The couple's antics slowed their pace. Within moments we had closed much of the distance.

The lady caught sight of our rapid approach, snagging his elbow in one hand and tugging him off the path to allow us to pass.

Then she turned back toward me. Recognition shot through me, followed by instinctive irritation. The lady from the ball. The one with the lemonade.

Of course, she would act without the slightest consideration for propriety. In fact, if there were a punch bowl available now, she would upend that as well.

And this gentleman, if he warranted the name at all, was engaging in, nay encouraging this behavior. They were well suited to one another, that was certain.

He was shorter, like her, though not quite as extreme. Instead of her curves though, he was more compact. His apparel was shabby beside her too. Beneath her then, possibly in trade. It was just as well that she made a match outside the gentry. She would never learn to conduct herself properly.

In my distracted perusal, I failed to note the two ladies approaching from the opposite direction on the path. My first warning was Mother's delighted hum of recognition.

The first of that group, I placed with little trouble, Lady Rycliffe, widow of the late Marquis of Rycliffe. She was well acknowledged as one of the most handsome ladies of the *ton*. The second took but a moment longer to recognize. Lady Davina Hasket, her sister-in-law. Lady Davina was easily one of the most eligible debutantes of the Season.

To my great astonishment, they greeted the lemonade chit amiably. Their actions shocked Mother as well if her choked cluck was any indication.

The situation had become much stickier with their arrival. Before, we could have passed by the girl and her suitor without acknowledgement. Now though, Mother will want the marchioness's notice.

The decision was taken from me when Lady Rycliffe greeted my mother in her usual thick, French accent. "Lady Grayson! It is so good to see you out and about. I hope you are much improved?"

My mother straightened, pleased with the recognition and concern.

"The megrims come and go. I was sorry to miss the ball last week though. Hugh assured me it was lovely."

The lemonade lady stiffened with the reminder of the ball, and Lady Davina covered a smirk behind her hand.

"Yes, quite lovely," I added. My tone came out more strangled than I intended.

The unknown gentleman shifted closer to his companion, shielding her from my view.

Tom, on the other hand, barely managed to cover a burst of laughter with a cough. I shot him a dangerous look, but he just grinned, rocking back on his heels.

"Lady Grayson, I don't believe you've had the pleasure of meeting my dear friend, Miss Katherine Summers. Miss Summers is the niece of Her Grace, the Duchess of Sutton. Miss Summers, this is Lady Grayson and her sons Lord Hugh Grayson and Mr. Tom Grayson."

And so I had her name. Niece of a duchess, that was something of a shock but did explain her presence the other night.

She performed a proper curtsy, much more graceful than anything she managed thus far. Through it all, she wore an unsightly flush, evidence that she was capable of shame at least.

"A pleasure to meet you, Lady Grayson, Lord Grayson, Mr. Grayson. May I introduce my brother, Mr. Christopher Summers?" She gestured toward the man still posted protectively between us.

She had not managed to attract a suitor, then. That was no surprise given her lack of decorum.

Her brother provided an appropriate bow in response. My mother tucked her chin like a discomfited turtle trying to escape a predator at the sight of him though. She did have a tendency to fret when presented with those outside the peerage. The megrims would surely make a reappearance soon.

The niceties observed, the ladies spoke for a few moments on the particularly fine weather. Miss Summers used the opportunity to right her bonnet and fuss with the ribbons, rather than contribute to the conversation in any meaningful way.

Her gown was a pale pink color that did not suit her coloring at all, particularly with the flush that still called her cheeks home. It sat tight on her bodice, entirely too obvious for such an occasion, and pulled on her hips in an entirely unflattering way.

"—do you not think so, Lord Grayson?" Lady Rycliffe asked.

"Hmm," I murmured. I had no notion what direction the conversation had taken, and I could only hope that my hum was interpreted correctly.

"Really? I distinctly recall you telling me that you preferred lemonade to dancing." Tom added with a cheeky grin. "In fact, I remember you told me the other day that you were served the best glass of lemonade you ever had at the ball the other night."

My teeth ground together in an effort not to clap my brother over the head. "No, I quite prefer dancing to drinks, Tom."

"I'm almost certain you had a great deal to say about the lemonade, and I heard nothing about dancing. But, perhaps I'm misremembering."

"Perhaps," I bit out.

Lady Rycliffe was making a valiant effort at a straight face. Lady Davina made no such attempt. Mother's mouth could not have pinched any tighter. She had no idea of Tom's true meaning, but she understood there was something she did not know.

Miss Summers on the other hand, had shrunk entirely behind her brother who shifted in a manner that might have been menacing if he were taller.

"If you would excuse us, I feel my megrim returning," Mother said, tightening her hand on my arm. We bid them adieu correctly, before turning toward the house.

We made it three steps before the tirade began, far too loud. "The impertinence of those two. It's hard to be believed. I cannot imagine what Lady Rycliffe and Lady Davina see in that chit. With that hideous gown. And her brother, clearly in trade. She has no business setting foot in a ballroom as fine as Her Grace's. In fact, I'm certain the smell of him is why my megrim has returned. People in trade have a certain scent about them."

Tom made an effort to shush her, but it was no use. She was quite skilled at dragging her feet when she had something to say that she wanted everyone to hear. Even if she knew it was inappropriate.

The walk back to Grayson house was slow and filled with a

great many complaints. By the time we returned, I had a megrim to call my own. And Mother returned to her rooms with even more afflictions than when we left.

~

AFTER SETTLING Mother in her rooms with her tonic, I found my way to the study with the intention of answering the letters that awaited me.

Unfortunately, Tom took it upon himself to sprawl across the desk, his boot clad feet on top. All my carefully sorted papers were upended into indistinguishable piles. He made free with my scotch as well if the bottle beside him was any indication.

"Bit behind on the correspondence, Brother?" he asked.

I refused to dignify his impertinence with a response, instead pouring my own glass and taking a seat across from him. I shoved his feet off with my hand, and he stumbled slightly. Unfortunately, he caught himself before landing on his face.

"So, Miss Summers. I take it she was your assailant the other night?"

"Indeed."

"I fail to see what all the whinging was about then."

"I do not whinge."

His only answer was a derisive snort. "I found her to be quite fetching, particularly around this region." He gestured toward his upper chest with cupped hands in an entirely inappropriate display.

"Really Tom, must you be so crude?"

"It comes naturally. Honestly though, you painted her to be some sort of hideous beast."

"Of course, she's not hideous. She's just... not as she ought."

"What ought she be?"

"I do not know? Statuesque, fair, graceful."

"She can hardly help her height or the color of her hair."

"Regardless, she displayed a complete lack of decorum and behaved in an entirely imprudent manner. Had we been alone and someone came upon us with her patting her hands all over my chest, we would have been forced to wed."

"A fate worse than death."

"Precisely."

"I'm positive you need not worry about that at any rate. Certainly, she heard Mother's ravings and was so offended that she will never speak to any of us ever again."

I could not suppress a wince at that memory. "That was badly done of her."

"Let us hope that Miss Summers is not a true friend of Lady Rycliffe and Lady Davina. Neither would take kindly to Mother's insults of their friend."

I could add nothing to that worry except a sigh. Mother really was impossible to check. "Nothing to be done for it now. Are you staying for dinner?"

"No, I'm headed to the club tonight, care to join me?"

"White's?"

"No Wayland's."

"Absolutely not."

"Hugh..."

It was beyond belief that he was pressing this issue. He knew my feelings on our brother's devious dealings. "No, I will not set foot in that den of iniquity."

"It's just a gaming hell. I dare say you would enjoy yourself."

"Never. And do not think that I will front you a single pound when Michael takes you for everything you have and then some."

"He's hardly going to bleed me dry. If he intended to leave

us destitute, he had years to do so. Winning my inheritance off me at his club is a much less efficient way to go about it."

"Do not joke about such things."

"For the life of me I cannot understand your issues with him."

"Leave it, Tom."

His only response was to finish the dregs of his glass and straighten his cravat.

"Very well. I'll stop by sometime in the next few days to see how Mother is recovering."

"Good night then."

I could not bring myself to wish him well. Tom's willingness to support Michael in the man's shameful efforts to swindle every gentleman of the *ton* out of their fortune was beyond belief.

In my irritation I swallowed back the remnants of my own scotch before pouring another. I finished that rather more quickly than I ought. In this state I would have no success with my correspondence. Instead, I wandered off to the billiards room for some practice, leaving the letters for another day.

Six

HUGH

THEY FASHIONED a dance floor on their grounds, quite ingenious really. The gardens surrounding the floor were lit by hundreds of torches. They were accompanied by tiny fireflies dancing between them. A massive stone staircase opened onto the dance floor. The banisters were wrapped in garlands covered in jasmine; the blooms perfumed the air.

The night air was unseasonably warm, leaving me covered in an annoying layer of sticky sweat. Rather than dancing, the members of the ton mingled beside the floor; each eagerly glancing toward the staircase leading from inside, waiting for someone. Though I had no idea why my peers were waiting with bated breath, I joined them in monitoring the staircase.

My efforts were in vain. I glanced away right when the quiet murmurs of the beau monde dissipated, leaving nothing behind but the crickets singing their approval.

Turning toward the source of all the excitement, the breath was knocked from my lungs. The masses parted, leaving only the two of us; the most exquisite woman I had ever seen and myself.

Her eyes, a cerulean swirl of sea and sky, caught the torch-light, sparkling just for me. Her midnight black curls were unbound and cascading down her back, ready for my fingers to slip through. The moonlight and torchlight warred for purchase on her pale skin, flickering gold and shining silver. Her wide mouth was bitten to an enticing rich rosewood, lips pressed together in a knowing smile.

I felt my own mouth mimicking hers. I knew it, too. This attraction was unlike any I had ever felt. Heat pooled low in my gut, and my heart hammered in response.

Her form, draped in red silk, was nothing short of sensual. The deep Bordeaux sleeves of her gown fell down her shoulders revealing miles of unblemished skin for my hungry gaze. And gaze I did, appreciating every curve she offered to me.

The silk gown rested low on her bosom and tight across her hips, draped elegantly across her slim waist with heavy skirts falling below. It was like nothing I had ever seen. It was everything I never knew I wanted. Never in my life had I wanted a gown pooled on the floor of my bedroom with such desperation.

With every second of perusal, she made her way closer to me. Her eyes locked on my form, warm with her own interest. Each breath brought her nearer. With each delicate stride, each blink, she became more and more familiar to me. She paused, just out of my reach, and, with a start, I placed her. Miss Katherine Summers.

My lungs protested the recognition, a choked gasp escaping. This magnificent, captivating creature before me could not be the improper girl in soaking lilac muslin I met before.

There was no inducement that could end my open-mouthed stare. Nothing except the act of her brushing past me, reaching a hand out to a gentleman behind me, the one I had not noticed.

Her bare elegant fingertips met a grasp that was not mine. She pulled the man to the floor just as the orchestra fingered the opening notes to waltz. Without hesitation, she pressed her sensuous curves to his form. In answer, he pulled her closer. Her small form tucked against his larger one, slotting together like missing halves.

The envy burned deep in my gut.

Their dance brought them closer to me. Then his dark familiar eyes met mine. And the fury exploded.

Michael.

My Katherine's luscious curves pressed tightly against my degenerate brother.

He was decked in his best finery, scrubbed and polished to a gentlemanly shine. One hand curled possessively over the curve of her hip while the other pressed her hand to his chest instead of to the side as was proper.

She rose on her toes, still managing the steps with an inhuman delicacy, whispering in his ear.

He smirked in my direction, and she cast her gaze behind her, meeting my own shocked expression. Instead of the knowing smile she offered me before, her lips were twisted into a cruel sneer.

Turning her attention back to her partner, she allowed him to press a kiss to her hand before dropping it to rest on his chest. The move freed his own to slide sensuously into her curls, settling against the back of her neck.

He pulled her wide, lush, lips to his with a hungry grin. Her own hands slid up his chest to tug him down to her. There she met his searing kiss with enthusiasm, tongue, and teeth.

The members of the ton *returned from wherever they had shuffled off to, once again surrounding the floor. None of the scandalized gasps or horrified exclamations that should have characterized the scene arrived, instead approving rumblings surrounded us.*

Michael and Katherine abandoned all pretense of dancing,

instead his hand slipped to the buttons lining her spine, working first one then the next open.

She turned to face me, allowing my brother free range of her back. Her dress was only pressed to her form by the forearm pinning it to her chest.

She met my gaze, and in a hauntingly, throaty, seductive tone she spoke, "You thought I was here for you? As if I could ever be yours. I'm here for the real viscount."

I AWOKE WITH A CHOKED GASP. My bedding and clothing soaked with sweat. I managed to haul myself toward the chamber pot before retching pitifully. The exercise proved futile, and I resorted to spitting the bile. I raked clammy hands through damp hair, trying to regulate my breathing.

Between shaky inhales I tried to recall the last time I dreamt of Michael.

It was clearly Tom's fault, his insistence on maintaining a relationship with the man seeped into my unconscious mind.

Miss Summers, too—it was all due to that conversation with Tom.

There was no need to think further on the matter. I rinsed my mouth with the water glass I kept by my bedside before lying back down.

Unfortunately, the images from my dream refuse to abate. Every time I closed my eyes they returned. The images alternated between sensuous silk-wrapped curves, glowing pale skin, amused blue-green eyes, and Michael's infuriating smirk.

It was little more than a quarter of an hour before I determined that sleep would be impossible.

I made a half-hearted attempt to dress, throwing on a shirt and breeches, before heading down to the study. Once there, I lit several candles before pulling out the letters from my solicitor once more.

Perhaps this time I could make sense of his reports since I would certainly not be getting further rest.

I had replaced the solicitor that Michael worked with three years ago for one who was much more amiable. Unfortunately, I was still forced to use the steward that Michael hired. There were no other reputable options in Kent, though I searched far and wide.

The man, Matthews, was brusque to the point of rudeness. He also had no interest in solving any tenant disputes and instead sent them to me for management.

I could hardly account for it. Certainly, Michael never handled these matters. My brother seemed fond of hiring boorish, and impertinent workers. I preferred to work with affable, good-humored folk whenever possible.

In my less charitable moments, I suspected that my brother encouraged them to make my life as difficult as possible when I took over.

The sheer volume of correspondence, creditors, and complaints I received was enough to drive anyone to madness.

Such was the case at the present. Matthews sent word of a tenant disagreement over some well or other with the neighboring landowner. How should I be expected to know to whom the well rightly belongs and who should pay the other for its usage? Should they not work that out amongst themselves?

Michael would never have been involved in such matters. Even if he did not instruct Matthews to send me complaints that he could easily have solved himself, I was positive he chose not to resolve these trivial issues and left them for me to handle.

I could feel the tension building behind my brow, threatening a megrim to rival Mother's.

Fortunately, the sun was beginning to brush the clouds. Fresh air and exercise might do me some good. Eagerly, I returned to my room and rang for Stevens to help me dress for riding.

At length, I was able to set off at a brisk pace free from the worries of my study.

Seven

KATE

THE INVITATIONS DRIED UP QUICKLY. Even Aunt Prudence, society darling, could not garner invitations for her unfortunate, clumsy niece. Before, invitations were addressed to both of us, now they were pointedly only addressed to her. It seemed that one unfortunate moment in a ballroom was enough to ensure I was ostracized.

The worst of it was that part of me felt nothing but relief, the part of me I would never reveal to my aunt or to Jules. Neither of them could ever understand. They were born to be a part of this world. I was born to the life of a country vicar's wife or perhaps the wife of a solicitor.

Embroidery, French, and dancing were of no use when the crops were flooding. None of those accomplishments would comfort a parishioner after a stillbirth. Were I to succeed in convincing a gentleman I possessed all the necessary skills for a society wife, he would surely be nothing but disappointed in under a year. My only hope was for Aunt Prudence to tire of me and return me to Lincolnshire where I belonged. There I could be of some help to Mother and Father with their flock. Or, perhaps act as an exceedingly unqualified governess to my sister's numerous offspring.

Unfortunately, my aunt seemed to take the dearth of invitations as a personal challenge. The less society wanted to see of me, the more she was determined to secure an invitation. She never went so far as to allow me to turn up uninvited, but if there was any ambiguity to be had in an invitation, she was sure to exploit it.

I had no proof, but I suspected that she browbeat her daughter-in-law into hosting a ball with the sole purpose of securing an invitation for me. The poor woman was mere months out of the childbed. I could not believe that she wanted to host such an event.

While my aunt ensured I received the invitation, she had no power to force gentlemen to ask me to dance. The entire night was spent propping up the wall—far away from the drinks table for obvious reasons. Even the company of Ladies Celine and Davina, both of whom were quite popular, did not entice the gentlemen to my side.

The only consolation was the lack of a certain viscount and his mother. Lord Hugh Grayson and Lady Grayson had proven themselves to be the cruelest sort that day in the park. She flung insults in my direction as she walked away, and he merely grunted in agreement.

At least the younger son tried to quiet her proclamations. Improper and uncultured I may have been, but I would never dream of spewing such venom at a person; particularly one with whom I was so little acquainted. Were any of my relations behaving thusly, I would certainly check them. Having witnessed such a display, I could hardly recall what I had initially found attractive about the man. Thick dark hair, intriguing gray eyes, and a handsome form were hardly enough to overcome such a poor character.

Tonight though, tonight my aunt had taken a different tactic. She took it into her head to host a dinner party before the whole of the *ton* retreated to their country estates for the winter holidays. She was determined to show me off to best effect, which apparently required me to display at the pianoforte after dinner.

She also decided the best way to overcome my foibles was to include both the viscount and his mother amongst tonight's numbers. After all, if Lord Grayson forgave my display at the Rosehill ball, surely the rest of the beau monde would as well. And, the two hadn't declined. Of course, no one declined my aunt's invitations.

A gown had been commissioned specifically for this evening, a missish white satin thing cut far too low on the bust. Aunt Prudence's maid had tightened my stays far past the point of comfort and I feared spilling from either end. My aunt's own delicate form prevented her from sympathizing with my fears. My hair had been stuffed with more baubles than my head could support. Overall, the effect was simultaneously over and underwhelming. I hadn't the heart to complain though, nor the time to make substantive changes. Guests were due to arrive in moments.

I took my place at my aunt's side just as the first carriage arrived. This one conveyed her son and daughter-in-law. My cousin and his wife were kind but not particularly interested in his mother's charity case, a situation which suited me perfectly.

They were followed by Lady James and her husband, the Baron James. I hadn't realized they received an invitation, and it took all my efforts to suppress a groan. Lady James hadn't taken any pains to apologize for the incident with the lemonade and, in fact, stepped on the hem of my gown in the modiste the other week. I could no longer excuse these events as accidental. She, of course, looked quite fetching in a rose-pink gown, quite outshining her elderly, portly, sweaty husband.

She and her husband preceded several other guests including Lady Rycliffe, Lady Davina, as well as her mother and brother, all of whom appeared to have stepped off a Parisian fashion plate.

Unfortunately, Juliet was unable to leave Aunt Sophie, whose condition had worsened still further.

Finally, well past fashionably late, the viscount and his mother arrived. I could excuse a slight to me, but to delay my aunt's dinner party... I gritted my teeth between greetings. It was beyond the pale.

Worse still, Aunt Prudence seated me next to Lady Grayson at dinner. I was forced to sit beside the woman whose scent could only be described as floral death, perhaps a bit of citrus for added complexity.

The smell put me off my dinner, which had been quite promising. My aunt did not hire inferior staff. I often thought, usually midbite, that her cook was well worth the humiliation that was a Season in town. I struggled for a bright side, the best I was able to manage was that I would hardly have been able to eat in the stays anyway.

Lady Grayson took no pains to speak to me, instead blatantly snubbing me when I attempted to engage her. I tried to excuse it as some hearing difficulty, but she seemed to have no difficulty comprehending her son on her other side.

Fortunately, Celine was seated to my right, she had no compunction quietly mocking the absurdities around us. My own appearance included. "Tell me, how many peacocks lost their lives for your headpiece?"

I had to disguise a laugh as a cough into my napkin.

"You would have to ask my aunt for confirmation, but I expect at least three. It's nothing to the number of whales who lost their baleen in an effort to contain my bust. Behold their success."

Celine did nothing to hide her chuckle as I made a subtle gesture with my fork toward my chest. Lady Grayson's choked swallow proved that she was not, indeed, suffering from hearing loss.

"Yes, their efforts do seem to be in vain. Why does your aunt insist on dressing you in gowns that would flatter her? Your figure is spectacular but quite her opposite. In Paris, you would need to beat the gentlemen back with a riding crop. Though I know of more than one man who would find that to be an incentive rather than a deterrent."

She timed this comment to coincide with a sip of wine, and I choked slightly in response. Fortunately, I was able to contain the wine in my mouth.

"Even though the fashions here are much behind, certainly your modiste could not have suggested this cut," she said.

"In spite of all my efforts and those of Mme. Dubois, my aunt was certain this would suit. I'm sure it would suit. Anyone else."

"Perhaps she will allow Dav and I to escort you to the modiste. We could find you something… more flattering."

"That would be lovely."

Her tone dropped lower before she added, "At least you're under your aunt's thumb. Lady Grayson has no such excuse for whatever it is that she's donned." There was no choked squawk from beside me but there was one on the other side of Celine from Davina who had paused her emphatic gesturing at her brother in favor of eavesdropping. "I've also discovered the source of her megrims—it is her perfume no doubt." Davina's second snort drew her brother's attention once more and they resumed their animated gesturing.

Eventually, supper came to a close. With Celine's help, I actually managed to enjoy myself if not the food. As expected, per his mother's explicit instructions, my cousin requested some musical entertainment for the evening.

I was supposed to use this opportunity to display my one accomplishment of note. What wasn't planned for was Lady James's eagerness to demonstrate her own talents on the pianoforte.

~

HUGH

The food looked excellent. Whether it tasted as good as it looked was a question for someone sitting farther away from Mother. Her signature scent had a cloying tendency to make food less appetizing. I now remembered why I sat opposite her when we dined at home.

Miss Summers had managed to dress and act with more decorum than she did at the park, and with less sensuality than in my dream. In fact, she made the opposite choice. Gone was the temptress in red; replaced by an unflattering cloud of white tulle. Her hair was filled with more baubles and trinkets than her neck should be capable of supporting.

Her Grace seated her niece next to Mother. It was likely in an effort to assure the *ton* that there was no ill-will from the lemonade incident. Of course, Mother's blatant snubbing of the girl would certainly have the opposite effect. Even though I reminded her that dismissing the girl would not go unnoticed by the duchess, she pointedly refused to turn in Miss Summers's direction.

Mother's scorn seemed to have no effect on the girl herself. The entire supper, she engaged in a whispered, giggled rapport with Lady Rycliffe. I would have expected more of Lady Rycliffe than she demonstrated tonight. Perhaps the rumors of her liaison with Michael were more accurate than I had credited. It would explain her complete lack of decorum and choice of friends.

Shortly after supper, and before the sexes separated, the Duke of Sutton requested a musical performance, and the purpose of the evening became clear. Miss Summers must possess moderate skill at the pianoforte and Her Grace was attempting to display her niece to the greatest advantage.

The plan backfired spectacularly when Lady James offered her talents. I had to cover a smirk with my handkerchief. She was an exceptional talent and all things accomplished. Surely Miss Summers could not be up to the task at that level.

That lady took a seat at a stunning pianoforte. Miss Summers even offered to turn the pages, proving that she was, at least, capable of behaving in polite society.

Lady James began a light and airy piece by Beethoven. Music not being my forte, I only recognized the composer, not the piece. She played with an unstudied air. The effect was quite becoming, overall. Were she unwed, and I a few years older, she would have been an excellent match for me. Her tall, statuesque form was pleasing, her light golden-brown hair suited her complexion and warm brown eyes well.

Somehow, the elderly, jowl-necked baron had managed to snag her. That was a travesty I could not countenance. Prior to her wedding, she had been quite publicly courting the new Duke of Rosehill. Everyone anticipated an engagement at any time, one day the courtship abruptly ended, and she was affianced to the baron.

Rosehill had looks, funds and a title far superior to that of James. Gossip and speculation still followed them both. Whether the failings came from Lady James or Rosehill was anyone's guess. Though, as far as I could see, she was flawless.

When the lady finished to great acclaim and applause, she was pressed to perform another piece. She chose something even lighter. I did not know the composer but the effect was enchanting.

When it came time for Miss Summers to demonstrate her talents, Lady James correctly offered her services as a page turner.

What followed managed to stun the previously inattentive audience into rapt silence, even my mother.

Miss Summers began softly. I believed it was a Mozart composition. While timid, her technique was clearly flawless, and though I loathed to admit it, her air was artless.

As the tempo picked up, she gained confidence; her fingers flew across keys like a butterfly's wings.

At some point, Lady James lost her place in the piece and ceased turning the pages at all. The loss did not affect Miss Summers in the slightest.

I had never seen such a performance in my life. Such a technically challenging piece should have read as showy, tedious, and pretentious. Particularly in such a situation.

Instead, the notes fell from her fingers like a strand of pearls. Each note led to the next on the strand in perfect succession, made more beautiful for its predecessor and embellished by its successor.

For all the girl was clumsy and indecorous in every other moment, she was clearly at home on the piano bench. My mouth hung open in astonishment, I could feel it. My eyes too, were wide and unblinking.

This was the woman from my dream. Confident. Graceful. Sensual. Her ill-fitting gown and ridiculous hair baubles faded away in the shadow of the clear delight written across her face. Her eyes were brighter and cheeks flushed with the effort of her display. The entire picture was every bit as enticing as the silk-clad goddess of my dreams.

As the piece came to a close, the tempo slowed and drifted off until the last note held out for the audience to admire. She was met with substantial, well-deserved applause. Even I could admit her talents were worthy of praise.

The stunned crowd was too astonished to request another piece.

When no ladies were willing to demonstrate in her wake, the gentlemen retired to the billiards room while the ladies gathered in the drawing room.

Eventually, the evening drew to an uncomfortable close. No one expected such a display from clumsy Miss Summers and as a result, they had no map to proceed from this point.

Eight

KATE

I KNEW IT WAS COMING. I should have known. Even still, the letter in front of me rang false.

Aunt Sophie was gone.

The ache in Juliet's heart was palpable in her letter. She loved my aunt as a mother in all but blood. She had lost a second mother.

Her father was hardly a comfort in the best of times. And, though Jules spoke little of it, he had all but disappeared in the months after Aunt Sophie's stillbirth. My friend was alone in the world once more.

My response was entirely insufficient to express my sorrow. Worse still, I had returned to Lincolnshire for winter —there was no hope of returning to her side for months.

She was left to mourn alone.

Winter turned to spring while I waited for the snow to clear. The previous spring had been notably wet. It delayed the planting and subsequent harvesting in late summer and fall.

Many of Father's parishioners were feeling those effects by the time I returned from town. This winter was even more harsh.

It was sometimes a week or more before the snow cleared enough for Mother and me to visit the needy with blankets and baskets of preserves and bread. It was all that we could spare ourselves.

Even Lizzie, my sister, and her husband Sydney, a farmer by trade, had difficulty keeping their four children full.

I was pleased that I had the foresight to clear Aunt Prudence's basket of scrap linens and notions before I returned to the country. The bits and bobs provided far more comfort here than they would have in an empty London townhome. I was able to provide some of the struggling families with extra gloves, hats, and blankets. They were warm, even if my stitches were crooked.

Kit remained in town for the winter, focusing on his studies, and I missed him fiercely. With him gone, it fell to me to assist Father with the maintenance of our cottage. Most mornings, I rose well before dawn to chop wood beside him.

I often thought of Aunt Prudence while I swung my ax. She would be horrified.

Her invitation to return to town came in early March. The cold persisted long into the spring and I could not be spared until after the planting. I could hardly leave when there was so much help needed here.

My return was again postponed by my cousin's second confinement. Aunt Prudence left London for the country to be by her daughter's side.

All these events conspired to ensure that I did not return to town until midsummer.

~

MY STOMACH TURNED into knots as the carriage shuddered to a stop outside of the James estate. Torches lit the steps that lead to the imposing black double doors.

The air was balmy, bordering on sticky. Reaching back, I felt my curls for any rebels that may have escaped their pin and ribbon bindings. Aunt Prudence's lady's maid performed a miracle, and they were all still shackled.

I was alone tonight. Aunt Prudence had been called to visit an unwell friend, leaving me unchaperoned. Rather than allow me to beg off, she arranged to have her son's wife fill the role, but they would meet me inside.

I was, however, thrilled with tonight's theme, royal jewels. Finally, I was able to abandon the pastels that suited me so poorly. And with my aunt's permission even. Tonight, I donned the gown I purchased last season when I went to the modiste with Ladies Celine and Davina.

The original intent for it had been some heretofore unannounced masquerade. This was better. The deep crimson—garnet—gown cut low on my bosom. Made of a shot silk, it shifted between scarlet and a shade just shy of black depending on the angle. The fabric grazed, hugged, caressed my curves, rather than covering them. Though the cut was low, the bodice wasn't immodest. I loved it.

I *felt* beautiful. Stunning. Gorgeous. Resplendent. Everything I had always wanted to feel.

My aunt even lent me her ruby hairpins for the occasion and her miraculous maid wove them with matching ribbon into my inky curls. They were tiny embers left burning in the coal of my ringlets.

Without her oversight, I was able to sneak a bit of rouge onto my lips. The lip color, the wine of my gown, my near translucent skin and perpetual flush came together for the first time. I was lovely.

Also, it seemed, late. I was nearly certain that the invitation said 9:30 p.m. The few stragglers milling about outside, the sheer number of carriages lining the drive, confirmed that I read the time wrong.

Ordinarily, I would have wavered, considered returning home—ball unattended—but tonight... tonight something special hovered in the air. Perhaps it was the gown. Or the lack of chaperone. Maybe it was the unexpected invitation from a lady I hadn't thought enjoyed my company. All I knew was that those doors were calling to me. Something enchanting and wonderful was waiting just beyond them.

With a deep breath, I closed my eyes and pressed them open.

HUGH

Lady James was an exceptional host. She managed to gather the best that the beau monde had to offer.

Tonight, her ballroom was filled but not uncomfortably so. She limited the guest list to only those most agreeable. She had chosen a black and white theme which displayed ladies and gentlemen to their best advantage.

Were she not already trapped in a most unfortunate marriage, I certainly would have thrown my hat into the ring. Her white silk gown shone almost silver in the candlelight.

Her husband, Lord James, had excellent taste in scotch and a free hand with both the bottle and the cigars. Even though a wife was not on the table, the evening was certainly enjoyable.

I danced an enjoyable set with Miss Cordelia Lucas. Though she was untitled, she had a substantial enough dowry that I could not discount her entirely. She had been light of foot and free with her smiles.

No other lady caught my eye in time for a second set, but the drinks table managed it. The scotch was truly exceptional.

In general, I found the crush and cacophony of balls to be a bit chaotic. Though the guest list was more exclusive, this one was no exception. It was a shock when, one by one, the voices began to dissipate, and the orchestra cut midnote. Until there was nothing left behind but deafening, palpable silence.

Turning, searching for the source of the disquiet, I was met with a dream. Or perhaps a nightmare.

Miss Summers, clad in the crimson fabric of that nightmare from all those months ago, was framed by the open archway at the top of the split staircase. Her eyes were wide, and her lip trapped between her teeth. She twirled her hands; they danced restlessly in front of her while each and every member of the *ton* stared at her in horror.

Disgust swirled in my gut. The chit had the sheer nerve and gall to display unease. After arriving well past fashionably late in a blood-red gown to a black and white themed event. What had she been aiming for?

Poor Lady James was certainly humiliated by her behavior. Her elegant evening and theme in tatters at Miss Summers's feet. The girl was so desperate for acknowledgement she had forgotten to have shame.

Worse still was the effect she had on me. Intellectually, I found her behavior abhorrent. The rest of me... That dream from months ago, all but forgotten, swam unbidden to the surface of my memory.

The living, breathing Miss Summers lacked the confidence of my imagination. The deep, clinging scarlet gown on her frame was every bit as seductive in person. Perhaps more so.

The red fabric burned black in the folds and drapes while the ornate chandelier flickered, reflecting off ruby hairpins. It highlighted, emphasized every single curve. The contour of her bosom, the nip of her waist, the arch of her back, the bend of her waist, the swell of her bottom, all sensually exaggerated. She was an audacious, luscious, calligraphic 'S.' Her every flourish embellished for dramatic effect, no matter how inappropriate the situation.

Not one of her previous gowns displayed her figure to such an advantage. That was certainly beneficial to my health. Never before had I experienced such a heady, contradictory combination of irritation and lust.

Across the ballroom, her eyes found mine. Too far to make out the color, they were still too wide, too big really, and haunting. I could not look away, could not breathe.

Seconds, minutes, an eternity later, she blinked; shuttering the connection between us.

Blood rushed through my ears, distorting the returning ballroom sounds. The scandalized whispers rose around me, indistinct.

Pointedly, I cut my gaze from her eyes and her form, turning back toward the drink table. If she wanted sympathy or acceptance for her poor behavior, she would need to look elsewhere.

Nine

JAMES PLACE, LONDON – JULY 1, 1813

KATE

MY INVITATION MADE a horrifying kind of sense now.

The situation bordered on comical. What lengths did Lady James go through in order to orchestrate this? A separate invitation with a specific time and theme. Did she snub Lady Rycliffe and Lady Davina to ensure they would be unable to foil her plot? Was my aunt's friend even ill? Lord, did she poison the woman?

Any possibly charitable explanation I could find vanished with a quick glance in her direction. She was bent at the waist cackling in a most unladylike fashion.

I couldn't help but hope she snorted a little when she laughed.

A blood stain in a sea of white, I was conspicuous in the worst possible way.

My feet froze, refusing to respond to commands; orders to flee, directives to fight were all ignored equally. Erratically, my gaze flicked from face-to-face, hoping desperately for a single friendly smile.

There was none to be had. No Celine, no Lady Davina, and if my cousin and his wife were present, they certainly weren't in the ballroom.

Expressions ranged from derision to cruel amusement, but there was nothing close to sympathy to be found. They were unfamiliar faces as well. She chose her audience well.

At last, I found a recognizable, imposing form. It was a wonder it took so long to pick him out. Lord Grayson stood several inches above the rest, with broad shoulders, a tight brow, and a familiar stern slash of a mouth.

My eyes found his, too far to discern the disapproving gray-blue gaze I knew too well. My eyes joined my feet in disobedience, refusing to abandon his.

Even across the ballroom and critical as always, he was captivating. Arrogant and self-important as well, but captivating, nonetheless.

Irritation hardened in my belly. What right did he have to wear that expression? There was burning fury there. Seething heat.

Slowly, the insults hidden beneath poorly feigned whispers beat their way into my consciousness. My eyelids shuttered against the hurtful claptrap. Words like "trollop," "light-skirt," and "Haymarket ware" wrapped around me. Cocooning me in venomous hate.

Less polite terms flitted past as well, things I had never heard as a vicar's daughter but understood regardless.

When I gathered enough courage to open my eyes once more, I found the viscount's back.

The cut direct.

I hadn't known until that exact moment, but I had been hoping for a rescue. Or, not even a rescue, a carefully blank expression would have been a welcome comfort. I should not have been surprised. At every available opportunity, the man had expressed disinterest at best, derision at worst.

Something about the combination of disappointment and expectation shocked me into action. I allowed a single calming breath before squaring my shoulders and settling a hand on the railing.

I was going to proceed as if nothing were amiss. And I would be damned before I fell down the stairs doing it.

In the end, it was the most graceful moment of my life, my descent down those steps. Were my pride not in pieces at the top, the satisfaction might have been overwhelming.

Whispers whirled across my path like autumn leaves in the wind as I made my way to Charlotte. She was undeserving of the title.

Of course, I referred to her with all due ceremony while I paid her addresses with alacrity. The bon *ton* could find fault with my apparel and my tardiness—she could humiliate me with those—but they would have no such repudiation of my behavior. I would not stoop to match her.

After an insufferably long delay, the orchestra had enough of my humiliation, shifting to signal readiness. Couples found their way onto the floor, the gentlemen handsome in black and the ladies lovely in white. The effect as they spun and swayed on the floor was enchanting. Their beauty made my choice in attire all the more inflammatory.

The *ton*'s gossip trailed me through the room, closer than my own shadow. I was not too proud to cling to the edges of the ballroom. It hardly mattered. There were no warm greetings or polite smiles to be had. Nothing but thinly veiled contemptuous sneers awaited me.

I caught a glimpse of myself in a mirror lining the wall. My once appealing flush of excitement was now splotchy evidence of my shame. My rouged lips, formerly enticing, now served to further paint me a fallen woman. My curls must have taken my humiliation as permission to misbehave, slipping slowly free from each pin to hang limp and unfashionable.

Spotting the refreshment table, I made for it in the desperate desire for some occupation for my hands. Something, anything that could serve to ease my discomfort.

Out of the corner of my eye, a broad, dark-haired gentleman followed the others out a back entry. Presumably, they were in search of less wholesome entertainment. At least the viscount's absence meant that I need not endure his repudiation any longer. I would not miss his scorn.

For two more sets, I called the wall home. Counting the moments before I could reasonably make an escape was my chief occupation.

No rescue was forthcoming. My cousin was nowhere to be seen.

In spite of my best efforts to blend in with the wall, my dress was made to stand out. I could not escape notice, no matter how I tried. Catching the edge of another insult hurled in my direction, I turned. One of the ruby pins slipped from my hair, dropping to the floor while a heavy curl fell free. With its escape, the rest of my coiffure teetered precariously at the back of my head. One wrong turn and the entirety would come tumbling down. A solitary pin dug into my scalp, threatening a dark, curly avalanche.

Slowly, delicately, I bent with my knees to retrieve it, unwilling to risk further censure by bending forward, displaying my assets. I managed it, but with the movement, the entire masterpiece collapsed on itself. The lengthy strands fell about my shoulders, pins and ribbons tangled within the mess.

By the grace of God, my disaster escaped all notice. All but one. Glancing as I stood up, I found Charlotte's gaze, hateful glee burning in her eyes.

Quickly, before I could raise further spectacle, I slipped through the back door the gentlemen had used; hoping desperately that there was a retiring room where I could return to some kind of order.

The richly carpeted hall was empty and refreshingly cool. Free from the ballroom, I recognized how overheated I had become. I supped on great welcoming gulps of air. Pressing a hand to my heart, I willed the throbbing, pounding rhythm to slow. Like the heat, I hadn't noticed its racing in the ballroom. I was too focused on perfecting my statue impression.

Finally free from the watchful eyes of the *ton*, I felt no particular hurry to sort my hair and return to the fray. Surely no one would miss me at my post against the wall.

Gradually, I became aware of heavy, jovial, masculine voices coming from a cracked elegant mahogany door. Once I recognized their presence, I caught the thick rich tobacco scent that permeated the air. Glasses clinked and drinks trickled into them. The notes of deep, hearty laughter floated above the dampened sounds of the orchestra and muffled conversation from the ballroom.

Buoyant chuckles and conversation became more distinctive in the hall as the rushing of my eardrums faded. Still, comprehension hovered out of reach until the letters of my own name floated past. "Kate Summers. Did you see what the chit was wearing? I wouldn't mind taking a tumble with her. Begging for it, she was."

Bile filled my mouth with a metallic tang. I didn't recognize the voice but the words, oh they were horrifying. Tears burned, welling, blurring my vision. I turned to search for a sanctuary. Somewhere. Anywhere.

Before I found a single step, a different voice joined in. A familiar voice. One with a haughty, derisive, pitch to its tenor. "You may want a tumble, but I could not stand it. She is simply too much. Everything she does, too bold, too brash, too loud. And her appearance, her eyes are unnervingly large, and her lips are far too wide. Oh, and the teeth, much too crooked. And the body... It is far too much. Everything about her."

I could not stay here. Not for a single second longer. I could not bear to hear Lord Grayson list yet another fault.

I sprinted in the opposite direction, toward the other end of the corridor, silent but for my breathing sounding harsh in my ears.

Grasping a random door handle, I yanked it open with all my might. Shoving my way inside sightlessly, I pulled it shut behind me. Blessed darkness and silence blanketed me from the horror of this night. Free from the bright lights and harsh sounds of the *ton* at last.

By degrees, my eyes adjusted to the single source of light; the moon streaming from a small window, high on the wall.

A closet, my haven proved to be a linen closet.

Sufficiently assured of privacy, I collapsed onto my bottom. Tucking my chin against my knees, I squeezed my eyes shut, tighter than ever before, forcing back tears between ragged gasps.

Again and again, over and over, round and around that hateful man's hateful words swirled through my mind.

I may be too much, but at least I am not too cruel. And he was too tall and too conceited anyway. And insolent, and supercilious, and pompous, and awful. Just awful.

Who would say such things about another person? He ate at my aunt's table. Should courtesy not dictate that he refrain from outwardly insulting her niece? And in front of eligible gentlemen too.

Aunt Prudence, how was I to tell her? I was ruined. There was not a single man in town who would even glance my way ever again. Not that I would wish for a gentleman who spoke the way they did tonight.

The moon streamed through the high window, casting light on my gown. My beautiful, horrible gown.

Some magical night this turned out to be. A bitter laugh escaped unbidden, burning as it burst free. That naive girl who opened those black doors this evening was gone. Dreams of romantic declarations, poetic words, elegant waltzes, and passionate kisses with handsome gentlemen were shattered on Charlotte's dance floor.

I had no interest in the attentions of men ever again. Not that I would ever receive them.

My tears finally gave way to anger. I used the moment to examine my hideaway. Lone straggling napkins and tablecloths were folded and stacked neatly on shelves to one side. The other side was piled high with empty silver store bags. All sacrificed to the evening's extravagances then.

No one would set foot inside my closet until the servants cleaned tonight, perhaps tomorrow. I was free to pluck the pins from my now tangled hair before working the knotted ribbon free. One by one, I pulled them loose and I was able to run my fingers through the curls. I twisted the lot into a simple style with the ribbon, tucking the pins into my bodice for safe keeping.

I was in need of an escape plan. It was impossible for me to stay until an appropriate hour. My disheveled coiffure would not go unnoticed. And with the way those gentlemen were speaking... There would be no hope of a polite excuse for my appearance. The *ton* would think the worst of me and there would be no disabusing them of that notion.

Certain that I was as presentable as I could make myself in a closet, I stood to leave. Twisting the handle in my grasp. It turned easily. Then it kept turning—too easily.

I pressed against the door. No success. I turned it again and pressed at the same time. Nothing. I pulled. Nothing. I turned and pulled harder.

At once the handle gave, pulling free from the door and sending me tumbling back to my bottom with a sharp thump. The handle still grasped in my hand. And the door was unopened. *Oh—Oh no! Please no!*

Ten

HUGH

I WAS HALFWAY through my speech before I realized it was rather unkind. A few words later, I was certain it would all but ruin the girl. But once the gates were opened, there was no holding back.

The gentlemen listened with rapt attention. Parker clapped me on the back approvingly. Westfield tipped his glass in my direction encouragingly. Laughter warmed the billiards room. With each word, their endorsement became more essential to me. A mandate. There was not a disappointed gaze to be found. It was heady, addicting.

Once I ran out of complaints, I could hardly recall what I had said. It would have been a struggle if pressed. No matter, no one was pressing me. Parker had followed, enumerating on the impolite activities he would perform on her bosom once freed from the gown.

I was not entirely certain that such things could be done. And if they could, I sincerely doubted they would. At least not outside of a brothel. They would certainly require some form of lubrication.

Across the room, Westfield announced the bottom of the scotch. As the closest man to the door, I was volunteered to fetch more. James directed me toward the study just down the hall.

The world tilted slightly when I stepped from the smoke-filled gaming room into the well-lit hall. I should, perhaps, limit myself to only one more drink, lest I say something I may regret.

Warm cheers followed as I trundled down the hall. I paused occasionally to rest a hand on the wall.

What had James said? Third door on the right. How many had I passed? Glancing back, I counted, one, two, ah—there it was.

Bracing one hand against the wall to steady myself, I turned the knob in my left. It pulled easily and I stumbled into the darkened room, tugging it closed behind me before stepping forward. My foot caught on a substantial, unidentifiable lump on the floor.

The lump swore, a feminine curse at that. At once, the near black room filled with girlish chatter, or—yelling.

My drink-addled brain struggled to comprehend the light, fast, furious words. "Wha?—"

"Lord Grayson?" The womanly lump asked. The notes were strangely familiar in the dark, but I could not place them.

"Yes?" I wasn't certain why it escaped as a question, but her answer—it was a woman, I was certain—was another curse. It was even less ladylike than the last.

The lump rose to standing, twirling around me to the door, scratching at it by the sound of it. A wordless cry of frustration followed her efforts.

"Why did you close the door? I told you not to close the door!"

"I don' remember that."

"Oh, good lord! Are you drunk?"

"No' quite."

She flopped gracelessly back to the floor with a resigned sigh. This time she collapsed into a patch of moonlight.

Miss Summers.

My stomach turned uneasily at the sight of her. "Wha' are you doin' in here?"

"The doorknob 's come off."

"Wha' ya' mean?"

"The. Door. Knob. Has. Come. Off. We're stuck."

Once again, my stomach gave a jolt. But the fog that had overtaken my mind cleared slightly, comprehension slowly dawning. "We're stuck?"

"Yes."

"But... I can't be stuck in here with you."

"Tell that to the doorknob." She raised her hand, passing the aforementioned knob.

"Did you try to put it back on?"

"No," she bit out while I turned to slot it back into the hole where it belonged. "That never occurred to me. Thank you so much for your wisdom, Lord Grayson."

My efforts proved fruitless long before her sarcastic tone registered.

"We cannot be trapped here together."

"Again, I refer your complaints to the doorknob." She snarked.

The swirl of drink had abandoned me thoroughly. Sobriety rushed forth with a sickening lurch. Surely, she must understand. We cannot be seen together. She would be ruined. I would be—No!

I pressed myself as far back as possible in the small closet, rushing toward the door with all my strength. Slamming into the wood with my entire weight.

Thud.

Nothing more. No splintering or cracking to be heard.

"What on earth are you doing?" She chirped.

I rammed myself against the frame once more. My shoulder screamed in protest. "We cannot be in here together."

"The servants will find us when they're cleaning up from the ball." She was not understanding.

"We cannot be *seen* in here together." I said the words more slowly. Locked alone in a closet was uncomfortable and unpleasant. Locked in a closet with an unmarried woman was a marriage sentence.

I could see the exact moment she comprehended my meaning. Followed a second later with, "No! Oh no!"

She rose abruptly, resuming her scrambling scratches at the door with no more success than my battering ram efforts.

For nearly half an hour, we struggled, digging and ramming to no effect. The solid mahogany was impenetrable. Our only measure of the time was the length of the orchestra sets, barely audible in our fortress.

Finally, her fingers raw and my shoulders unusable, she collapsed back to the ground in the strip of moonlight once again.

She did look rather fetching, all rumpled in the silvery-blue light. Light! Moonlight! The window!

There it was, salvation. A small latch tucked at the bottom of the tiny window. It would open! To be perfectly honest, I was more than willing to break the glass to escape, but avoiding that effort was all the better. There was but one flaw in the escape plan I was formulating. In spite of my height, the window still eclipsed my reach by a foot or more.

Along the side, there were shelves that lined the wall, abutting the wall where my salvation lay. I grabbed the topmost shelf, pressing a foot to the lowest.

Snap!

I barely managed to lift my foot from the ground before it cracked off the wall, broken. The remaining shelves would not support my weight even if I could reach them.

"What are you doing?" She interjected, irritation thick in her tone.

"The window!"

"What about it?"

I turned back toward her, gesturing to our salvation. "It opens, we can climb out."

Wordlessly, she plucked herself off the ground, finding my side. She sized up our escape. "You'll never fit through there. Your shoulders are much too broad."

"You are all complaints and no suggestions. What do you propose then?" It was an irritated, snappish comment and it was unfair. She had been right at every turn.

"Do you suppose you could lift me?"

"What?"

"I could probably fit."

"You want me to lift you?"

"Do you have a better idea?

I waited nearly a full minute for inspiration to strike. Nothing came. "Fine."

Wordlessly, she positioned herself below the window while I eyed her from behind. She was shorter than I remembered. The top of her curls barely reached my shoulders. In my memory she had been taller, sturdier.

In the moonlight, her curves, though impressive, were delicate and less caricatured. Her bold, brash countenance had overtaken her physical form in my mind, made her stronger, more substantial.

Faced with her petite form, I gripped her waist as gently as I was able while maintaining a grip. Through the gossamer fabric, I felt the edge of her long stays. I had never touched a lady's unmentionables. The thought of them on her was... intriguing.

Brushing the intrusive thoughts aside, I tightened my grasp, lifting her clear off the ground with ease. A quiet gasp escaped her.

"Did I hurt you?"

"No," she murmured, distracted. I could feel her stretch toward the window, but my view was limited to red silk. "Can you step closer to the wall?"

Following her instruction, I pressed her against the wall and myself more firmly against her. She smelled lovely, feminine and floral. One inhale and I was addicted, jasmine and orange blossoms and something indefinable.

Above me, she made a tiny grunt, struggling to reach the latch. Damn! I had no business having such a reaction to that sound. To her scent. To the smooth curve of her waist under my fingers. To the cascading curls brushing against my cheek.

They must have come free during the scuffle. The tresses were long and inky like midnight, softer and cooler than the silk of her dress. Did all women have hair like that?

"Can you lift me any higher?" Her question brought me back to myself, to the situation at hand. I could. I could lift her much higher. But... in order to do so, I would need to grip her bottom.

"I... uh... I can, but..."

Silence. "Oh." I caught the end of a thick swallow. "Can you? I mean... Perhaps my legs instead? That might be slightly less... intimate."

I coughed out something that sounded affirmative. Loosening one hand from her waist, supporting her easily with the other. I slipped my free hand down to grasp a thigh. A shapely thigh. The other quickly followed, pressing her still higher.

Still trapped in floral scented, wine-colored silk, I heard

the click of the latch and a triumphant sound. The window above creaked with disuse as it slid open.

She pulled herself upward, making an inch or two of progress before she was beyond the reach of my help, struggling to pull herself farther.

I moved both hands down to her calves, trying to press her higher. The silky fabric slipped against her stockings, and she slipped a few inches before my grip tightened enough to catch her.

Without asking for permission, I slipped one hand then the other beneath the folds of her skirt to grasp her silk clad legs.

I earned a disgruntled sound for my efforts before she tugged once again at the windowsill.

That was the precise moment, with my hands beneath her skirt and my face pressed in the crest of her thighs, that I heard it.

The brush of the opening door against the carpeting echoed in our prison.

Light from the hall spilled into the room, bathing the wall in front of us in a bright glow. Trapped in the light, we both froze, unable to move, to separate.

From behind me, I heard a throaty chuckle. A second. A third.

"I see you took my suggestions to heart, Grayson. I didn't mean right this second," Parker said. Loathsome toad.

"Well now," another voice chimed in. "I see what was taking the scotch so long. Well-done lad! If I had known the reward, I would have gone to fetch it myself." Westfield, a letch if there ever was one.

Carefully, I knelt down, depositing Miss Summers on the ground. She turned to face me, even more disheveled in the bright hall light. Her expression wavered between resignation and contrition.

"Grayson! I didn't think you would defile the chit in the midst of my wife's ball!" James added. "Come on man, what happened to too much to tumble with?"

I watched the hurt slip across Miss Summers's face before disappearing. I shut my eyes against it, willing it to stay away.

Before I turned to face our audience, I heard a ladylike voice join the chorus of raucous laughter. "What are you all doing out here—Oh! Miss Summers! Lord Grayson!"

I did not recognize the lady. I did not have to, I knew what it meant. The men, perhaps with some inducement, could be convinced to forget the entire scene before them. But a woman... There was no way I was leaving the closet without a fiancée.

Eleven

HUGH

THE DAMNED COAT was too tight. It pulled my shoulders together uncomfortably even though I was certain it fit when I purchased it some weeks ago.

I fought not to fidget in the face of the glare I received from the bride's brother.

My bride.

Her brother failed to comprehend the finality of the situation. Or so it seemed. Neither did he feel it necessary to explain why, precisely, he was so displeased with this union. It was a far greater match than Miss Summers had any right to aspire to, at least without her bit of conniving.

At first, I had thought Miss Summers was every bit a victim of the same situation I had been; but upon further reflection, I realized how deliberate, how contrived, it had all been.

"You are what?" Mother screeched on that day, the morning after my life became something I did not recognize.

"I am engaged. To Miss Summers." I repeated.

"What on earth for?"

"She was compromised."

"By whom?"

I bit back a sigh. "By me, Mother."

"So, the brazen hussy seduced you?"

"Mother..." I breathed out a sigh, hoping to disguise it. "We were inadvertently trapped together, alone. And found together."

"Oh! Of course, she did not seduce you. She was too ill-bred to manage it. Your taste is too fine. She had to use other means."

"It was an accident."

"That is precisely what she wants you to think, my dear boy. Women like *her* are always strategizing. Always trying to move up in society where they have no business being and no one wants them."

"She is the niece of a duchess."

"And who is her father? Her mother?"

"I suppose. You truly believe it is possible?"

"I believe it is probable! Why do you think she came to town last year? And to return after her showing last season? Certainly, she knew the only way she would find a husband was entrapment."

"But... It was a coincidence..."

"Was it? Or did she lure you there? And, when you were trapped together, did she insist on appropriate distance? Or did she position the two of you so your circumstances would be even more scandalous. So there would be no hope that you would escape with your honor?"

"It is not possible."

"I suspect she had some sort of signal. Ensuring that

someone would find you at the worst possible moment. She is a devious wretch."

"But…"

"And where was her chaperone?"

"I do not… her cousin was there. He agreed to the marriage on her father's behalf. But there was no…"

"Precisely! She orchestrated this entire thing to entrap you. You must throw her off, Hugh, you must!"

"I cannot. You know I cannot. Not with my honor intact. It would bring shame on the entire family. I would never make a suitable match anyway if I begged off. And you would be punished by society as well for my mistake. None of your friends would be able to receive you. And Tom…"

"Oh, Hugh. My darling boy, we will get through this together. I will be here for you, to expose her schemes and plots. And once she bears you a son… you can send her to Kent, and you need not see her again. She can even stay in the dower house, there is no need for her in the main house at all."

I could not reply. It was so clear now, what had been so muddled under drink and lust and shock last night. I was marrying a duplicitous, deceitful shrew; and that insidious, underhanded harlot would be my wife. She would bear my children, and they would be saddled with her too big eyes and too brash countenance. And, at only two and twenty, my life was over.

AND NOW, in mere moments, my fiancée would reap her rewards. A title and fortune to be envied. Yet, still her brother had the sheer nerve to act as though she were some prize. A catch and not the spinster second daughter of the second son of an earl—not particularly well-regarded.

Mr. Christopher Summers had approached the settlement

negotiations as a practice for one of his law courses, rather than a polite discourse between gentlemen—or a gentleman and a future farmer. He argued every point, ensuring I received almost no benefit from this sham of a marriage—the one ruining my life.

I had to marry the girl regardless of the settlement; my honor brokered no alternative. But to be accused of marrying her for a fortune... It was too much.

As viscount, I had no need of her fortune. I had not even realized she possessed one until I saw the documents that arrived from her father. Ironically, if the *ton* had been aware of her portion, she might have attracted notice earlier. There was more than one cash-strapped gentleman willing to overlook her temperament and appearance for the £10,000 she brought to the marriage. I, however, was not one of those men—not that I had any access to it, regardless.

No, Mr. Summers did not like me, did not respect me, and was quite certain that I would make his sister very unhappy, indeed. He should have addressed his concerns to her as she orchestrated this entire sham. Now I could feel his glower on the back of my neck, burning through me. I wished that my bride would disabuse him of that notion. She was about to receive everything she had schemed so hard for, the least she could do was call off her dog.

My betrothed was clad in yet another unfortunate gown. This one was a peachy shade that offset her natural flush poorly. Once again, it was covered in too much lace and too many ribbons. Her hair was just as awful, decked again in too many baubles.

In the months that I had managed to delay this wedding, she had worn nothing like that red gown. Nothing that would give me a spark of hope for this marriage. It was equally a relief and a disappointment. I could almost forget the effect she had on me in that closet. For that brief moment when I found her, not too much, but instead perfection itself. It was a trick of the moonlight, a fabrication of drink and proximity, nothing more.

Beside me in the church, covered in flounces and frippery in a garish gown, she was every bit the too much I remembered her to be. Her forgery that night made her all the more hateful. That one second where I felt something akin to relief when her cousin ordered us wed, had never resurfaced. The lingering scent of jasmine and orange blossoms when my head found my pillow that night—morning—vanished. The ghostly contours of her waist in my grasp, the one that had me clenching my fists around nothing but bedsheets, was only an apparition. And the black-red swirl of silk that burned behind closed lids was an illusion, a fiction, some kind of trick to entrap and ensnare me.

And behold her success. She stood beside me while the vicar droned on about marriage being a remedy to sin. Was it still a remedy against sin if it was brought forth in furtherance of a sinful, deceitful, agenda? I could hardly ask the skinny, hooked nose fellow as he rambling on.

I was barely able to hear the clergyman's words over the rushing of my ears. In spite of such difficulties, I must have been able to comprehend the words because my blood froze for a moment, desperately listening for an objection at the appropriate time.

Instead, all I heard was an ill-timed cough from Tom— probably on purpose. He, at least, seemed to find this entire debacle to be a source of great amusement.

The rushing returned with a vengeance, so severe that I nearly missed my cue but for the curious stares from the vicar. And my bride.

"I—" My chest was so tight and my voice so hoarse that I had to clear my throat before continuing. "I will."

Miss Summers shut her eyes, relief perhaps. Surely, she

could not think I would jilt her now. Such a thing would ruin me as well as her. As a gentleman, I could never throw off a bride.

Her own "I will" was little more than a whisper. She refused to meet my gaze through the entire ordeal.

Finally, her hateful brother handed her to the vicar, who passed her to me in turn. The process was accompanied by another frown from her brother, as though this mess was my fault.

I repeated the words monotonously. I promised to love and to cherish with my gut twisting with shame and uneasy deceit. Her repetition was clear but, again, barely above a whisper. She stared at the floor and her mouth was twisted into some unreadable knot.

At the vicar's direction, I twisted the simple gold band on her finger.

Together, we knelt before the man bestowing prayers and blessings on deaf ears. Time passed slowly, seconds felt like minutes, and minutes felt like hours. At last, we were given leave to rise and sign the register.

And just like that, it was done.

I was an unhappily married man, surrounded by those offering congratulations. A glance to my side confirmed that my bride was missing. Turning back, I found her with her brother. His hands were on her cheeks while he whispered something to her. She closed her eyes, tipping her head back to allow him to press an affectionate kiss to her forehead.

It was a bizarrely intimate scene that I interrupted. I caught the end of his words to her. "Be brave, little Katie."

And her answer, "I love you too, Kit."

She turned her attention back to me, offering her hand—the one without a ring—to place in the crook of my arm. I guided her, my wife, out of the church and into my—our—carriage.

Twelve

KATE

KATHERINE, Lady Grayson. Viscountess. The words tasted
foreign on my tongue and, in my mind, just as they had since
the moment I tried them on. In spite of Kit's assurances, I was
his little Katie no longer.

Desperate for something to look at other than my
husband, I spun the delicate gold band around my finger. Not
a ring, it was a more effective trap than even the thickest of
shackles. I was his now, until death did us part. A life sentence
for the sin of hiding in the wrong closet.

Apparently, my bridegroom felt no more need for conversation than I did. He peered out of the carriage window at the
passing London streets. Assured of his preoccupation, I
glanced at him under lowered lashes.

It shouldn't have been possible for him to have grown
more broad, but he certainly seemed like he did, hulking across
from me. The stitches on the shoulders of his tailcoat agreed
with me, straining under the bulk of his shoulders and biceps.

He had cut his hair for the day. It had been brushed back

with a bit of pomade, but it was defying him, a few pieces flopping in front of his eyes. His ice gray eyes... I thought he looked at me with distaste before, but it was nothing compared to the hatred he viewed me with now. Those eyes were topped by that permanently furrowed forehead. A single canyon formed, a line carved between the two dark, straight brows. Forget a smile, I couldn't recall actually seeing his lips in the months we had been betrothed. Instead, I found them pressed tight together into a steely gash. Somehow even the dimple on his chin seemed to deepen in disapproval of our circumstances. I suspected that the clenching of his jaw had something to do with it.

There was no question; my husband hated me.

He hated me, and I was to spend the rest of my life under his power, begging for tiny scraps of affection. I tried to draw a calming breath but the gown Aunt Prudence insisted on cut deep into the top of my breasts with each inhale. The sharp tulle sliced into my skin, protesting my need for air. Worse still, the thing was as hideously uncomfortable as it was plain hideous.

In truth, the color was the least flattering aspect of the gown, but the lace and ribbons did nothing to improve matters. Kit, in a desperate attempt at levity, had spent the morning comparing me to various citrus and stone fruits. The numerous sparkly baubles stuck in my hair added to the cacophony. They were making a valiant attempt to escape my head. Powerless to remedy the situation, I resolved to keep my head steady until I could find a mirror to fix, or better yet, remove them entirely.

Far too soon, we arrived outside of Aunt Prudence's home. The wedding breakfast... I alternately wished it to be over and for it to be never ending. I had no desire to attend, to wear an unfortunate gown whilst receiving false congratulations and ignoring sneers from the *ton*. But... after this meal, the rest of my life would begin in earnest. And that was a horrifying prospect.

THE WEDDING BREAKFAST had been a comedy of errors beyond even Shakespeare's imagination. My new husband glared at everyone. My brother seethed at my bridegroom. Lady James's eye seemed to twitch every time I was congratulated; her plot to ensure I was removed from the marriage mart a success, but not in the manner which she had intended. My new mother-in-law had swallowed a lemon and could not muster the effort to toady to my titled aunt and cousins. Aunt Prudence remained blissfully ignorant of the tension—as she had for the entire length of our engagement—accepting compliments on the event with alacrity. Lady Rycliffe was desperately trying and failing to find a way to get the two of us alone to give me "the talk," deeming my aunt's version insufficient and inaccurate. Lady Davina and her brother were engaged in some sort of tiff that involved a number of emphatic hand gestures. I was fairly certain those had nothing to do with me or my nuptials. And my new brother-in-law, Tom, was desperately trying and failing to diffuse.

I could not decide whether to laugh or cry.

Unfortunately, after the breakfast, my arrival at Grayson House was less a comedy and more a tragedy. The servants were welcoming and kind, and the house was well maintained —if somewhat distastefully decorated. That was where the good news ended.

The viscount disappeared immediately on our arrival, presumably to his study. He did not feel the need to offer an explanation for his whereabouts.

Unfortunately, his mother insisted on joining my tour. Weston, the butler, served as a guide since the house was seemingly between head housekeepers. A pretty red-haired maid, Anna, accompanied us. She was a few years my senior and grew up on the country estate but had volunteered to join her mother in welcoming me. Mrs. Hudson, the cook and Anna's mother, was clearly beloved by everyone and welcomed me with open arms and a plate of delectable lemon tarts.

Just as I was beginning to feel a little more at ease, Lady Grayson reminded us of her presence with her usual wordless choking sound.

Her taste clearly differed from mine, the various furnishings she had chosen served more as ostentatious displays than any practical purpose. It was my place as viscountess to redecorate. *Wasn't it?* I'd been told by all and sundry that it was expected. My mother-in-law seemed less than pleased with that idea when Anna mentioned fetching some upholstery samples the next time she went to market.

"Surely the new viscountess is not so high in her instep as all that. She is a simple country girl and has no understanding of London furnishings and fashions and can have no need to make changes."

Anna waited a beat before continuing on the tour without reply. Dining room, ballroom, billiard room, music room—no pianoforte to be found—library, and drawing room all passed with no further comment on any improvements. The viscount's study door was shut firmly, lending credence to my previous assumption that he was hiding there.

The tour moved to guest bedrooms, each step bringing us closer to the thing I feared most.

"Now for your new chambers. Hugh told me you wished for the adjoining rooms and had no qualms about who may occupy those rooms at present. I certainly hope they are to your taste," the dowager said in a pinched tone.

One glance inside confirmed I had understood her implication correctly. These had once been my new mother-in-law's rooms, not long vacated if the scent of lilacs and death were any indication.

Did that mean...? Did my new husband typically share adjoining chambers with his mother? Was that the done thing? Anna, catching my puzzled expression, gave a surreptitious shake of her head.

That was something of a relief then. They had been vacated in preparation for the wedding night. My wedding night... My stomach gave an unhappy jolt at that thought. Not for the first time, I wished Celine and I had found a few moments alone. Aunt Prudence's depiction of events seemed unpleasant at best.

"Would you like some time to rest before you dress for dinner?" Anna asked, seemingly sensing my rising panic.

"Yes, please. What time is dinner typically served?"

"Seven. Shall I come back at six? His Lordship indicated you do not have a maid of your own. I can have a notice placed right away."

"Yes, thank you," I said.

After an eternity, they left, the door clicking behind them. I waited a full minute before turning the key, still in the lock, and rushing to the window. I threw it open, heedless of the November chill. Shoving my entire head and chest out the window, I took desperate great heaving gulps of air. It was both in an attempt to ease my distress and to clear my sinuses of that woman's lingering scent.

Dipping back inside, I reached behind, trying and failing to undo the miles of tiny buttons pinning me into the itchy, overembellished gown. Before I could rip the thing in my effort to escape, I caught a knock at the door. Closing my eyes against the panic, I took one last breath of fresh air before shutting the window and turning to open the door once more.

It was a relief to find only Anna. "I thought you might need assistance?" she asked.

"Yes, thank you. It has been something of an over-whelming day and I didn't consider…"

"Not to worry! Would you like the window back open? The room is a bit stuffy."

"Yes, thank you," I said.

I wasn't even embarrassed to have been caught, just relieved for a further source of fresh air. She flitted over to the window, throwing it open, before returning to my side.

"I've started to unpack some of your things. Do you have a preference for which nightdress?" Oh, good lord. The night-dresses Aunt Prudence had insisted on. They were every bit as frilly and uncomfortable as the wedding gown.

"I think my shift will do. Thank you." She undid the buttons with ease before loosening my stays.

"Would you like me to take your hair down as well?"

"Yes, please." She directed me toward the vanity, urging me into the seat in front of the mirror. One by one she worked the pins, baubles, and ribbons free, before taking the comb I had sent ahead and running it through my curls. Her efforts were gentle, sure, and so soothing. She finished up without a word, turning to leave.

"Anna?"

"Yes, my lady?"

"No need to put a notice out. If you'd like the promotion that is?"

"I beg your pardon?"

"Have you any interest in the position of lady's maid?"

"Of course, but I'm not qualified!"

"Don't tell anyone, but I'm not qualified to be a viscount-ess. I think we're well-suited."

"Are you certain?"

"Yes, as long as you call me Kate. I'd quite like for someone to still call me Kate."

"Oh, but I couldn't."

"Please?"

"Yes, my—Kate." She offered a quick curtsy before leaving me. At last unburdened by my gown and hair baubles and with the cloying scent slowly dissipating, I curled on the garish floral comforter and fell asleep.

Thirteen

KATE

FAR TOO SOON, Anna returned. It was something of a shock that I slept at all, let alone as soundly as I had.

She suggested one of the least objectionable gowns that my aunt had allowed me to pack. It was simple and unadorned in navy with as modest a neckline as my ample chest would allow for. Unlike some of the others, it fit well enough that it wasn't actively painful. That was not to say that it was flattering, but at least I wouldn't spend the evening wishing to claw my skin off.

Anna then performed some sort of witchcraft with my hair. I had no idea how she pinned it, but it seemed less inclined to fall out immediately after she finished than it usually did.

"This is lovely, Anna, thank you. Or, I suppose, Hudson?"

"Anna is fine. Hudson may be confusing with Mama."

"All right then. I suppose I've dawdled rather long enough, have I not?"

"Lady Grayson—the dowager viscountess—does value punctuality."

"She is to dine with us then?"

Anna offered a sympathetic shrug in lieu of a response. I could do little more than sigh while trailing her along the unfamiliar halls. She deposited me just inside the garish drawing room. I was apparently the first to arrive.

Finally alone, I took a moment to inspect the place. It was filled with golds and bright reds as far as the eye could see. And a few forest green accents were added to the cacophony. Upon closer inspection, the gold detailing on the furnishings had worn poorly, it was faded and peeling at the edges. That was one of the many reasons I preferred natural finishes.

After less than a day it was already apparent that any attempts to redecorate would result in a battle with my predecessor. Still, I could not be expected to spend the rest of my life surrounded by this vulgar juxtaposition. I wandered over to the large window overlooking Park Street. The view, at least, was pleasant.

The curtains, likely once a fashionable, if discordant, brocade, were faded and threadbare in places. It seemed they, too, were chosen with style, rather than durability or longevity, in mind. I hoped that was not a precedent I would be expected to maintain. I could not see myself choosing something of questionable quality simply because it was fashionable—such a thing was too wasteful to consider.

I couldn't recall any of the furnishings from my family home being discarded. The one time Mama had redecorated, the curtains and accessories were all given to one of the local tenants, still in excellent repair. These could not be donated; they would fall to pieces if glanced at the wrong way.

A hacking, pointed cough from the doorway alerted me to Lady Grayson's presence. Once again, I reminded myself that no good could come from purposefully alienating the woman. I would need her guidance if I was to succeed in my new role.

"Good evening. I was just admiring the view. I hope you had a chance to rest? It was quite a busy morning."

"Of course. The view," she replied with a pinched mouth and narrowed gaze.

Yes, I was sizing up your curtains for the rubbish bin, at least I have the decency to pretend otherwise.

I was saved from a response by the arrival of the viscount. *Hugh?* He hadn't given me leave to address him as such, but surely, in private... It felt much too late to ask. Could I go the rest of my life without addressing him at all? It would be far less shameful than making a wrong choice and receiving a correction.

He merely grunted in response to my greeting. In the months of our betrothal, he seemed to develop an ability to see through me, rather than look at me. It was discerting and any hopes I had that our vows might lessen that tendency were doused in that moment. Something about the greeting made my stomach curl uneasily, and I tucked my hands behind my back to stop the fidget that was building.

This man was to be the father of my children, a cold, unfeeling wraith determined to pay not the slightest bit of attention to his new bride. Suddenly the rest of my life seemed quite long indeed.

Before the silence could stretch even further, a footman arrived to usher us into the dining room.

"Thank you...?"

"Timothy, my lady."

"Timothy. I appreciate the reminder. There have been a lot of new faces today."

"Of course. Please don't hesitate to let any of us know if there's something we can do to make your adjustment more comfortable."

Lady Grayson huffed in irritation ahead of us.

"I cannot think of anything just now, but I appreciate the offer." I answered, ignoring her response entirely.

By the time I arrived in the ostentatious dining room with the ridiculously oversized table, the dowager was already hovering at the foot of the table. Her son stood at the head, leaving one seat in the middle.

Was I not? Should that spot not belong to me?

I paused, looking in askance at Timothy who was gesturing awkwardly with the other footman beside her. Clearly, all were at a loss.

Without comment, I moved to stand beside the middle seat, unwilling to cause a scene over this. That remained the case until I caught sight of the smug, self-satisfied expression on Lady Grayson's face. I took a deep breath, pressing the irritation down deeper. Not a fight for tonight.

My husband and his mother certainly did not converse overmuch at the table, there must have been space to fit sixteen. This could not be an enjoyable practice for anyone. I watched as the poor footmen scurried back and forth with each course. This was just silly.

The food, though, was exceptional. Perhaps the best I'd ever eaten. Rich soups, roasted vegetables, tender meat graced my plate, each bite was so flavorful I thought I might die of happiness. My marriage of less than twelve hours may have been a disaster, but this food might just make up for that misery.

I thought I was managing to disguise my euphoric delight adequately, but I must have failed.

"You seem to be enjoying the food?" It was the first words my husband had spoken to me since our vows. The words themselves were neutral but the tone told me they were not a compliment.

"Yes, your cook is quite talented." I had to nearly shout my response which only garnered me a hum of acknowledgement. I waited a full minute, hoping for another attempt at conversation before asking, "is it usually just the two of you for dinner?"

"Sometimes Tom joins now that he is finished with his schooling."

"Oh, that is lovely. My sister, her husband, and their children are frequent dinner guests at home. We did not see Kit as much as we would have liked, of course, with him in town for his studies."

"I did not realize your sister was married. I suppose that explains how your aunt ended up with you," he said. I parsed that statement for a second, trying to determine if there was an insult beneath the comment. I was fairly certain there was, but I chose to ignore it.

The dowager asked, "Is your sister's husband in trade like your brother?"

"Sydney is a farmer."

I knew the response my answer would garner, and I was correct, pursed lips and a disagreeable noiseless whine.

My husband pinched the bridge of his nose between his thumb and his forefinger. All the while, I was left to grit my teeth at the insult to my family. Sydney, while untitled, was certainly a better man than my husband and it grated at me to see him insulted so. I had wished desperately for a marriage like my sister's, dreamed of a husband who respected and adored me. Night after night, I hoped for a man who was as kind and gentle with his children. Lizzie's husband was intelligent, charitable, and handsome, everything I had wished for in a man.

Not... *this.*

～

HUGH

That answer was not going to appease Mother. Nor would the haughty tone. And were the noises while she ate really necessary? The soft little hums and moans—they were very distracting. At least the gown she had chosen for dinner was less unfortunate than her wedding gown.

I had spent the entire afternoon in the study, avoiding my new wife. It was cowardly and unkind, I knew, but I truly did not know the protocol for this moment. And tonight... That was a worry at the forefront of my mind.

I had not anticipated marrying at two and twenty. I always thought I would have more... experience before bedding a wife. But a brothel seemed tawdry and there was never anyone appropriate that I had more than a passing attraction toward.

It was not as though Father had time to discuss it with me before he passed. I certainly could not ask Michael. His suggestions would be completely inappropriate for a lady. A viscountess. I had a viscountess.

I had just sworn to love and cherish this relative stranger until death us do part. *With my body, I thee worship*, that part was clear. The how though, that was murkier. My only relief was that she was surely as inexperienced as me.

While I had been ruminating—not panicking—about this evening's upcoming events, the conversation had halted. My wife's little noises of enjoyment dropped away as well. Now, all that remained was the scraping and clattering of cutlery on plates.

Irritation nipped at me at Katherine's pathetic expression. I felt bad for the chit. And I had no idea how to bring back any sort of conversation. The formerly delicious shepherd's pie turned gummy and tasteless with a single glance at the miserable look on my wife's face.

For someone who wanted this marriage desperately

enough to trick me into it, she certainly did not look the part of a delighted bride. Particularly now, when she was meant to be celebrating her successes. Perhaps Mother was wrong, it was a rather elaborate plot. One that certainly could have ended worse for Katherine.

She had curled in on herself, moving food around on her plate without really consuming any. This was not the attitude of someone crowing over their victory. Once again, I was struck by how small she was. Could her feet touch the floor under her chair?

Weston came in, tray laden with pudding, and took one look at my solemn bride and made a gesture at me, silently ordering me to talk to her.

"So, Miss Summers, do you have any evening habits that you partake in?" I asked. Weston made a pointed cough, and I glanced over at him—confused. He raised his brows pointedly and it finally dawned on me. "I mean, Katherine? Is Katherine all right?"

"Katherine is fine, or Kate. I usually practice if we're not entertaining."

"Practice?"

"The pianoforte. I don't believe I saw an instrument earlier, though. I will have to find some other occupation. The library looks to be most impressive."

A memory ghosted through my mind, her fingers moving dexterously over the keys with graceful ease. That was a disappointment, watching her play might have eased the tension a bit.

Still, I seized on her other topic. "The library was a pet project of my grandfather. He was a great reader from what I understand. I believe Michael did a great deal to it while he was managing the estate."

"Michael?"

Mother's eyes narrowed at me for that slip. She detested

any reminder of the man. Now, I was left to explain a relation to my wife, one I certainly should have disclosed prior to reciting our vows. Such a connection to a gambling magnate would surely have given me pause...

"My, uh, elder brother."

"Oh, I am so sorry for your loss. I had no idea." She turned to my mother, wide eyed. "Please accept my condolences."

It took a moment to understand why she was apologizing. I was so used to the situation that it hadn't occurred to me to clarify.

"My *natural* elder brother. He is still with us."

"Oh... Was he at the wedding? There were so many faces, I cannot recall."

"No, I had not informed him of our nuptials."

"Oh," she drawled slowly, dragging the syllable along behind her thoughts. Finally it seemed to sink in. Perhaps a later date would be better to provide her with the rest of the details.

Mother's lips had all but disappeared at Michael's mention, and I did not think she could manage further explanation without a megrim.

"Are you in the habit of some after dinner activity?" Katherine asked, abandoning fraught topics.

"Nothing particularly noteworthy."

"I see," she said, her expression crestfallen once more. What had I done this time? I do not think I would be well suited to such a melancholy wife. I had not thought to expect that out of her. What was I supposed to do with her tonight?

Fourteen

KATE

Dinner was a long, drawn-out affair with none of the gay chatter and easy teasing of home. Even when I dined with Aunt Prudence there was discourse.

But this silence interspersed with pointed comments from my mother-in-law and irritated sighs from my husband—Hugh. I was determined to refer to him by his name, in my own mind at least. And he had asked to call me by my Christian name, so surely, I could do the same.

I had never met anyone as skilled at shuttering a conversation as Hugh. We were in this marriage, for better or worse. He could at least attempt to converse like a civilized being.

As painful as the meal was, I hoped it would never end. Because what came after... Well, Aunt Prudence made *that* sound unpleasant at best.

In spite of my prayers to the contrary, eventually we ran out of courses. There was little point in separating the sexes given our number, so we all retired to the drawing room as one.

My fingers itched for piano keys, something to cut the

tension and distract myself from events soon to transpire. The unease was palpable. Every person in this room, every person in the house really, knew precisely what was to happen in a few short hours and we were all carefully avoiding the subject.

Helpfully, Hugh poured me a glass of sherry when he fetched his own drink. I should learn his preferences, which would be appropriate for a wife.

I took a healthy sip and liquid fire dragged down my throat. It was a soothing burn, distracting from the edginess that was overcoming me. I hadn't noticed earlier, but a clock rested above the mantel, and it felt like an eternity between each tick.

At last, I could take the silence no longer. "I understand the plan is to travel to Kent after the New Year?"

"Yes," Hugh answered, offering me nothing else.

I tried again. "It's nice that the distance allows for travel in winter. Lincolnshire is much too far, the journey can turn treacherous."

"That explains why your farmer did not attend the wedding," Lady Grayson added.

I chose to ignore the implicit slight, continuing, "that and travel is difficult with four little ones. My sister also suspects she has another on the way, but it is too soon to be certain."

"Four children? How long has your sister been wed?"

"Just five years, but she has always wished for a large family. We are all quite pleased for her. The children are just precious as well."

The dowager straightened at that news. Perhaps potential grandchildren were the key to her approval. Hugh said nothing, pouring himself a second drink. It wasn't until he pulled the glass from my hand that I noticed I had emptied my own as well. He handed me a refill without comment, returning to his perch near the drinks.

"Healthy?" Lady Grayson questioned.

"Oh yes, and smart as well. The eldest idolizes my brother, and he is determined to follow him into the law."

That earned me a *hmph* and no further questioning.

The silence stretched on, broken only by the ticking of the clock. Finally, after the 2,764[th] tick, I could stand it no longer.

I rose, startling the others. "I think, perhaps, I will retire for the evening."

Hugh's jaw clenched, and he swallowed hard. His mother's lips pursed in that, now familiar, sucked-a-lemon way that she had. My husband stood, presumably to escort me.

"I can manage the way, thank you."

He nodded at my side, throat bobbing once again. His hand found my shoulder. He started, pausing for a moment before continuing softly, words meant for only the two of us, "I shall see you later?" His voice was thick, harsh.

For the first time I considered that, just maybe, he was as nervous as I was. His head was cocked, and his back curved slightly making him smaller than usual. The effort was foreign on him, and the effect was strangely comforting. His slate blue eyes searched mine, searching for I didn't know what.

His efforts, more than anything else, were a relief. That he asked, instead of assuming as was his right, soothed some of my trepidation. I nodded, more confident than I felt and he reciprocated, straightening once more.

For a moment, I had forgotten just how tall and broad he was—my husband. One complaint I should not have was an unattractive husband. He towered over me, mint and vanilla scent surrounding and enveloping me. The hand on my shoulder was warm, hot almost, and burning an imposing print through the gossamer fabric of my gown. He swallowed once more, before releasing his grip, freeing me to my toilette.

~

THE ROOM HAD BEEN AIRED OUT SLIGHTLY in my absence. November chill battled for dominance with the heat from the roaring fire. An oversized copper tub of steaming water had been placed to the one side behind a screen, and I nearly cried at the thoughtfulness of the gesture. I set about pulling the pins from my hair, marveling at Anna's talent. She had managed to restrain my slippery locks through the whole of dinner, a previously unimaginable feat. The woman herself arrived shortly thereafter, bearing the fragrant jasmine soap I brought with me. She took over the task seamlessly before helping me from my gown and into the tub. The water stung as I entered; normally, I would find it too hot, but I appreciated the distraction tonight.

On the other side of the screen, Anna fussed with my night dresses, clearly searching for the least objectionable option. They were all garish. Aunt Prudence had ordered four, each more hideous than the last. I wasn't entirely certain how I would be able to sleep strangled in ribbons and scratched by lace. But, I was given to understand that sleep wasn't their intended purpose.

"Kate?"

"Yes?"

"I don't suppose there are any less..."

"Vulgar options?"

"That wasn't the word I was going to use."

"It's the one you meant though."

"Well, yes."

"My old one is in the other trunk that hasn't been unpacked yet. It's seen a bit of wear but at least I won't be attacked by it. I don't suppose you know anything about removing ribbons and lace?"

I heard the trunk creak open, followed by a rustling and a soft sound of triumph. "I can try," she answered, distractedly, with more question than confidence in her tone. "The ribbons seem doable but the lace, some of it appears to be structural."

"I feared as much." I dragged the soap up and down my skin, luxuriating in the fragrant scent. "How long do you suppose I have?"

"Perhaps a quarter of an hour or so? His lordship asked Stevens to fetch water for him as well."

Hugh ordered the bath for me? That was unexpectedly thoughtful. Bolstered by the confidence of that gesture, I rose to dry off.

Anna helped me into the nightdress, guiding me over to the vanity. She set about running a brush gently through my hair. Ordinarily I wore it back, braided. Is that how one wore their hair on their wedding night? I caught her questioning gaze in the mirror, clearly neither of us had that answer ready.

"Down? I think down."

I nodded. Even if that was incorrect, I quite liked my hair, and it was one of the few things Hugh hadn't listed as a fault.

I had done my best to forget that unkind speech, and the memory of it now sickened me. A man who hated my body had vowed to worship it this morning. And tonight we were to...

Mistaking my stricken expression for one of nerves, Anna rushed to comfort me. "Do not fret. I don't know all that goes on between husband and wife of course, but his lordship will be kind to you. I'm sure of it."

I gave her the surest smile I could manage. It felt weak and weary to me, but she accepted it.

Finally, she ran out of activities to distract me with. I bade her goodnight and did my best to ignore her sympathetic expression as she closed the door.

I found the bed, now scented more of fresh winter air than whatever it was the dowager preferred. Wiping damp palms on the bed coverings, I determined that they would be the first things to go.

Was this how I was supposed to await him? Or was the chair better? Perhaps the vanity?

My teeth caught the edge of my lip hard, ripping a layer of skin off. When did I start biting it? Determinedly I clenched my teeth against each other, leaving no room for cheek or lip between them.

Suddenly, a knock sounded on the door from the adjoining room, harsh and cold in the silence. Closing my eyes, I inhaled deeply, releasing it slowly, before responding, "come in."

~

HUGH

I made my way back to my bed on unsteady legs.

That was... I understood now, what all the talk was about. It certainly would not be a chore to bed my wife. Not at all.

I flopped on the turned down covers, tracing a finger along my lips. I was struck once again by how small my wife was when I walked in. Seated on Mother's ugly bed coverings, she took up nearly no space in her simple white nightgown.

For the first time, I saw her hair loose. It was longer than I had thought, a silky dark curtain down her back. Her skin was flushed, her lips bitten, eyes bright.

And I could read every nervous thought that flitted through her head. Her eyes widened when she took in my banyan, lingering on the opening of my neck, gaze flitting down farther before landing on my bare feet.

Hers were bare as well, ten delicate toes available for viewing. Ankles too. Even in the relatively modest nightdress, it was more skin than I had ever enjoyed before.

Finally, I sat beside her, slipping my hand atop hers on the bed. She flipped her palm up, lacing our fingers together. Hers were short with flat blunt tips and close clipped nails. It was a wonder she could stretch her hand wide enough to reach the keys on the pianoforte.

It took a long moment before I could speak, this was not a place to allow nervous silence to overtake me. In this, I must lead. "Did your aunt talk to you?"

She nodded, staring at our entwined fingers.

"You will let me know if I hurt you?"

Again a nod.

I urged her back, and we became one. At first it was awkward. The rhythm had not been as instinctive as I expected. And her small hand, still laced with mine, tightened at first entry. She made no complaints though, tucking her face into my shoulder instead.

I suspected there had been some pain but she said nothing. I could only hope it was not too significant.

Her hair was soft when I tangled my free hand in it. The unwieldy movements quickly became familiar, pleasant, plea-surable, euphoric, *everything*. Far too soon it was over, I was panting my release into her hair.

Everything inside me screamed against leaving her. But that was the done thing. It would be improper to pull her to me, to fall asleep with her hair brushing my chin and her curves tucked into my side.

Even now, settled in my own bed, I wanted to return. Instead, I forced myself to crawl beneath my own covers. It was far too long before sleep found me and when it did, it came with the scent of jasmine.

Fifteen

KATE

I AWOKE to the rustle of Anna with a breakfast tray in the sitting room. My sleep was poor and filled with fits and starts. Last night was not as terrible as I feared, in some moments it was even pleasurable, but it was nothing like what I hoped for. I hadn't acknowledged it consciously, at least not until after he left, but I dreamed of easy touches and warm, tender kisses. It did not seem that those would be a part of my future.

A small part of my heart ached for what I would never know. Buttoning that piece of myself away, I knew I could mourn that loss later. When I was settled in this house, this role, this life. Or perhaps, those things might come with time and familiarity.

Today, I needed to begin the impossible task of becoming a viscountess. It was apparent after yesterday that no help would come from my mother-in-law's corner. With no path before me, I decided to begin with solving the most irksome problems first. The bedclothes needed to go. Preferably today. Ideally in flames.

Anna poked her head around the corner, lifting the tray with both hands in wordless explanation. I sat up, tucking the appalling bed coverings around me.

"I did not know whether you preferred coffee or tea or how you took them, so I brought both and the fixings."

"Black tea usually. Unless there is drinking chocolate."

"There can be."

"You're a treasure."

"Do you prefer to take your breakfast in bed? Or in the breakfast parlor?"

"I've never taken it in bed before. I will probably prefer it downstairs except on special occasions. I was wondering, are there any guest bedrooms I might be able to exchange bed coverings with?"

"Of course! But I thought you might wish to redecorate to suit your tastes."

"Yes, but I think this should not wait that long."

"Understood. I can bring you the ones that might fit."

"That's all right. I ought to get used to the layout of the house."

"Very well, is there anything else I can do for you this morning?"

"I don't suppose you know what I am supposed to be doing?"

"Her ladyship is usually abed until much later. She occasionally meets with Mother to plan menus. There are a few of us who have been here for a number of years, so the household is relatively self-sufficient."

That was inconvenient. I could not imagine it would be a lengthy task to select new bed coverings, and I had a desperate need for occupation today.

"Would it be too much to trouble you for a bath again?"

"It's already set up in the other room."

"Treasure," I called after her as she made her way to the hall.

"Let me know when you wish to dress, my lady."

∼

I WANDERED into a third guest room trailed by Anna and Timothy. This one overlooked the back of the property and was decorated with navy and cobalt brocade. It was by far the least objectionable bedding set I found thus far, and it was likely going to be my choice. It seemed as though the dowager hadn't gotten her hands on this room.

Trailing a finger over the cool silk, I made my way to the windows to inspect the curtains as well. Best to swap all available fabrics in the hopes of removing my predecessor's scent that still permeated my room.

Just below me, in the courtyard, I caught the day's first glimpse of my husband. Clad in shirtsleeves with some sort of sword in his hand. He fought an invisible enemy. His shirt was transparent with sweat. How that could be in the chilly November air, I could not say. His broad shoulders supported the heavy sword with ease. His movements were graceful, dance-like. He slashed and thrust and twirled. The movements were nothing like the awkward thrusting of last night. This was practiced.

Not for the first time I wondered if last night had been anything but. I had never heard of a gentleman in his twenties who hadn't partaken at a brothel but... That thought warmed me slightly, that my husband and I might have that in common, that we might learn together.

A tactful cough came from over my shoulder as Anna appeared at my side.

"Ahh, I should have known."

"I don't—"

"The maids all have that reaction too. You should see him with Tom and Michael, no one can decide who to admire more."

I hadn't yet met Michael, but Tom... Tall, and slightly lanky with youth, his eyes were bright, and his smile was always ready, so unlike my husband. I could understand the appeal.

"Do they do that often?"

"Tom joins him when he has time. Michael hasn't been here in years."

"Was there a falling out? I seem to have put my foot in it last night."

"I heard something to that effect," she said. Timothy cleared his throat—the culprit. "Her ladyship was not fond of him, so he spent a great deal of his youth in the kitchens with us. When his father passed, Hugh was just eleven, not prepared to take on the estate. Michael managed it until he came of age. There was some discord over Michael's future plans."

"Future plans?"

"Michael owns Wayland's. The gaming hell. His lordship does not approve. He thinks it tarnishes the family name."

"But Michael doesn't carry the family name, does he?"

Anna offered a mere shrug and headshake in response. I could see my mother-in-law rejecting a small boy due to his parentage. She seemed the type. But for Hugh to cut off his own brother over the possibility of an unfortunate connection... that was worrying.

Would my family, too, become unfortunate connections to be discarded? She was already displeased with Kit's and Sydney's occupations.

I pulled my gaze away from my husband. Gesturing to the bed coverings, "these will do until I can select something more to my taste."

"Of course, my lady." Timothy set about immediately stripping the bed, piling everything into a basket to be washed. A quick glance below told me that Hugh was still hacking and slashing away at his nonexistent enemy.

~

HUGH

I spent the best part of the day performing footwork drills and point control. It had become a more regular occupation since my engagement. The months had honed my skill, the practice had become ritualistic. It was the work of mere minutes before my mind emptied and my body took over. I could think of little beyond the cool air rushing through my lungs and the burn of my muscles.

Unfortunately, today the burn was in a slightly different location—and I knew the reason. Every advance twinged usually. The cadence was reminiscent of a different rhythm in a different location.

Katherine, with her floral essence and silky curls and breathy sighs... How was I to think of anything else? How did anyone achieve anything when they had a wife? I have a vague memory that I had not always found her so appealing. Clearly, I had been a foolish dolt.

It was only my carefully held control that prevented me from seeking her out, hauling her over a shoulder, and carrying her back to the bedroom. In my fantasy she shrieked with delight.

The rest of the day was spent in my study, far away from my too tempting wife. When the time came for dinner, I arrived in the drawing room to the vision of my wife perched politely on the settee with a book.

Objectively, I knew the sight would not have been so

arresting before last night, but now it was... alluring. She did not hear my arrival, and I was free to observe her unnoticed.

Katherine leaned slightly to one side against the arm of the settee, one foot tucked underneath her leg with a slipper abandoned below her. Her gown was a dark, jade green, with little but a strip of lace where the bodice met the skirt for embellishment. Like the navy she had worn last night, it suited. Her coiffure was pinned back with simple elegance, no baubles to be seen. In the dying daylight and the flickering of the fire, I thought I could just make out a flush on one shoulder, irritation from my bristles, perhaps. That was equal parts warming and worrying. I would have to be careful with her delicate skin, but the marks—they named her as mine.

Whatever her novel, it held her interest quite thoroughly. Not once did she give any indication that she noticed me from my perch against the doorframe. Page after page passed in silent study.

When I could take it no longer, I shifted, making purposeful rustles. She started, her back shooting ramrod straight and her foot slipping down to join its companion on the floor. There was something disconcerting about the gesture, unnatural. I missed her previous ease.

Before I could speak a word, urge her to relax, I heard Mother's stern, precise footsteps from down the hall. I, too, straightened, pulling away from the door and farther into the room. It was something of a surprise to see Mother today. I expected with all the excitement yesterday that she might have one of her megrims this evening. But here she was, entering in all her formidable glory.

Once Mother had been situated in a chair by the fire, we remained in an overpronounced silence until one of the footmen called us to dinner. Katherine stepped around me and into the dining room, not waiting for me to hand Mother up or escort them both.

My irritation at the rude gesture dissipated at once when I saw what changes she had made. Instead of the full sixteen-person place setting Mother preferred, she had adjusted the table down to seat just four. It was intimate, appealing. I could see the benefit of it when I dropped Mother off at her place between the head and foot. Mother made a choked wordless noise upon entry and again in finding the spot that had always been her usurped.

In retrospect, I realized that Mother had been in the wrong place last night. And that her former seat belonged to Katherine now. The adjustment would surely be difficult for Mother. Perhaps Katherine could have been kinder in making her point. But, knowing Mother, kindness would not have resulted in the necessary behavioral amendments. I mentally applauded my wife's ingenuity.

Sixteen

HUGH

A FEW DAYS LATER, Katherine's first visitor arrived as soon as could reasonably be termed appropriate. I believe she mentioned something about her friend during dinner last night, but I could not recall precisely.

The girl wore a gray gown of half-mourning. That explained why I did not recognize her from the wedding or Season. She was pretty, taller than Katherine, but lacking the luscious curves I was rapidly developing an obsession with.

Our greeting, though brief, showed the girl to be well-mannered and decorous. I slipped off to my study while Katherine provided a tour of her new home.

I had not paid attention to the second entrance to my study, the one into the library, when I arrived. In a fortuitous circumstance, it was cracked open slightly. I had the opportunity to hear the raptures our visitor expressed at the sight of our library.

"Kate, it is wonderful! You do not mind if I live here, right? Perhaps a little nest of blankets by the fire just there?"

"I knew I would not be able to peel you away from this room. That's why I saved it for last."

I ought to get up, close the door, and allow them their privacy. I even made it so far as rising to the door but curiosity ate at me and I lingered instead. Listening.

"I've asked Anna to bring the tea tray in here," Katherine said in a conspiratorial tone.

"You are my favorite person in the entire world."

"I am hoping you'll be able to take a look at some of my gowns before you become too lost to the world."

"Oh dear, did Her Grace help with your trousseau?"

"Help is a word... Not the one I would use."

"That unfortunate?" The girl asked.

Before Katherine responded, I heard a knock at the library door and the clatter of one of the maids and footmen with a tray followed by the rustle of fabric. The gowns?

"Oh my, that is unfortunate."

"Aunt Prudence has never met a lace or a ribbon she found wanting," Katherine explained.

"So, it would seem..." The knock of wooden hangers against each other interrupted the rustle of lace and ribbon. "I could add a bit behind this lace, here, to make it more comfortable. To remove it entirely... I don't believe there is enough fabric in the bodice. The skirt would end up attached in the middle of your bosom."

"Flattering..." Katherine's tone was dry and sharp and brand new to me.

"Indeed. This nightgown, I may be able to work with this one..." A nightgown? Intriguing.

"Turn it over."

"Oh dear. Why only on the back?"

"I've no idea."

"And your aunt thought this would... entice? I do not know much about the desires of men but that seems like a lot of frippery. How, exactly, did she manage to marry off her daughter?"

"Impeccable breeding, a massive dowry, and the face of an angel."

"I suppose that would do it. Kate, you said they were unfortunate, but I had no idea. Why did you not say anything?"

"You were caring for Aunt Sophie, and then you were in mourning. Besides, they were not all this unfortunate. My engagement seemed to bring out her worst taste."

"Perhaps some of Sophie's gowns?"

"Absolutely not. I can have new gowns made. But I know those are your only options."

I had never heard that tone out of my wife, sharp and insistent. It was strangely... erotic.

"But they would certainly suit your figure more than mine. And these cannot possibly be comfortable."

"I did inherit the family bust... Still, I have faith in your efforts. You absolutely must take a look at the embroidery thread and sewing notions I brought with me. Take whatever you need."

"I could not possibly."

"You will leave here with at least one book and as many sewing notions as you can carry," Katherine insisted.

"Kate..."

"Jules... Please? Let me help. I had Aunt Prudence, flawed though her efforts may be, her intentions were pure. You're to navigate the Season with no one to guide you."

"If you are certain..."

"I am, now drink your tea and stop trying to give me things you need."

Her friend offered a put upon sigh that I was almost certain was false. Katherine's answering chuckle confirmed it.

"How is marriage treating you?" Instead of the elations and raptures I expected, my wife sighed. "Kate?"

"It's just... a lot of change. And Christmas is upon us, and it will be my first without my family." Katherine's answer was small, sorrowful. I had not considered that she might be having difficulty adjusting. Surely that would ease with time.

"Will Kit not be joining you?"

"I had not asked," Katherine said. "Lady Grayson certainly would not approve."

"Surely she could not object to you including your brother in the festivities."

"She objects to everything I do."

Certainly, that was a falsehood. Obviously, Mother had not yet warmed to Katherine. But she could not possibly object to the small changes my wife had made to the house.

"I am positive that is untrue. Who could object to you? Perhaps she is having difficulty adjusting herself. It must be quite a change for her, to go from mistress of her home to a guest in it. Have you tried to include her? Seek her advice on matters?"

I quite liked this friend, all very sensible suggestions.

"I suppose I should try to do that. Enough about me. How are your efforts to prepare for your Season?" Katherine asked.

Did ladies not discuss the marital bed? At least in careful euphemisms? Feedback would have been appreciated.

"As well as can be expected. I will never finish all my tailoring and improvements in time."

The conversation never returned to our marriage. I lingered, listening through a mind-dulling discussion of sewing notions and embroidery techniques. Hovering until long after all speech had ceased and Katherine's friend had taken to casing the bookshelves, punctuated only by brief expressions of delight at whatever she found.

At last, I turned to the shelf where I stored the drinks, pouring the scotch with a heavy hand. I was certainly not brooding while I sat behind the great wooden desk, feet propped atop, wondering why Katherine had directed her friend away from questions about our marriage with such determination.

KATE

Juliet's visit was such a relief. Even though she confirmed what I already knew about the unfortunate nature of the gowns and nightdresses that my aunt had insisted on. She was a breath of fresh air.

Unfortunately, she also provided me with a source of some sympathy for Lady Grayson. It would be difficult to watch the home I'd decorated and loved, full of things I had carefully cultivated, ransacked for parts. Of course, now I was left with the actual task of trying to include her while still carving a place for myself in a house that seemed to have no space for me.

That was the chafing feeling I hadn't been able to identify. Not until now. Nothing here was mine. Not my bedroom, slightly improved by new bedding, but still not mine. Not my closet, still filled with unflattering colors, itchy lace, and tangled ribbons.

I hadn't noticed, not until Jules eased the ache that had formed, but I missed my family. I longed for my home. These were unproductive feelings. This was my new family and my new home. I just had to find a way to make both of them *feel* like mine.

Between over-small bites of partridge—the first thing that Mrs. Hudson had made that was not to my taste—I threw the question to my companions. "Lady Juliet reminded me that

Christmas is nearly upon us. Do you have any particular family traditions?"

It was Hugh who answered, distractedly pushing the partridge around on his plate—we won't be having that again, then. "Tom will join us on Christmas Eve and stay until Boxing Day."

"That's wonderful. Does Michael join as well?"

The dowager choked on the overdry bird, but Hugh gave a curt, "no." As if that were all there was to the discussion. Did the man have anywhere else to go? It was not as though he chose his parentage.

Since Jules put the idea in my head this afternoon, I was desperate to host Kit for Christmas. In retrospect, I probably should have left the infamous Michael out of the discussion to ease the way for my own ends. "Do you suppose there might be room for one more? I would like to invite my brother while he remains in town."

Both responded at the same time. The dowager's insistent, "absolutely not, there will be no room at all," overshadowed her son's more measured response.

"I see no reason why you should not. It is Christmas after all." It was the first time my husband had sided with me over his mother. It warmed something inside me, all the way to my toes. Distracted with my delight, I took a normal-sized bite of partridge and had to choke it down.

She was undeterred by her son's response. "The servants will want time off for the holidays. They cannot be feeding and caring for the whole of Lincolnshire whilst understaffed."

Hugh swallowed hard against his bite of poultry. Without looking at me, he responded, "Apologies, Mother would know better than I what the staff can manage. I should defer to her superior expertise. Perhaps it would be better if you did not invite him."

At once the few bites I had managed to choke down

turned hard and cold in my stomach. Quickly, I buried my gaze in my plate, fighting back tears. His answer was all the crueler for the previous "yes"—more hateful for the seconds of hopeful cheer that had begun to rise.

Biting comments ran through my mind. To the dowager, "Is the staff not well trained enough to handle a single additional visitor?" "Would my brother be more welcome if he had a title?"

And to my husband, "why is your brother's presence more important than mine?" "Was your original answer only a yes because your mother hadn't responded yet?"

Then I remembered Juliet's comments from earlier. It would be a difficult holiday for my mother-in-law, her first without the title of mistress of the house. I could survive one Christmas without Kit. He would come next year when I would be more sure of my place.

I swallowed back the tears filling my throat. I was still unequal to the task of meeting my husband's gaze. "Of course, the staff should be with their families on the holiday. I would not wish to overtax anyone."

The rest of the dinner was endless. I ached to hide away in my room—as much as it was my room—needing to be free from the confines of this table.

It took nearly five minutes to wrest my gaze from the unfortunate partridge on my plate. Eyes first landing on my husband, whose own study of his plate put mine to shame. Then to the dowager. *She* met me with a haughty expression, one brow lifted, and she raised her fork, a bite of unpalatable partridge on it, taking the bite, and chewing with pursed lips. She, alone, enjoyed the dinner. She even gave her shoulders a subtle back and forth of superiority before glancing back down at her plate with a smirk, returning with another fork-full.

I grabbed my nearby wine and took a thick swallow,

stuffing my irritation and hurt further down. Nothing in the world could have induced me to sit in the drawing room with the two of them that night. Fortunately, I was able to plead a headache without lying. More fortunately still, for the first time since our marriage vows, my husband saw fit to leave me alone that night.

Seventeen

GRAYSON HOUSE, LONDON — DECEMBER
25, 1813

HUGH

CHRISTMAS ARRIVED TOO QUICKLY. Katherine seemed to settle into her role as mistress of the house well enough. Though there was the occasional struggle with Mother. Her friend visited nearly twice weekly, always in the library, and always leaving with at least one book, usually three or four. I never had the good fortune to be able to listen at the door again.

Now that I understood my wife's gown selection a bit better, I was less put-off by the ribbons and lace. She visited the modiste one day nearly a week ago with Ladies Celine and Davina. I had high hopes for a new wardrobe from that trip in the near future.

At night, she was warm and soft and sweet smelling, and every moment was lovely.

Today though, after church she visited with her brother instead of returning home. I did not begrudge the effort, particularly after my faux pas with Mother the other night.

When she returned, she was quiet, withdrawn—nearly

sullen. I tried to remind myself of her conversation the other day. She missed her family. This was a great deal of change. Throughout the day, she rallied, and by the time Tom arrived she was in her usual subdued good humor.

Mrs. Hudson made a truly excellent roast, and I was particularly looking forward to the Christmas pudding.

Tom, having learned quickly that his role was to fill conversation, asked Katherine, "so, Kate, did Kit return to Lincolnshire for the holidays? It's quite a long trip, is it not?"

"No, he remains in town."

"He had somewhere else to be for Christmas dinner then?"

"I believe he found a friend who could accommodate him."

"Why did you not have him here? I know you have not had Anna's Christmas pudding, but that alone should have been enough incentive to attend. I dream of it all year long."

I could take no more. "Tom..."

At my warning tone he looked to me, confusion plain on his furrowed brow. He stared at me, a beat too long, before turning back to Katherine. Then his gaze shifted to Mother, who gave her roast far more attention that even such an excellent cut was due. Finally, he turned back to me, something accusatory in his expression. Or perhaps that was my own guilt.

"Apologies, Kate," he said. "I hope you will be sure to include him next year. I enjoyed speaking with him at your wedding breakfast. He seems an interesting fellow."

My wife offered nothing more than a half-hearted nod in response. Clearly recognizing Mother's previous explanation for the reed thin excuse that it was. Suddenly the roast was somewhat less delectable.

At length she answered. "Perhaps, but I believe he will

finish his studies before next Christmas. Currently, he plans to practice closer to home to be near our parents."

"You should invite your entire family. It would be nice to have a big group some time. It has been just the three of us for years. And before that we only had the occasional addition of Michael."

"That is a nice idea, but I wouldn't want to overtax anyone."

"What do you mean?"

"The servants, it would be too much to have such a large group visit."

"I see." There was confirmed suspicion in Tom's tone. "Easter then."

Unable to take the forlorn expression on my wife's face a moment longer, I interjected, "Yes, definitely Easter."

Katherine's gaze finally abandoned her plate, meeting mine, eyes wide with something akin to hope. For a long moment, no one moved. I, at least, was waiting for Mother to present an issue to that arrangement. Even she must have felt displeasure in Tom's expression and tone because, while she made no agreement, she also did not argue the issue.

Finally, at long last, the pudding was brought out. Pudding cured all ills, particularly this Christmas pudding— Anna's Tom indicated? I thought she was a maid now, not a cook. Regardless of who was responsible, it was every bit as delicious as I remembered. Even Katherine seemed to brighten at the taste.

"CARE TO EXPLAIN why your wife thinks one additional guest will overtax the servants beyond reason?" Tom accused —not even waiting for me to pour the drinks.

"Mother may have suggested it would be too much."

"And you did not step in and assure Kate that it would not?"

"What do I know of the capacity of servants?"

"Enough to know that one additional person could not possibly cause much difficulty. Particularly since the person would not even require a room for the night. Mrs. Hudson would never hear of leaving someone out on a holiday, and you know it. She would rap your knuckles with a spoon right now if she knew you had let that girl's brother be left to find some other home for Christmas." He took a thick swallow of the port I poured while he ranted.

"I'll thank you not to refer to my wife as 'that girl.'"

"Really Hugh? That is the part you take issue with? Tonight was badly done. Kate has left her home, her family, everything she knows to join this family, and you won't allow her the comfort of her brother at supper on the holiday?"

"Mother said—"

"Oh, Mother said, did she? Well, I suppose since Kate married Mother, she should have final say. And oh, I forgot Mother is viscount as well, so of course you could not consult the servants yourself to confirm her flimsy excuse."

"Tom—"

"No, Hugh. You've married Kate—your allegiance should be to her."

"But—"

"Damn it, Hugh. What, what excuse could you possibly have?"

"I did not intend to marry Katherine. She was compromised. I had no choice."

"What has that to do with anything? She is your wife, your viscountess. Treat her as such!"

"This is none of your concern, Tom. You should not be involved."

"I became involved when I watched your wife on the verge of tears at supper."

"She was hardly on the verge of tears. And I am finished discussing the matter."

"Fine, but you owe your wife an apology."

"Tom!"

"I'm finished. This is good port."

The vintage was of fine quality, but it tasted like vinegar in my mouth.

Eighteen

THORNTON HALL, KENT — DECEMBER 27, 1813

KATE

MY HONEYMOON... How strange it sounded.

Even though I had nearly a month of marriage to my name, the entire endeavor felt like a surreal dream from which I could not wake.

Tom had spirited my mother-in-law away the day before Hugh and I left for the country. She was set to take in the waters in Bath for her megrims. Given that I was the primary cause of her megrims, I had high hopes that Bath would revive her but little confidence in the longevity of her cure when she returned to town. Why the waters in Bath were any different to the waters at nearby Margate, who was to say? My preference was for their distance.

It was a relief to experience the overwhelming house without her judgmental gaze. And overwhelming it was, massive and stunning in equal measure. The exterior was a well-maintained red brick with slate roofing. It jutted from the center of a circular drive, imposing in its size—it was easily five times the size of my parents's vicarage.

The interior was clearly Agatha's doing, unfortunately. Once again, filled with expensive furnishings of poor quality designed entirely with fashion in mind. But there was one advantage the home offered that the London house did not.

A pianoforte.

I nearly cried at the sight of the magnificent instrument. It was made of a rich, warm wood with delicate inlays and decor. My husband and his mother may not care for music, but someone in the not-too distant past was an aficionado.

There was a thick layer of dust over the entire instrument, and I blew it away from the keys before tapping down on the middle c.

I could not hold back a wince—out of tune. That was to be expected. That could be remedied. Already, my fingers itched to grace the keys once more, but I forced myself to wait. It would be all the sweeter for tuning.

The London house suffered for lack of a housekeeper. It was clear from the state of the music room that this home was in the same desperate need.

Anna and the rest of the staff who joined us in the country had been hard at work already, airing out my boudoir of the lingering stench of death and lilacs that followed the dowager. It was much too large a home to maintain only when the family was in residence. It required regular love and care.

With the staff seeing to far too many duties, and my husband meeting with his solicitor, I was left to explore on my own. I was grateful for the reprieve. For the few moments his absence afforded me to be Kate, thoroughly overwhelmed by her new position and home, instead of Lady Grayson, Viscountess.

I almost laughed when I stumbled into the library. Jules thought the library in town was impressive... I would need to invite her for a visit. Though I would certainly never see her again when I did. She would be buried in the mountain of tomes, never to be seen again.

Hours later and exploration unfinished, I meandered in the direction that I recalled the dining room to be. I had directed an informal meal; everyone was much too busy to manage a full supper.

The dining room, that was overwrought as well. Another oversized table certainly capable of seating at least twenty. There hadn't been time to see about shrinking it down, so I ordered my place setting next to Hugh. Incorrect, it may be, but I was not willing to shout at my husband an entire meal.

He was already seated when I arrived, looking in askance at the setting at his side. I sat myself, not wishing to disturb the footman for such formalities.

Braced as I was for disapproval, he shocked me with a grin. It was crooked, and made his eyes crinkle in the corners. There was a dimple on the upturned side. Inanely, I wondered if he had dimples in both cheeks or just the one.

It was a punch to the gut, how handsome he was at that moment. He was beautiful—blindingly so. Now that the steely slash of his mouth had relaxed, I could see his lower lip was fuller than his upper. I had the absurd desire to taste it.

He had taken the notion of a casual dinner to heart as well, wearing only a waistcoat with his shirtsleeves rolled to his elbows, no cravat to be found. His hair was ruffled, tousled, as if he'd run his fingers through it more than once.

I knew I was staring, likely in an incredibly insipid fashion, but *good lord*. How was I to speak, to think, to breathe next to *that*? In slow motion, I could see the grin start to fall, no doubt self-consciousness shifting in at the corners.

More than anything I had wanted in weeks, months, since that night in the closet, perhaps before, I wanted that grin back.

"Sorry, I don't think I've ever seen you smile quite like that."

"Surely that's not true," he said, grin slipping further away.

"Don't stop, I like it."

He blinked, parsing my words for a moment, before the grin returned, even more brilliant than before. This time he added a crooked brow to the mix, pleased with himself. He straightened too, running a hand through his hair, preening. For me? It wasn't my gut that received this punch this time. Instead, it hit lower, in a completely new way.

I liked that too.

I felt an answering smile blooming on my face. Without warning, without bidding, words from months ago flashed through my mind, "her lips are too big."

My heart sank, and I caught my oversized lower lip between my teeth before it could offend, sliding my gaze down to my plate.

Beneath the table, I felt a bump against my knee. Hugh had nudged my knee with his own, teasing or friendly perhaps. His effort had the desired effect, and I met his eyes once more.

"What happened? Where did you go just then?" His eyes were wide, earnest.

"Sorry, I just remembered something someone said one time. Shall I ring for dinner? I suspect they're distracted with opening the house and lost track of time." I tried for an unaffected air, but it rang hollow to me.

"All right." His tone lowered in response, drawing out the word hesitantly. Clearly, he was unsatisfied with my answer but unwilling to press me. Good.

Objectively I knew I could not hold one drunken speech against him for the rest of our lives, it would not make my situation anymore tenable. But something about the words had found a home in my mind, flitting past at the most inopportune times and slicing deep. Death by a thousand cuts of my own making.

~

TRY AS I MIGHT, the jovial grin from earlier was gone. Truthfully, I could not bring myself to exert myself for its return.

The next morning, I awoke with renewed determination. If I could not succeed as a wife, surely I could succeed as a viscountess.

As usual, my husband was nowhere to be found. Presumably hiding in the study or practicing his fencing drills on the grounds somewhere.

No matter, I was determined to pay a visit to the vicarage. I needed information, and the vicar's wife was certain to have it.

When I found Anna, she had kindly taken to dusting. The task was far below her current duties, but she made no issue of it. She was, however, easily persuaded to abandon it in favor of escorting me to my destination.

The vicarage was no more than a mile away, and there was nothing more than a light dusting of snow blowing past us on the tree-lined pathway. When we passed the stables, Anna promised to introduce me to the horses on our way back.

The vicarage itself was formed of the same red bricks as the house and well loved. It featured a small rose garden that I was certain would be breathtaking in peak season. We were ushered into the small, cheerful sitting room quickly. There we met a small, pretty woman who had definitely seen some fifty years but certainly not more than sixty. She had hints of gray at her temples under her cap and warm, honey-colored eyes. Physically, she was nothing like my mother. But her presence, the essence of her bursting forth from her smile... She shared my mother's heart.

Perhaps the role cultivated such a countenance, or perhaps such a countenance was drawn to the role. Mrs. Sarah Hughes, I quickly learned, had served this parish with her husband for more than thirty-five years. She preferred her tea with far too much sugar and a splash of milk. Anna's lemon tarts were well missed in the parish. Little Mariah Bell, not so little anymore, had grown quite pretty and married the butcher's son. In addition to these gems, I learned any number of other things about any number of other people I had yet to meet. Perfect.

"So, Mrs. Hughes, I am hoping you might be able to help me. You see, the estate is in desperate need of a housekeeper. Mrs. Hudson is running herself ragged trying to do those duties as well as cook. Do you know of anyone looking for work who might be qualified?"

She tapped her chin thoughtfully for a moment before answering. "You should speak to Mrs. Lydia Tanner. She was housekeeper over at the old Revello estate until she wed. Her eldest is out of the house now, and I expect she might be bopping around at home looking for trouble to get into."

"That's just the sort of person I'm looking for. Thank you! I expect we will need at least another maid and footman for this house, do you have any suggestions there?

"Oh, I think young Matthew Smithson is looking. He broke his leg badly a few years ago and has difficulty with the farming tasks. Though, footman in a house that size might be too much for him," she said.

"I'll speak with him. Get his thoughts on the matter, perhaps if he's given opportunities to sit, he can manage."

"That's good, though her ladyship will not approve. Well, I suppose you're her ladyship now, aren't you? I'll have a further think on the maid."

"Thank you. I'd like to begin visiting tenants as soon as

possible, perhaps you can provide some direction there as well? Where I should start? Who might need items that I can provide them, food, blankets, and the like?"

"Of course, dear. I must admit, when I heard the viscount took a wife, I would never have expected you," she said in a teasing laugh.

Though I knew the words to be true, and though I'd heard them throughout my engagement, they still stung. Especially when I had thought Mrs. Hughes and I were forming the beginnings of an easy friendship in the few minutes we'd known each other.

"That seems to be the consensus." Though I could hear the bitter undertone in my voice, I didn't think she would be able to detect it.

"Yes, I feared the worst, but you're a delight."

I froze for a moment, waiting for her to continue, to drag me back down.

"She is, isn't she?" Anna added, cheerfully.

My heart swelled twice its normal size and a lump rose in my throat as I fought back grateful tears.

"Thank you. I am trying but I do hope you'll let me know where I can improve." My words were thick with emotion, and Mrs. Hughes offered a warm, comforting smile.

"Well, you cannot possibly be worse than the dowager. But I promise to tell you when you're being daft. Yes?"

A laugh burst from my chest, deep and grateful. "Yes, please."

"Good, have another cup of tea, dear. Tea cures all ills."

"Yes, Mrs. Hughes."

"You're learning already. That is always the correct response." With another laugh, I took a grateful sip.

I wiled away the afternoon, in this vicarage that felt like home. With the woman who was not my mother, but comforted me the way my mother did. And the girl who was rapidly becoming a sister to me.

For the first time since I stepped out of the carriage at Lady James's ball, it seemed as though everything might actually be all right.

Nineteen

THORNTON HALL, KENT – DECEMBER 28, 1813

HUGH

I WAS DEVELOPING one of Mother's megrims—lord, I hoped those were not heritable. It had been two hours of back and forth with Mr. Matthews, the steward of Thornton Hall. Two hours of listed problems, and needed improvements. And two hours of insisting that there are not enough funds coming in to fix the problems and execute the improvements. A claim which was patently absurd because I sent more than enough funds to cover such things every month.

I wished I had been able to let him go along with the solicitor Michael hired during his tenure.

Mr. Forsyth, my solicitor, was always amiable and pleasant to meet with.

Mr. Matthews was always one complaint after another, and "Michael did it this way," and "Michael left instructions that the irrigation system was of the utmost importance." *Michael is not here, and Michael is not viscount.*

Finally, after another hour filled with pointless arguments, he agreed to return later in the week with documentation. As though one could trust the books of a man hired by a notorious gambler, liar, and cheat.

My wife was nowhere to be found for luncheon and one of the footmen told me that she went to visit the vicarage. That was a surprise. I could count on one hand, perhaps one finger, the number of times Mother sought out Mr. and Mrs. Hughes. Perhaps it was something to do with Katherine's upbringing.

Wandering through the halls of my estate, my muscles were tight, tensed for some unknown action. I needed exercise. In town, my chosen activity was always fencing.

The one diversion that the country allowed that the city did not. Riding. Not just riding; galloping across the countryside, heedless of those around you. Racing for miles while the wind rushed through your hair.

Occupation found, I changed and set off for the stables—for Perseus. I ordered the blood bay stallion saddled. I allowed him a moment to readjust to me, it had been some time since we saw each other. Then we were galloping across the fields.

My muscles tensed and released in time with his. Orchards and fields passed in a blur. Finally, Perseus decided he was finished with his gallop. He was a stubborn one. He loved to sprint across the open land until he did not. Without another horse to push him on when he was done there was no dissuading him.

I dismounted next to a pond, allowing him a few moments to refresh himself. We were somewhere on the Smith farm, perhaps the northeast corner? The field beside me was almost entirely underwater, the edges swirled with a mixture of frost and mud. The drainage must be abysmal here. Perhaps Mr. Matthews had a small point regarding the irrigation issues. That field would not be plantable in the spring as it stood.

Silently, I vowed to take another look at the books to see if funds could be provided for such improvements. I had no idea what such a thing would cost though, surely a substantial sum.

At last, Perseus had sated himself at the pond, but he kicked at the ground in protest when I attempted to mount him. He really did best with his lady love to show off for, Andromeda. I tugged him reluctantly along until we reached the road, where he finally allowed me up.

We walked along at a stubbornly slow pace past the old mill. It had certainly seen better days, two of the blades were broken off completely and another was damaged quite beyond repair. Perhaps Mr. Matthews had a large point. My burgeoning megrim was returning with a vengeance.

MY RIDE back to the house was considerably longer. It was approaching supper when I finally returned. I stepped inside, with no staff to be found, I was left to hang my hat on my own. I trailed down the hall, fully intending to dress for dinner when I heard it. A bright, allegro piece—Mozart perhaps—from the pianoforte in the music room.

Katherine.

I had almost forgotten her penchant for the piano. But now, notes slipping one right after another in perfect measure in a dance of fingers, and I remembered. Nothing in the world could have kept me from her in that moment. My body recalled the enchanting sight of her playing; dragging me, compelling me forward.

In the hallway just outside the music room, I found the entirety of the household staff. They curved around the entry to the room, staring, awestruck, at the sight and sound of my wife. When they caught a glimpse of me, they startled before scurrying off to whatever duties they had been neglecting. I could hardly blame them for stopping to appreciate her.

Alone in the hall at last, I moved to the open doorway. Framed by the massive windows, the sun setting behind her, my wife was lost to her keys. Her wide eyes were closed, dark lashes spilling onto flushed cheeks. Her dexterous fingers moved, seemingly of their own volition, across the keys quick and light as a bird's wings. Her playing was passionate but unstudied. There was no performance here, no artifice in her. She had not even noticed her previous audience's arrival or departure, and she did not know me now. She was lost to the music, and it was breathtaking.

She wore a dark rose gown tonight. It had no embellishment save a small scrap of lace at the bodice. Her gowns had improved substantially since the modiste delivered them a few days before we left town. They fit to distraction, cupping her generous bosom, highlighting her nipped waist, before hinting at the luscious hips and thighs below. Her hair was loosely twisted away from her face, it too was unadorned. The silky strands caught the fading light behind her, each curl a silky ribbon.

I could bask in this sight every single day for the rest of my life and never tire of it.

For the first time, without caveat, I knew with every piece of my soul, that my wife was exquisitely, stunningly, mind-numbingly beautiful. Not sensuous, like in my dream, not alluring, the way she was at Lady James's ball—though she was those things too—but she was just unbearably beautiful. And she was mine. Forever.

⁓

I HOVERED IN THE DOORWAY, far longer than I ought, before Stevens pulled me away to dress for dinner. Katherine never once noticed me, too lost in the notes around her.

Already seated in the dining room when I arrived, she was once again settled beside me instead of in her proper position at the other end of the table. I much preferred her by my side. She was still in that dark, red-pink gown that highlighted curves without detracting from her natural beauty. Her cheeks were still flushed from her exertions. Glancing up from her place setting, she offered me a small, tightlipped smile.

"Hello," my voice cracked, and I had to clear my throat before continuing. "I heard you playing earlier. Did you have someone in to tune it?"

"Oh, I'm sorry. Should I not have?"

"Of course you should. We should see about getting an instrument for the London house as well. I had nearly forgotten your exceptional talent."

The footman arrived with the soup. She remained silent until he left before dipping her spoon. "I would never say no to a piano, but I'm certain 'exceptional' is far beyond my talents."

"It is not." Her eyes snapped to me, a turbulent turquoise in the light of the tapers. I could not fully read her expression. I expected a pleased response but there was an edge that I had not anticipated and could not name.

"I understand you went to the vicarage today." I said, changing the unexpectedly tumultuous subject.

"Yes, we are in desperate need of a housekeeper, at least one maid and a footman as well. Mrs. Hughes was able to point me in the direction of both a housekeeper and footman."

"That will save us the effort of putting a notice out. I would not have thought to consult her."

"Mama always knows who is hiring or who is in need of employment. I also thought to start making charitable visits to tenants. Vicars' wives always know who is in need of what."

She was going to visit the tenants? I had heard of such things of course, but it was never something Mother did. The idea of my wife, caring for my tenants, making a home here; it caused a warmth to swell in my chest. "That is a good notion. Have you given thought to improvements you might wish to make to the house?"

"Some. Anything that can be purchased locally, I would like to do so. It will take longer but it is good for the community, and I believe the quality will be better. I've always found that local craftsmen have a sense of pride in their work, particularly when they know it will be displayed to great advantage." Her posture loosened as she spoke, relaxing into her convictions. I could not disagree with her assessment.

Still, I had hoped she would make changes to her bedroom sooner rather than later. It was... disconcerting, to visit her in what had been Mother's chambers. Mother's scent had not had the opportunity to dissipate last night and it was something of a distress. One night and I had begun to miss the jasmine and orange blossom essence that permeated Katherine's room in London. And her person if I were honest.

"You went riding, I understand."

"Yes, I inspected a few of the farms." While racing through them at a gallop. "Do you ride?"

She hesitated for a moment, as though the simple question was a trap. "Yes, I enjoy riding." Katherine finally added, slowly, parsing each word as she spoke.

"Perhaps some time you might join me?" She merely nodded in answer, turning distractedly to the footman as he brought in the pheasant.

Though it was perhaps more than we had spoken at once in the entirety of our marriage, I could not help but lament the uneasy silence when it returned. Somehow, I had said the wrong thing. Again. What it was or why it was wrong remained a mystery. But I did seem to possess a talent for it.

Twenty

KATE

COUNTRY LIVING SUITED ME. I made friends with the tenants, hired a housekeeper, began replacing furnishings, had somewhat stilted supper conversations with my husband, and settled into something like a life. But ever looming was the threat of town, of returning to the strict social protocols, of living with Agatha once again. I feared *that* most of all.

When the time came, I was not ready for it. The carriage sped across the countryside with alarming ease. Never before had I prayed for a rut or downed tree on a journey, but I did that day. No catastrophe of the sort befell us.

We arrived back in town only a day before Tom returned with Agatha. One final reprieve.

Once again, we had a quiet supper, just the two of us. An idea had been nagging me for the past week or so. It consisted of one part desire to mend fences, and two parts desire to have Tom act as a buffer between Agatha and myself. Positive this would be my last opportunity, I finally broached it. "In the country, my parents always hosted a weekly dinner where any family nearby was expected to attend. Do you think perhaps we could try that here? Invite Tom weekly?"

My husband answered distractedly, moving his asparagus around his plate more than eating it. "Certainly, that sounds like a fine idea."

Now for the real trick... "I was wondering, if it would, perhaps, be a nice gesture to invite Michael? I would like to meet him."

His eyes snapped from his plate to mine, expression unreadable. "You wish to invite Michael?"

"Yes." No wavering, no hedging. I knew little of the man, but what I did was intriguing. Mrs. Hughes and the other tenants spoke exceedingly highly of him. Anna considered him to be one of her dearest friends. And Agatha seemed to hate the man with every fiber of her being which was quite the endorsement as far as I was concerned.

"Why?"

"I would like to get to know all of your family."

His gaze returned to his plate with the kind of focus I rarely saw without a saber in his hand. "I suppose you may invite him. Although I must warn you, he will not attend."

"Still, he should be afforded the opportunity, he is family after all."

Hugh offered a barely audible huff at that comment. "You will be the one to tell Mother," he directed.

"Of course." It was a fair, if unappetizing assignment. Content with a goal achieved, I returned to my own supper.

HE WAS ACTUALLY ATTENDING. Michael had agreed to attend.

I had to admit to some surprise. While the tone of my invitation had been somewhere between begging and manipulation, the man owed me nothing.

When I received a folded and sealed response from Anna this morning at the breakfast table, I nearly fell over.

"Michael is attending supper? You're certain?" Anna flushed, the words burst from her rapidly. She pulled the note from my hand, eyes stuttering rapidly over the page before flipping the note over, searching the empty back for something.

"What?"

"I'm sorry. That was unbearably rude. I just—I hadn't thought he would..." Her face and her chest now matched the flames of her hair. Suddenly I thought I might be missing something essential.

"Anna, is everything all right?"

"What?" she asked distractedly, still flipping the single page front to back, searching for information that was not there to be found. "Oh, yes. Everything is fine. I just thought he might..."

"Might what? Anna, what am I missing?"

Finally, she set the pages down beside me at the table with a resigned sigh. Her expression was more forlorn than I had ever seen before. In fact, I had never seen Anna anything other than cheerful. It was disconcerting.

"I thought he might bring someone with him."

"Who? Was there someone I should have invited?"

"No. No one."

"Anna?"

"I just... I hoped he might bring Augie with him."

What's an augie? "Augie?"

"Augustus Ainsley, the old stable master's son. He was a footman here before he left to help Michael at Wayland's."

Oh... That's an Augie—must be a handsome one.

"I see... Should I amend the invitation?"

"Oh, no. He would never join a formal dinner. I just

thought he might join us downstairs in the kitchens. I haven't seen him since his father passed, you see. It would be nice to catch up."

"There's nothing in the response to suggest that he would not bring his friend with him, particularly if he does not wish for a place setting."

"I suppose you're right." Her flush was receding slightly, leaving behind the prettiest blush on just the apples of her cheeks.

"Anna? Perhaps Mary can attend to me tonight? You might have some time to freshen up?"

"Oh, I'm certain that won't be necessary. There's nothing in the response that implies that Augie will attend either. All that besides, he's just an old friend. I don't know why I'm in such a state over it."

"A handsome old friend, I suspect?"

"Am I that obvious?" She buried her face in her hands and the words were muffled but clear.

"You're the picture of subtlety." I propped my chin on my hand, fixing her with wide interested eyes. "Tell me everything."

Her head popped back up, unable to hold back a grin. "He's so handsome. And kind. And funny. And smart. And wonderful."

"Handsome, kind, funny, smart, and wonderful? He would have to be all that and more to deserve you. It's settled. Mary will attend to me tonight."

"Oh, but what if he doesn't attend at all?"

"Then I shall make it clear he is to attend the next week."

"Next week?"

"These suppers will be weekly. At least until you're wed to your handsome, kind, funny, smart, wonderful gentleman."

Her face was alight with hope, even as she attempted to decline my offer. I would personally drag the man to the house by his ear if necessary. If anyone deserved to experience the hopeful delight clear in her countenance, it was Anna.

IF I FORGOT to let Agatha know that her stepson was dining with us tonight, it was entirely accidental. If I hovered by the window, eagerly awaiting the arrival of an unfamiliar carriage, it was entirely coincidental.

When said carriage—a fine carriage indeed—pulled up just outside, my heart stopped for a moment. It started again when not one, but two gentlemen descended from inside.

Biting back an unbearably pleased smile on Anna's behalf, I was entirely able to ignore Agatha's berating of Timothy. Michael had brought his friend for Anna. That, alone, was enough to endear him to me.

I could make out little in the way of detail in the dim lamp light. The two men wavered outside, the taller one gesturing toward the alley toward the kitchens. After some discussion, that gentleman lifted his hat to straighten his hair before righting it again. Then he scampered to the alley, the other man calling something after him. Now alone, he stared at the door with a sigh. The shorter one was Michael then.

I hovered just outside of Agatha's vision, barely suppressing the instinct to pace. Because I was listening for it, I heard the sounds of Weston opening the door and greeting the man. Hugh and Agatha gave no indication they noticed anything out of the ordinary in the slightest.

When I could stand it no longer, I made my way to the hallway. There I saw Weston with his arms around a man, I had never seen Weston be anything other than implacably professional. I could not stop the, "oh," that escaped at the sight of the warm familiarity between the men. The gentleman —Michael—turned to me at the sound.

He was shorter than my husband by at least a few inches, and his build was smaller and wiry. The way he carried himself... It was easier, freer than Hugh's precise perfection. His complexion was a shade or two darker than his brother's, with an olive undertone. His hair was dark, like my husband's, but warmer, a mahogany to Hugh's walnut. Where Hugh's eyes were that slate gray, Michael's were a melty chocolate. In every way my husband was cool, unapproachable; a stark contrast to his brother's welcoming warmth.

Michael was more like Tom in countenance, easy and loose-limbed in his bow, though he lacked the eager energy of youth that Tom brought to every interaction. He turned slightly, moving more fully into the light, I bit back a gasp at the state of his eye. I hadn't noticed in the shadows of the hall, but one eye was dark and swollen heavily with injury.

It was clear now, in spite of how approachable this man appeared, there was an edge to him. A confidence filled his frame, born of trials and tribulations I know nothing of. There was a weariness too, likely born of the same. He sized me up with the same intensity that I examined him. I wondered where I measured. If I was as much of a disappointment to him as I was to my own husband.

Suddenly, I felt a large hand land possessively on my lower back, hot and hard; my husband staking a claim. I should feel irritation at the gesture, Hugh had never felt the need to mark me before. Why would his brother bring out that instinct?

Finally, Michael spoke, "Hugh, good to see you." His voice was honey warm, higher in pitch than Hugh. There was an amusement in the tone, buried deep. He found Hugh's possessiveness entertaining. Hugh must have read it as well. His hand slid from my lower back around to tighten his fingers around my waist, his arm branding a strip across my back. Michael shifted on his feet, leaning back slightly, bringing his eye back into the light.

Instead of greeting his brother, Hugh spit out a flustered, "what on earth happened to your eye?"

Michael winced, as if only just remembering the injury himself. It seemed unlikely to me, it was severe, if he could see out of the eye at all I would be astounded.

At first, he offered only a crooked smirk in answer. When he spoke, there was a teasing lilt to his voice. "Do you know, it was the strangest thing. I was promenading in Hyde Park, as I like to do. Out of nowhere, this enormous swan dove straight from the sky at me. Beak first! Went right for my eye. Honestly, it's a miracle I wasn't killed."

I could no more restrain my giggle at that speech than I could stop the sun from rising in the morning. It was an effort to restrain a full snorting laugh. I knew he was mocking my husband. And I knew Hugh would not appreciate my amusement. But really, who could blame me?

Reminded of my existence, a person rather than a lamp he was claiming for his own, my husband replied. "Katherine, this is my brother Michael. Michael, this is Katherine Grayson, my wife."

"Pleasure to meet you, Lady Grayson," he answered with a proper bow.

Buoyed by his joke, I corrected him to Kate. With Weston's pointed cough, I directed everyone back to the drawing room.

Unfortunately, a few steps outside the room, Agatha's displeasure with a footman became apparent. And she had no idea who was waiting for her in the hall.

Twenty-One

GRAYSON HOUSE, LONDON - JANUARY 12, 1814

KATE

HUGH and I entered the drawing room first and were met with the sights and sounds of Agatha berating Timothy.

Behind me from the doorframe I heard something like a scuffle. I turned in time to see Weston offer a grin and a saucy wave before closing the doors behind Michael.

He surveyed the room quietly, taking in the situation with calculating eyes—eye. I could see the moment he marked the changes I made to the room. His expression was still unreadable, careful.

Agatha caught sight of me and shifted her ire from Timothy to me. "I suppose in the backwater county you hail from, they eat out of their hands like rodents?"

It was preferable to her abusing innocent staff, but the insult to my home smarted. She hadn't noticed Michael, hovering near the door, not willing to entirely abandon the exit. I bit back a retort for a moment, waiting for Hugh.

Any hope I had that the protective, possessive gesture from the hall would carry into the drawing room vanished.

143

Hugh had made his way to the sideboard, pouring a drink, entirely refusing to acknowledge his mother's vitriol.

Instead, it was Michael who came to my rescue, stepping into the room, drawing Agatha's attention. "Good evening, Lady Grayson. It's a pleasure to see you again. I hope you're in fine health."

It was a far more deferential speech than the woman deserved, especially with what I was given to understand about their relationship. Her eyes abandoned me and slid to his person with utter revulsion. They narrowed, as though he was an insect crushed and oozing under her shoe. Instead of the usual lemon-pursuing, her mouth twisted into a snarl. Her brows were drawn over beady eyes that were shuttered flat, dead, evil.

"What are you doing here?"

Five simple words. It should not be possible to spit so much contempt into five words, but she managed it. Oh lord, I should have warned her, told her. I should not have organized this in the first place. This poor man, here for dinner at my beckoning, was about to suffer abuse beyond what I thought her capable.

Instead of shrinking, as I would have done, or raging as most men would in the face of such hatred, he leaned back against the wall with purposeful casualness. As if such venom were entirely commonplace.

He answered, almost cheerful in his tone, "I was invited."

And then I realized. It *was* commonplace. It was every day. When had Agatha married his father? Surely, he could not have been more than six or seven years of age... Suddenly my heart ached for the boy this man had been.

She turned back to me, the only conceivable culprit. "Who would do that? Katherine? Did you invite this knave into my home?"

Words escaped me, still trapped in the unbearable sadness

for the boy who was no more. Before I could formulate a response, Michael shook his head from across the room.

"I was led to believe this was a family gathering. I am family, am I not?" That was certain to make the matter worse, but he adopted a cheeky grin. He was courting her ire. Encouraging it. Relishing in it.

"You're not! You're nothing but a street urchin my husband took pity on. And look how that turned out. A villain stealing the fortunes of respectable gentlemen, praying on their good natures! I should have had you thrown from the house when I first arrived, back to the sewers with the rats where you belong."

Michael remained unaffected, or, more likely, continued to feign it well. Hugh sighed, for a brief, brilliant second I thought that this—surely this—would be too much, that he would step in.

Instead, he drained a glass of something alcoholic, refilled it and handed a second glass to his brother. He knew. He expected it. And he let me invite his brother anyway. Now, he made no move to check his mother. If he could allow that speech, that utterly hateful, vile speech, to stand... Hugh would never defend me. I was utterly alone in this battle. Always.

Michael, clearly anticipating this reaction, just continued to rile her up. "But they're so easy to steal from. I'll do my best not to spread fleas over the furnishings while I'm here, Agatha."

Though she would not, I appreciated the casual address. The lady herself inhaled, drawing breath for another burst of flames. I could not allow a guest to be spoken to that way in my home, it was unconscionable. Before I could respond, the door flew open and Tom strolled in, casual and unaware, into the midst of a death battle.

His gaze flitted from brother to mother to brother to me.

Assessing the situation, the easy smile tugging at his lips did not falter for a second. He greeted us all with his usual affability. It hit me again that he was used to this, too. Playing the part of shield, deflecting blows between brother and mother. Of course, he was so skilled at sheltering me from his mother's outbursts, which were nothing compared to these.

Suddenly the too-long curls, loose, long limbs, free grin, and easy, enthusiastic manners took on a whole new meaning. This man had single-handedly stitched this family together for his entire life. Before I respected him, but now I was awestruck. He was brilliant.

"What happened to your eye, Brother?" he asked Michael. I appreciated all the more the way he freely made use of relation, the open affection in the tone.

"Satin shortage at the modiste."

Michael's response eased the last of the tension from the three of us. Hugh was still determined to find peace at the bottom of a bottle, and Agatha could do little more than *humph*.

After a brief back and forth over the satin and lace, poor Timothy returned to invite us to supper.

Since returning from my honeymoon, I had maintained an eighty percent success rate in securing my rightful place at the foot of the table from Agatha. I would not fail tonight. Timothy, always on my side, was more determined than usual to ensure I won the battle. I assume Agatha's berating had something to do with his efforts. He actually turned the chair to me, leaving her to huff and pout to her designated seat. Michael, having witnessed my immature but satisfying display, raised the wine at his place setting in a silent toast to my effort. I was forced to bite back a laugh.

Tom was in fine form, managing the conversation with a deft hand. At least the conversation from Michael and I. Occasionally Agatha would throw out a barely concealed insult.

Hugh remained stubbornly silent, drinking his supper rather than eating it.

When the time came for the sexes to separate, Michael chose to beg off. I could hardly blame him after his reception. Instead of separating, Agatha demanded Tom's attention tonight, and I was able to watch my wretched husband drink himself to an early grave the entire night.

Twenty-Two

GRAYSON HOUSE, LONDON – JANUARY 15, 1814

HUGH

I FELT LIKE DEATH. But really, who could blame me, drinking was the only way through that disaster of a dinner. At some point, I fell asleep in my study.

Now awake, my head seemed to be making a valiant effort to leave my neck. I supposed sleeping on a desk would do that. Stevens had been by at some point in the not-too distant past if the lukewarm tea was evidence. He had made his displeasure known quite thoroughly as well—impertinent valet— knocking far louder than necessary, and dropping the tray from a dizzying height right next to my head.

My head was full of wool and the memories were hazy. I recalled a great deal of Michael flirting with my wife. Mother was in fine form as well, that much was very clear.

And before dinner... The ledgers. I finally received documents from the bank, and they match Forsyth's numbers. Someone was cheating me to the tune of hundreds of pounds. I needed another drink, but the bottle seemed to have wandered over to the bookshelf on its own. Stevens probably helped it along.

In the midst of trying to force down a few bites of dry toast without heaving it all back up on the desk, Tom clattered his way in, throwing the door open until it slammed against the adjacent bookcase.

Could he possibly be louder? "You look like shite." Or cruder?

"Thank you."

"I did not come here to compliment you. I came here to tell you off. Last night was badly done." Oh perfect, a lecture from my baby brother.

"I didn't do it."

"You didn't do *anything*. You just watched and drank while your mother insulted your brother and your wife both," he scolded.

"It was bound to be a disaster. I do not know why anyone was surprised."

"That was worse than ever, and you know it."

"I did warn her."

"No one could have prepared her for that. And it didn't need to be that bad. You could have stepped in."

"I had other things on my mind."

"What on earth could have been more important?"

"You do not know anything, Tom. You have no responsibilities. No one to whom you are accountable. You show up when you are inclined and then you leave when you have finished eating."

"I do not live here, Hugh. What precisely am I not doing that I am meant to do?"

"Nothing. I am simply not in the mood for a patronizing lecture from a child."

"You are being an arse. Tell me."

I could not hold back the sigh. I needed to tell someone—the truth was eating away at me. "There's money missing."

He blinked slowly, processing. "From where? How much?"

"Thornton. A few hundred, maybe a thousand."

"Shillings?" I leveled him a look that ought to have refuted his wishful thinking. "Explain then."

"Forsyth, our solicitor, is reporting an amount sent to Thornton. Matthews, the steward, is reporting receiving a smaller amount. Banking documents match Forsyth, so I'm inclined to believe him."

"Matthews has been with the estate for nearly two decades. How far do the discrepancies go back?"

He grabbed a random ledger, turning through the pages at an alarming pace. As if he would find the answer in his flipping.

"Two years at least, maybe farther. I haven't gone that far back."

"Well, let's figure that out at least, hand me the ledgers. It seems unlikely Matthews suddenly started pocketing funds after so many years."

"I made it to January of 1812 before supper last night."

"Leave these here," he said, gesturing to the ledgers. "Go clean up. You smell the bottom of a bottle."

"Thanks ever so." He waved me off, nose already buried in columns of numbers and dates.

Suddenly, my younger brother did not seem so young. "Tom?" He peeked his head up. "Thank you." He shrugged a shoulder, before turning back to the book, taking a sip of my tea before making a face at the temperature.

Dragging myself up the steps I had not managed the night before. I found a tepid wash basin awaiting me. Stevens. The man was incredibly skilled at making his displeasure clear without a word.

In an ill-considered maneuver, I dunked my entire head in the basin. It was effective at washing away the lingering effects of drink and sleep, in the most unpleasant manner possible.

Throwing my head back, I patted around with closed eyes for a linen to dry with. Finding nothing, I ripped my shirt over my head, dragging the damp fabric over my face to dry. I tossed it, still damp, in a corner. At least Stevens would need to deal with that, punishment for the cold basin.

My clothes were already set out. I should have rung for the man, but I was still peeved at him. I dressed with brutal efficiency before the wind abandoned my sails.

Perched on the edge of my bed, I stared at the door to Katherine's room. Something like guilt twisted in my chest. I should have put my foot down. I knew last night was bound to be a disaster, but I was too distracted to properly explain the situation to her when she asked.

And Michael... Tom wasn't precisely wrong. Mother had been in fine form. Historically, her insults had been more veiled and couched under an air of plausible deniability. Nothing about last night could be excused away as anything other than outright hostility. Such a poor showing, for my Katherine's first time hosting a dinner.

I had not the slightest hint of her this morning, none of that sweet orange blossom scent to be found. Why had I been in such a hurry to return to town from Kent?

I had thought to confirm a misunderstanding with the ledgers. Instead, I had confirmed that *someone* was swindling me. Now I wished like hell we had just stayed in the country.

Here there was no pianoforte, no intimate dinners between the two of us, no smiles just for me. It seemed Katherine was an entirely different person in town. And, to my great surprise, I found I quite liked the Katherine of Kent.

It was just everything else about Kent I hated. Tenants requiring new roofs, mills in need of repair, fields in need of irrigation, everyone wanted something from me. Always. Except her.

She never asked anything of me, my wife. Perhaps that was why I agreed to the damn dinner with so little thought. It was the very first thing she had asked of me. At least since she asked to have her brother for Christmas dinner.

Finally, I dragged myself up. Couldn't leave Tom alone with the ledgers for too long.

Stepping into the hall, I ran headfirst into Katherine. She did that thing she always does when I am close. Stared at my chest with interest before tipping her head back, back, back to meet my gaze. As if she was surprised at the size of me every time. It was charming as hell.

"Oh, I'm so sorry. I am glad I caught you though. Do you know Michael's favorite dish? No, of course you don't. I'll ask Mrs. Hudson. I'm inviting him back next week. And the week after. And every week thereafter." The words rushed from her, almost faster than she could enunciate.

"You wish a repeat of last night?"

"Yes. I intend to get to know your other brother. And if I have to do it one week at a time, then that is what I shall do. Oh, and I'm inviting him to the ball."

"What ball?"

"The ball I'm hosting. I told you." My head was too full of cotton to follow her rapid clip.

"All right," I answered distractedly. She nodded, pert and fetching, before dancing around me and down the hall. I blinked inanely after her, before heading down the stairs for the study.

Finding Tom in much the same position I left him, but with the addition of a plate of Shrewsbury cakes, I settled back into my seat with a sigh.

"Did you know Katherine was hosting a ball?"

"Yes. Did you not?"

"No..."

"Hugh..."

"What? And she decided she wants a repeat of last night. Weekly. You are attending."

"But—"

"No, you are essential to the prevention of bloodshed."

"Did she say why?"

"She wants to get to know him. Whatever that means."

"I suspect that it means she wishes to get to know him. She took great interest in me the few times we had tea."

"You've had tea?"

"Hugh..." He sighed.

"What?"

"Nothing. I expect you'll figure it out sooner or later."

Twenty-Three

GRAYSON HOUSE, LONDON - MARCH 4, 1814

KATE

AT LEAST THE *ton* chose to attend... My first ball.

Of course, it was a fair bet that the masses were hoping to witness my failure and humiliation. Or witness whether I donned a scandalous red gown.

I did not.

A few friendly faces made the effort as well, Ladies Celine and Davina, and Jules were all present.

Jules even had her first dance with her new fiancé. Her father arranged a match between her and the Duke of Rose-hill. They were both lovely dancers and a beautiful couple by all accounts. But the sparks I hoped would fly between them were more like snowflakes.

The food, as always, was exceptional and remarked on by all. The updates I made to the ballroom were lovely. Overall, I was pleased with the enchanting effect of the jasmine perfuming the room and the roses adding a splash of color.

Instead of red, I chose an emerald-green dress. It fit well, nipping in slightly to emphasize my waist while remaining tasteful. Anna dressed my hair to perfection with a simple ribbon. I was determined to prove that I could comport myself with the dignity befitting a viscountess.

Even Agatha could find little to complain about at the actual event. The days and weeks leading up to it were something of a different story. The workers were megrim inducing, my improvements were ruining her carefully cultivated aesthetic, the guest list was missing this person or other. Or it should not have included that person.

Since we returned to town, Hugh had become even more distant. It was not uncommon to see him only at dinner and for a brief, though increasingly pleasurable, marital congress. Otherwise, he was hiding out in his study the rest of the day. Today though, I was certain it would be different. It had to be.

Tonight, he dressed in his finest tailcoat, the one he wore for our wedding. He donned a brocade waistcoat to match my gown. Inattentive he may be, but he certainly could not be accused of being anything other than handsome. If it was possible, he may have actually gotten broader in his shoulders. I suspected that fencing was the culprit.

He had surveyed my efforts with a disinterested eye, making no comment. I tried not to let it bother me, but this, more than all the other household improvements I had made with little reaction, stung.

He did his duty, opening the ball with me. A waltz, our first.

Our first dance, actually.

For all that I had insisted to Juliet that a dance would be just the thing for her and her fiancé to awaken the first flutterings of attraction, I had little hope for my own first dance. Hugh was confident in the ballroom, sliding me into place with the ease that came from years of tutelage. I had no such advantage, but nearly two decades bent over the keys of the pianoforte had imbued me with an impeccable sense of rhythm and I had impressed the tutor Aunt Prudence had hired.

The instructor hadn't felt like *this* though, hard and warm and steady and smelling faintly of mint and vanilla. Given the height difference between my husband and I, my gaze met his clavicle more than his eyes, but he dipped his chin to meet my eyes. He had one of my gloved hands tucked in his, the other sat possessively low on my waist, bordering on inappropriately intimate.

Feeling bold, I commented, "I've not waltzed often, but I believe your hand is a bit familiar, my lord. You'll scandalize our guests."

His answering smirk was the kind of wicked I'd never seen before, certainly not on him, easy, crooked and devilishly familiar. Tonight, his eyes were more blue than gray, and dark in the candlelight, almost navy. In lieu of words, his hand slipped a fraction lower, scandalous. "Hugh!"

His response was low, and deep, and graveled in an entirely new way, "You are my wife, Katherine. Certainly, the *ton* will forgive me this one indulgence."

How he timed that comment to the first notes, I'll never know. He guided me easily with his heavy, hot, hand on the small of my back, in spite of my stunned sluggishness.

It took several bars for me to regain coherent thought from that comment. "You know they will not."

He turned his attention over to our joined hands, clenching, flexing, before slotting our fingers together. Incorrect. "With the way you look tonight, I cannot bring myself to care overmuch." The hand claiming my waist pulled me in closer, dangerously close. His breath dusting over my neck with every exhale. In spite of months of marriage, in spite of our audience, it was somehow the most intimate position we'd been in.

In a barely audible whisper, breathed more than spoken into my ear, he added, "you're too stunning."

It was *that*, that one word, that broke the spell he had cast on me, "*too*." Ice washed through my veins, and I stiffened in his arms. He pulled back, trying to catch my gaze, to search for answers, but I knew, if my eyes left his cravat, the tears would be inevitable. "Katherine?"

"Yes?" The word sounded tinny and false, even he could hear it, if the tightening of his grasp on my waist was any indication. Before he could question me further, I rushed to provide an explanation—anything but the truth. "I just remembered I forgot to have Mrs. Hudson make a few sandwiches without cucumber. Aunt Prudence loathes cucumber."

He made a sound low in his throat, an acknowledgment, an expression of disbelief but determination not to question further.

The song continued for several more minutes, but the intimacy was gone, shattered on the floor in the distance between us. When it finally ended, we broke for the requisite applause, strangers once more. Any hopes I had for the rest of the evening were dashed, disappearing with Tom in the study. Abandoning me to the beau monde, friends and enemies alike.

Tom was something of a disappointment in this. I had counted on him to do his duty. Ease ruffled feathers, perhaps dance with a wallflower or two. After all, they could have no serious designs on him, he was a second son and barely of age, but it would brighten their nights. And Michael had not seen fit to arrive at all.

Or so I thought. Several sets spent mingling later, the man himself slipped, awkward and disheveled, from behind the heavy velvet curtains lining the walls. He was probably trying to avoid drawing my notice to his late arrival.

Try as I might, I could not find it within me to be irritated.

In all honesty, I did not put the odds of him attending very high. Now, I was somewhat disappointed with myself for that. In spite of the fairly massive inconvenience they must be causing, he had yet to miss a weekly dinner. Week after week he subjected himself to at least the possibility of Agatha's venom. He had proved himself a fine ally.

Now though, he was late, dusty, and his eye was once again an unnatural purplish color. It was somewhat amusing, but I could allow him to think so.

"Hours late and eye blackened. I look forward to the explanation I shall receive tomorrow."

"Would you believe I was attacked by a rabid swan?" He really needed to maintain a list.

"No. I expect you'll be wanting something stronger than lemonade. Hugh and Tom are in the study with the good scotch." He gave me a grateful nod and scurried off in that direction. Probably worried I would press him into service as a dance partner. I really did think he and Lady Rycliffe would find each other amusing though.

Noting the sandwich tray was running low, I spun to locate Anna only to come face-to-face with Lady James. In a deep red gown.

The irony was not lost on me, nor the rest of the *ton*, I was sure. Still, the sight of elegantly draped red silk was hardly enough to wound me now. She was flanked by Mr. Parker, one of the many gentlemen who seemed to flock to her at these events. Her husband, however, was nowhere to be seen. "Lady Grayson, how lovely to see you. And looking so well. Married life seems to suit you. Perhaps not your husband though since you seem to have misplaced him." She arched an elegant brow whilst sipping her lemonade with a pointed stare.

"Baroness," I replied with a perfectly correct nod. Still, I allowed the word to hang between us, reminding us both of our respective stations. Channeling every bit of gumption I possessed, I continued, "I have not seen your husband tonight either? Is he unwell? It was so kind of him to send Mr. Parker to accompany you in his absence." I could not raise a singular brow and I knew better than to attempt it.

She blinked once, twice, before determining that my statement was indeed intended as a slight. The contempt slid over her features, eyes darkening, lips pursing. Better still, now that the veil had been lifted, I caught the tell-tale feigned step, the exaggerated lean, the faked trip.

And I sidestepped.

Instead of her intended target, my bosom, her lemonade glass landed with a crash at our feet. The orchestra stopped abruptly, the entire assemblage spun toward us in absolute silence. There, for all and sundry to see was Lady James, frozen midtrip, broken glass at our feet. And Her Grace, the Dowager Duchess of Rosehill, in a feather-encrusted silvery gown, was soaked in lemonade. She was easily one of the highest-ranking peers in the room. And there was no mistaking it, no shifting blame. It was obvious to all that the drink had come from Lady James's hand.

She came to the same conclusion, the horror shifting to her features in slow motion. Her eyes darted, desperate for a culprit to come forward, only to find none.

At last, taking pity on her, I broke the silence. "Oh dear, Your Grace, please come with me, let us see if we can repair the damage. Everyone, please do be careful just there until the staff has a moment to clean it. There's broken glass."

As if summoned, Timothy arrived with a dustpan, a bucket of water, and a rag for the glass and sticky mess.

Ladies Celine and Davina accompanied me to the retiring room in an effort to help. Her Grace was in remarkably good humor about the entire thing, at least, I think she was. She had a tendency to use five words when one would do and nearly all of them had three or more syllables. Still, there was nothing to be done about it, so their entire party left for the evening.

At some point, my husband and his wayward brother returned, but only the younger. Michael never made another appearance. Hugh was only in time to claim the last set. He spoke across the line from me, "Where is everyone?"

By everyone, he surely meant the people who had disbursed with the Rosehill party, Lady James and Mr. Parker, and the other gawkers.

"There was an incident with the lemonade."

"Who did you accost this time?" His tone was unreadable, but the slash of his mouth was quirked infinitesimally higher on the right side.

"Alas, the ballroom was bereft of surly viscounts to dampen. I left the honor to Lady James, and she chose a duchess instead."

"Lady James? Would not have thought it of her." And just like that the high of the evening rushed out of me again. The implied "it was entirely expected of you," remained unsaid.

"Yes, well... Did you and your brothers enjoy yourselves with the scotch?"

"More or less, Michael had a... favor to ask, and we had to borrow one of your guests."

"Borrow? Which one?" I asked, scanning the room for missing persons.

"Westfield."

"Oh, that was a favor," I said, relieved. "I should have realized when I didn't spend the entire evening shepherding him away from the debutantes."

"Good, I was worried you would be a bit peeved."

"Not about that." *Just about everything else.*

"You did well, Katherine. It seems the evening was a success." That would have warmed me, pleased me, if I thought he cared even the slightest bit about the success of the evening.

I merely nodded and left him to interpret my meaning.

With that the set came to a close, Aunt Prudence left with a kiss on my cheek. Agatha wandered to bed with another megrim and the night was done.

Nothing left but a mess to clean up.

Twenty-Four

GRAYSON HOUSE, LONDON - MARCH 5, 1814

HUGH

DREAMS OF JASMINE-SCENTED CURLS, tantalizing waists, and emerald silk gave way to a pounding headache and slight nausea—too much of the good scotch. I ordered my tea while still abed, an unusual practice for me. But the thought of the bright, unforgiving breakfast room was too much to stomach. My ginger tea went down unbearably slowly, and every sip was a risk. Memories of the night before came back in hazy fits and starts.

My shoulder twinged—that was from hauling Westfield. I had a vague notion of coercing the man from the billiard room with the promise of inappropriately young, female flesh then dragging him bodily to the library for Michael. He was heavier than he looked, and his weight was uneven, centered low. Hopefully, Michael had not left bloodstains in the library.

Did Michael have a blackened eye again? Tom brought ledgers with him? That felt right, but the why and their contents remained just out of reach, foggy and unwieldy.

Then there was Katherine, nothing about her memory was

vague or nebulous. That green satin was nearly as tempting as the red. It caressed her curves the way I wished I could.

Our marital encounters had not allowed for that but... some day. She was warm and floral scented in my arms. Dark curls trying to escape a matching green ribbon without success, I knew from experience they were softer than the finest of silks. The jade of her gown had shone in her eyes, more green than blue last night. Still, they were bright and large as always, and framed with impossibly dark lashes that cast shadows on her alabaster skin, which was flushed with excitement. Her wide, sensuous lips had been bitten to a darker rose than usual.

From my vantage point several inches above her head, I had been able to see straight down the top of her gown. I was a lecherous cretin for looking, but oh, was it worth it. Her breasts rose and fell with each labored breath, enticing, distracting. She had been delicate in my arms, following the press of my hands with ease and grace.

We had enjoyed a brief moment of flirtation, a hint of something more. Then she shut down once again. It seemed to occur with frightening regularity. Every time we took a step forward, we took two back, and she began discussing cucumber sandwiches or some other nonsense. I could brush last night off as nerves, but the time before? And the one before that? Something was there, in front of me, just out of reach.

EVENTUALLY THE NEED for food outweighed the potential revolt my digestive system was staging. Unfortunately, the coup nearly began when I rounded the corner to the breakfast room to see Katherine and Michael, heads bent toward each other, giggling.

With a pointed cough, I shut down their merriment and they turned toward me in unison. It was Michael who broke the silence. "Good morning, Hugh. Too much of the good scotch last evening?"

In lieu of a response, I made my way over to the sideboard and began to pile a plate high with food I had no intention of eating. Chances were, the best I would manage was dry toast, but that did not stop me. What point I was making with that display and accompanying grunt was anyone's guess.

"I just came by to apologize to your lovely wife. I was unaccountably late last night, and my eye is really unconscionable," he added.

With no more food to add to my pile, I was left to take a seat. Now that I had the whole mess in front of me, the mixed smells were adding to the tenuousness of my grasp on my stomach. Faced with the unappetizing choice of eating or the unappealing choice of conversing, I was forced to choose the latter.

"What was the reason for the eye this time? I cannot recall," Katherine asked Michael.

"Runaway carriage filled with puppies. One of the poor beasts stepped on my eye in their gratitude for my daring rescue."

"You're a credit to the race of men. It's astounding you managed to retain the eye," I muttered.

I took a pointed bite of toast, accompanying it with a glare. He had no business visiting my wife at this hour. It was nearly half a minute before I realized I had been chewing the bite for far too long, avoiding the inevitable. With no other choice, I swallowed it down and it hit my stomach like lead.

"Yes, you sound infinitely pleased," he said.

"Positively dancing inside."

"Though I do think I would look quite dashing with an eyepatch. Kate, what do you think?" he asked.

"Katherine has no opinion on your looks, dashing or otherwise. I presume you have managed to deliver your apology?"

"What do you think Kate, have I made a sufficient go of it?" he asked her.

"I suppose it will do for present. And I think you would make a smart pirate, swashbuckling across the seven seas, taking no prisoners."

The toast threatened to make a reappearance. Why had Michael and I been getting along so well lately? He was positively unbearable.

"Very well then, it seems my work here is done." He rose and offered Katherine an exaggerated bow. "Avast and shiver me timbers m'lady. Hugh."

"You're an atrocious pirate."

"Go back to bed, Hugh. You're being an arse." He said, trailing down the hall in the opposite direction of the front door before I could make a retort. Something about giving him the last word smarted more than it ought.

Kate stood and rang the bell. A servant arrived quickly, a quiet request made, and she returned to the table but chose the seat beside me rather than her previous position at the other end. With one hand, she slid her half-empty teacup and saucer in front of her. Taking a delicate sip with a speculative expression, she surveyed the damage to my person. In mere minutes, the red-haired servant girl arrived with a cup of black coffee in one hand and a glass of something thick, off-white, and creamy with black flecks in it.

"Absolutely not," I said.

"It's an old Scottish remedy. A traveling trapper who stayed with us through a long snowstorm, swore by it."

"Not even if this were the only food-like offering left in the country."

"Hugh."

"Katherine."

"It's just buttermilk, heated and thickened with a bit of corn flour with some salt and pepper for taste."

"That is even more revolting than what I thought it was."

"What did you think it was?"

"I won't drink it."

"Well, I won't sit here and subject myself to your bad temper. Particularly if you refuse to do anything about it. Enjoy your breakfast." She set her now empty teacup back in the saucer with a pointed clatter before rising to leave.

"Katherine, wait. I am sorry, that was unforgivably rude. Even if you are attempting to poison me, I can see it was done with the best of intentions."

"Honestly, if I were going to kill you, that is hardly the manner I would choose." She said it in such an easy tone that it took a moment for the full meaning of her words to arrange themselves in my mind. By that time, she was already halfway to the door.

"Katherine?"

She made no effort to turn and, instead, I was left with nothing but the image of swirling, sky blue skirts around the corner. I peered warily at the concoction, it was beginning to cool, and the steam was condensing on the sides of the glass. I took an uneasy sniff and once again my insides mutinied.

A brief glance at my plate was all that's needed to determine that relief was miles away at present. Without giving myself an opportunity to think, or worse smell it, I closed my eyes and held my nose and downed the glass in a few short gulps.

Immediately, I chased it with the entire cup of coffee, burning my throat on the way down. Concoction successfully gone, I waited a full minute for it to make a return. Surprisingly, it stayed put.

A few minutes later, to my immense surprise, my stomach

settled, and I could make headway with the toast. In less than an hour, I was bathed and dressed and prepared for Tom's ledgers.

I WAS NOT PREPARED for Tom's ledgers. Not even the slightest.

Twenty-Five

HUGH

I HAD TAKEN to staring at my father's portrait in the study. Searching, uselessly, for any sign in his expression of the disaster he left in his wake.

We were desolated when he passed. Months, possibly weeks of creditors coming for us from every available angle. Hell, he could have been thrown in debtor's prison.

But there was not one single indication of it in his painted countenance. Honestly, his expression was unreadable, except for the mirth in his smirk; as though it was amusing, what he could have done to us.

And Michael, my wretch of an elder brother, had saved us all. He did it without a single word. And I could not reconcile my feelings on that. Guilt warred with wounded pride and suspicion until all that was left was a swirl of indigestion.

Why had he not said anything? Was he waiting for some opportune moment? Should that not have come when I cut ties with him over the club? Or had it truly been a kindness? His pride?

I had not told Tom of my findings, not yet. I did not have the words to explain what I could not countenance. All I knew was that Michael had somehow taken the estate from the brink of ruin to prosperity in only a few years. And, it seemed, he had done it at the gaming tables.

He had left funds set up for everything: estate maintenance and improvements, funds for tenant emergencies, irrigation systems, Mother's modiste bills, hell—he had set up dowries for Tom's and my future children. And it was gone. All of it. Every single fund had dwindled to almost nothing.

I was not skilled enough to manage money the way that Michael had, but I wasn't this bad. I was being cheated, badly. And for the first time, I was beginning to suspect that it wasn't Mathews, the man Michael hired.

Two Viscount Graysons managed to bring Thornton Hall and Grayson House to ruin. And in under a decade too. It was impressive, really, when one considered it. The one man without the title, seemed to be the only one capable of caring for it. That was just... ironic, bitterly so.

I was in quite the mess, and I hadn't the faintest idea of what to do about it.

"I FORGOT to tell you Juliet will be joining us in the country," Katherine informed me at one of our, now weekly, dinners, handing me the potatoes as she did so. For the life of me I could not recall which of her friends that was. The one with the overwrought brows? Or the one with the bird's nest hair? A different one I could not recollect at all?

"Who?" I asked distractedly, only half listening. My mind was still in my study, still buried in the decades of ledgers. Still absorbing the apparent truths they held.

"Lady Juliet." Unhelpful.

"Have I met her?"

Instead of a response, I received the grinding of a wooden chair on a wooden floor. That sound penetrated my contemplation. Silverware clattered when the table shuddered with the motion of my wife's abrupt rise.

She strode out of the room in a flurry of skirts with little more than an "excuse me, gentlemen." Such rudeness, and in front of my family too.

Tom and Michael were openly gaping at me, seeking an explanation for her sudden departure. "Must be feeling poorly." I answered their unasked question with a shrug. Who could say why women did the things they did?

"Hugh..." Tom responded, somewhat exasperated in his tone.

"What?"

Tom and Michael were now exchanging significant glances and head nods. Before Michael stood and followed Katherine's exit.

"Do you suppose it's the roast?" I hoped it was not sitting poorly, I just took a bite a moment ago and I was not interested in experiencing whatever was wrong with Katherine or Michael.

"Hugh, your wife is upset with you." Tom over enunciated the words, as if I would not comprehend their meaning. I understood the definitions perfectly of course, but there was no evidence that Katherine was unhappy with me. She had said nothing of the sort.

"Why should she be upset with me? I did not cook the roast." Tom's hand came up to pinch the bridge of his nose between thumb and forefinger, as though he had one of Mother's megrims. Another symptom? I set my own fork down and pushed my plate away. I could not risk eating anything further.

My brother dragged an exaggerated breath before responding. "She is upset because you have been married for months and you do not know the name of her dearest friend. The one you met numerous times."

"Why should she be upset about that? I am a busy man. I meet lots of people. Is it the one with the hair or the one with the brows?"

"Hugh—that's not the—the hair. But you have met the girl multiple times. I have met her, and I only dine here once a week."

"I think she's the one who hides in the library. Scurries out of here with arms full of books as though we will run out if she does not take them all at once."

"Yes, that's the one. But Hugh, Kate is upset because you do not take an interest in the things that are important to her."

"That is not true."

"When was the last time you spent actual time together?"

If I had not been questioned, I certainly could have come up with any number of times. Once Tom asked the question, all instances escaped my mind. Without permission, time continued to march on, and without giving me a chance to think, Tom crowed his triumph "See?"

"Perhaps I have been a bit preoccupied sorting out these ledgers, but I am a viscount. I have many demands on my time."

"You spent three hours thrashing me with a sword this afternoon."

"Clearing my mind."

"I am just suggesting perhaps you should clear your mind with your wife. I hear wives are good for that sort of thing."

"What do you know of that?"

"Rumors, nothing more."

His typically ruddy face flushed even harder at his response. Too much time in the theater district, clearly. Before I could even attempt to explain French Letters to him,

Michael and Katherine returned. Probably for the best, as I was not certain how one used them.

Katherine returned to her seat, flushed quite fetchingly, before announcing, "Michael will be joining us in the country as well."

Tom choked, midsip. I could feel my face twist into what was surely an inane expression.

When words finally returned, they were equally inane. "He is?"

The response was a simultaneous "yes" from both of them. No room to broker discussion. Nothing like a request.

Twenty-Six

THORNTON HALL, KENT – APRIL 15, 1814

KATE

THEY WERE AT IT AGAIN. Michael and Juliet, heads bent together over a card table, murmuring softly.

I had never, not once in our lives, seen her so happy. Even worse, now that I knew what her joy looked like, I realized that I had never seen it on her. Gone was that way she had about her, the one I always assumed was just Juliet. The perpetual tension in her muscles, prepared to spring into action in any second, was nowhere to be seen. Instead, there was a new languidness to her movements.

She and Michael were feigning some sort of gaming lesson. There was little in the way of teaching going on. That seemed to be the usual case. Michael, a seasoned gambler, should have found the entire thing dreadfully dull. Instead, he looked at her as though she held the answer to every one of life's questions.

My favorite moments were the ones I caught when he thought no one was looking. The naked love in his eyes, and it could only be love, was unbearably heartbreaking and sweet to see. He looked at her the way I always wanted a husband to look at me. To see that expression on his usually guarded face... There were times it was all I could do to refrain from squealing in delight.

It was love.

There was no doubt in my mind that both of them were desperately in love. I had seen it on Lizzie's face and on her husband Sydney's face. Mother and Father, too, wore that expression often.

I was thrilled for my friend, unbearably thrilled. The only problem was their affection and consideration for each other threw my own marriage into sharp contrast.

Hugh did nothing but hide in his study, day in and day out. It was as though he could not stand the sight of me. Except at night, at night he came with more and more demanding, provocative touches.

I managed the disappointment well enough, visiting the vicarage and seeing to the tenants, making improvements to the estate.

It was true that I would never have the kind of life I had dreamed of, with a husband who looked at me with a fraction of the adoration Michael wore, but I was carving out a life here.

There was a satisfaction that came with running a household. Each incremental improvement brought with it more pride and a sense of belonging.

I had developed something like a friendship with several of the tenants. True, it was not a real friendship because they were too deferential of my rank for me to truly confide in them. But I enjoyed their company, and they enjoyed mine. And I did count Anna amongst my real friends. Michael, too, would soon join those ranks, I was certain of it.

It was different from the life I envisioned, but that need

not mean it was a bad life. And, once we were blessed with children, I need not feel quite so lonely.

A giddy part of me, a part that was certainly rushing ahead, considered that Jules and my children could be cousins in truth, the way we were cousins only in our hearts.

In the meantime, I left Michael and Juliet to their courtship.

~

HUGH

"And you are absolutely certain of these figures?"

"Yes!" The man, Matthews, exclaimed with no small amount of exasperation.

"Sir, one of you is lying to me. I would think you would want me to be assured that it is not you."

He had arrived at my summons a few hours ago with every single bank draft for the last five years. He had stomped his way into my office, in muddy boots and trousers, refused a seat, and turned progressively more purple in color the angrier he got.

"I don't need to toady to you. I won't be polite when I'm being accused of a crime I didn't commit. If you'll remember, *my lord*, I am the one who pointed out the discrepancy." If it were possible to infuse more disgust in the term "my lord," I did not know how to do it.

"You did not point it out, you merely complained that you did not have the money you wanted."

"Needed."

"Needed," I corrected, barely suppressing an eye roll.

"Don't know why I'm even dealing with you. I know Michael is in residence. He'd have this sorted."

"Michael is not the viscount."

"Oh, believe me, the whole of Kent is well aware. You've made that abundantly clear—you're nothing like Michael."

"Mr. Matthews, that is enough."

"I am just saying Michael set up the accounts. He knows what they were intended for. And I don't know why you're still accusing me. You have the bank drafts right there. You can confirm them at your leisure. But if you want to plant that field, you needed to have sorted out the irrigation last fall."

"Thank you for your timely input."

"It was timely, when I sent you a letter about it last spring, and the fall before that, and for the two years prior to that."

"Yes. Thank you. I think you best be off now."

He huffed in answer. Stomping out the door and tracking muddy boot prints back the way he came. Leaving the ledgers and drafts behind for my perusal.

I already knew they matched what he sent previously. I had all but memorized the ledgers I had in town. The drafts looked legitimate too, completed in Forsyth's neat yet distinctive hand.

That man's handwriting was nearly as familiar to me as my own. And Matthews's sloppy scrawl was exactly as it always was.

I would need to send these bank drafts for confirmation. But I was nearly certain that Forsyth was the one cheating me.

It would be the man I hired.

Michael would never hire a man who would cheat him. He was too clever for such a thing. He would save our family from destitution without a word. Because Michael might have been viscount. Matthews knew it. The tenants adored him. The *ton* loved him, not in spite of his degenerate ways, but because of them. He could do no wrong in Tom's eyes. Even Katherine seemed to prefer his company to mine.

Turning to face my father's portrait, still infuriatingly easy in countenance, I could not press down the feeling of disgust.

time in it than Michael and the servants' young children. Mother found the activity undignified and ungentlemanly. On more than one occasion, I watched from the schoolroom with envy as they splashed about, laughing too loudly. Once in a while, Tom and I would sneak out to join them. It was some of the few truly happy memories I had with Michael.

Stroke after stroke, I pulled myself across the lake. Though strengthened by hours with sword in hand, swimming utilized the muscles in a different way and the resulting stretch tugged pleasantly.

Distracted as I was by thoughts of the estate, and the hypnotic rhythm of legs and arms and breath, I did not hear the frantic flailing approaching.

Without warning, my shoulders were trapped in a hot steel band. My panicked breath was more water than air. Rearing back whilst choking, shoving against my attacker, kicking and thrashing.

Nothing worked.

The terror cleared slightly, and I could see—Michael. Dragging me, yanking me, pulling me toward shore. His one-armed strokes were more slaps against the water than any sort of technique, and he was kicking frantically beneath the surface.

This side of the bank was shallower, more sludge than water, but Michael was undeterred, dragging us through the muck. Tom waded in, pulling me free from Michael's branding hold. I collapsed onto all fours at the grassy edge, coughing and choking. There was a fair bit of swearing as well.

At my side, there was a soft, small, warm hand—my wife.

Katherine brushed my hair back from my face gently, rubbing my upper back as I hacked half the lake out of my lungs. After several minutes of shuddering, wracking coughs, I could breathe again. Turning I saw Michael, still prone on the bank.

"What the devil are you doing?" I intended for it to be a shout, but it was more wheeze, my chest still recovering from my near-drowning at his hands.

He was still taking desperate gasps as well, as he choked out, "is he breathing? Is he breathing?"

I managed to shake off Katherine and Tom, pushing to stand.

"Michael! What the hell?" That time I managed the necessary volume. He shoves himself to standing, brushing off Lady Juliet and the red-headed servant.

He grabbed both of my shoulders in his hands, grip harsh, bruising. Seemingly surveying me for injury. I was uncertain how effective his efforts were as his eyes were clouded with terror. "You're all right? You're unharmed?"

"Of course, I am unharmed. I was swimming. What are you doing? You nearly killed me!" He continued inspecting me for injury in spite of my rising protests.

It was Tom who interrupted Michael from his seat in the mud. "Hugh, let it go."

I glanced his way, prepared to share some of my ire with him. It was his expression that cut through everything. His brow furrowed, and his eyes shuddered. His lower lip was clenched in his teeth, blinking back tears.

Katherine tried to tug me away on her own before Tom joined her. Between the two of them, they managed it. Lady Juliet approached Michael from behind, a hand on his shoulder and a whisper of his name. That was all it took for him to return to reason. He turned away from us, back toward her.

~

MRS. HUDSON ARRIVED with blankets mere moments later, tutting at the lot of us in that motherly way of hers.

I bathed and changed and through it all, Tom's crestfallen face was burned in my memory. Katherine too, her eyes had been wide and sorrowful and her mouth, usually full and lovely, had pulled together into a sad pinched pout. The nagging feeling that I missed something vital was poking at the back of my mind, refusing to leave me in peace.

Scrubbed raw and pink, I dressed and made my way to my study, where I was fairly certain Michael could not attempt to drown me. Tom was already there, seated on the desk, legs swinging back and forth against the floor. The position was one I recalled him adopting often as a boy. He had grown too tall for it, and his heels hit the floor on the downswing and toes on the up. He had an overfull glass of something clear and the bottle within arm's reach. He stared at Father's portrait on the wall, his expression one I had never seen before.

At the sound of my approach, he turned to me and raised an empty glass and patted the desk beside him with his free hand. I joined him, leaning against the desk instead of perching upon it fully.

For a long moment, he just examined Father's portrait. The one I had spent the last weeks contemplating. It had been so long, I could not remember if the likeness was any good. That, more than anything else, saddened me.

Tom turned away, pouring a second glass and passing it over. Gin. It was an unusual choice for him; he thought it tasted of pine needles. It was never my first choice either. But, at the first bite of it in my mouth, I understood.

Father drank gin.

It tasted like he smelled: citrus, juniper, and cardamom. The burn was comforting now, with the recollection fresh.

I finished more than half my glass before Tom spoke. "I never asked. How could I never ask?"

"What do you mean?"

"I knew he drowned. I knew Michael found him. But I

didn't—not like that. Somehow, in my mind, he was just sleeping by the bank. Which I now realize may have been the most inane thought I've ever had."

The request for explanation was on the tip of my tongue when his meaning took hold. The floor dropped from under me. That nagging thought. The expression on Tom's face. The one on Katherine's. Michael's terror. The understanding was horrifying.

All this time, more than a decade later, some small part of me still felt the same way I had at eleven. I could have saved my father. Michael had not tried, had not cared. He was unfeeling and unconcerned in Father's final moments. What a joke.

Having witnessed Michael's horrified frenzy this afternoon, I knew with certainty down to my bones that he had done far more than I could have to save Father. That he had been anything but apathetic. That he was still haunted by the memories.

"Do you know, I honestly forgot he died in that lake? Some son I am," I said. Tom glanced at me before returning to the painting.

"I don't think just anyone in the lake would have caused that reaction, Hugh."

There was a part of me that I was not proud of that wanted to feign ignorance at Tom's words. "Michael and I do not have that kind of relationship, Tom."

"You could. I think, if nothing else, today proves that." Before I had a moment to argue, to explain that he gave us both too much credit, there was a knock. Katherine with a tea service.

She, too, had cleaned up somewhat, changed into a new gown.

Tom seemed to take her arrival as a cue to leave, grabbing a sandwich with an easy, "thank you, Kate," as he hopped off the desk. His expression was once again smoothed into one of easy familiarity as he swept out the door. As if our conversation was of no more importance than the dinner menu.

Sometimes, I wondered if I truly knew my brother at all. His perceptive nature and the ease with which he hid his feelings were discomfiting.

Katherine set the tea service on the desk behind me, rounding it and joining me in leaning against the desk, peering up at the portrait.

"Is that him?"

"Yes."

"Is it a fair likeness?" I should lie and say that it was. She had no way of knowing.

Instead, for reasons I could not explain, I answered truthfully, "Do you know? I cannot actually remember. I suppose it must be, for it is quite similar to the one at Grayson House."

"I think it must be. You look like him. All three of you."

"I am not sure that is true."

"It is. See, you have his gray eyes. You and Michael both have his dark hair. Michael and Tom have his furrowed brow. Tom has his nose."

"Poor Tom."

"Hush, it's charming. Gives him character. He would be far too pretty for the ladies without it."

"Is such a thing possible?"

"Oh yes, ladies don't want a man prettier than they are. Too much competition."

"I'll tell him you said so."

"Oh, I've told him so myself on more than one occasion." Purposefully, she settled her hand over mine where it rested on the desk while still observing Father's portrait. "Your father drowned?"

"Yes."

"Michael pulled him out?"

"So it would seem. I was not ready for answers when it

happened. I suppose it never felt like the right time after. At some point, I must have decided the answers I made up to comfort myself were the truth."

"It must have been terribly difficult, growing up without him."

I had not thought so, not after the first few months. Those days when the sun continued to rise and set. Winter turned to spring, to summer, and fall, before becoming winter once more. But in this moment, I felt his absence keenly, a gaping wound that had been present so long I forgot its existence until reminded of it.

I felt a soft pressure at my shoulder and turned to see a head of dark curls resting there. Her hand, the one not pressed into mine, came around her body to wrap around my forearm, tightening.

I swallowed hard against the knot that was forming, unbidden and unwelcome. It was, perhaps, the single most comforting gesture I had ever received. I pressed a gentle kiss to the top of the curls and received a tighter squeeze in answer. We remained there, her head pressed against my shoulder, until long after the tea grew cold and the bell rang to dress for supper.

And, when the heat of her temple was replaced by a damp cold emptiness, I could not help but think that Katherine may not have been the wife I wanted. But she may very well have been the wife I needed.

Twenty-Eight

THORNTON HALL, KENT – JUNE 3, 1814

HUGH

I WAS GOING to be responsible for my brother's next blackened eye. Perhaps two.

Incredulous, I watched from my study window with a slack jaw while a rain-soaked and disheveled Lady Juliet curled into my equally waterlogged, reprobate of a brother's arms as he guided her inside. Lord, the girl looked thoroughly tupped.

He managed to sneak her in with no one but me the wiser —as far as I could discern anyway. I allowed him a few moments to change before ringing for Stevens.

"Do you know where my brother and Lady Juliet head off to each day, Stevens?" I pressed him.

He flinched, starting several times before settling on, "No, my lord."

It was such a comfort to know that my valet, the one servant intended to be solely my confidant, was attempting to lie, poorly, on my brother's behalf. Was there anyone in my employ not in service to him? With a sigh, I sent him off to fetch Michael.

Stevens all but tossed my brother into the study when I bade him entry. Likely as displeased with Michael's behavior as I was.

"Close the door," I directed Michael. Something about scolding a man so many years my senior required a lower register than my voice usually occupied. "Have a seat," I added.

In a fit of pique, Michael chose to lean against the bookshelves opposite me instead. He found a book and flipped through it disinterestedly. It was a mere prop designed to infuriate me.

Unfortunately, the effort worked, and I aborted several attempts to begin my lecture before I found any words that were acceptable of a gentleman.

At last, I settled on, "She's engaged, Michael."

His flipping ceased. In fact, all movement ceased. Instead, my brother, so frequently in motion, was frozen, a statue.

Of course, when he reanimated, he was once again my ingrate of a brother. "Who is engaged, Hugh?"

And that was the end of my composure. "You know damn well who! She is engaged and a guest here under my protection."

"Oh, Lady Juliet? I hadn't heard she was affianced. What of it?" he asked with feigned confusion.

"You spend hours each day with her. Alone. I assumed you were in the rose garden, but I learned today that none of the servants know where you take her. Tell me!"

"Here and there," he replied with feigned nonchalance.

"Damn it all, Michael. This is not a joke. If anyone were to catch even a hint of this... you would ruin that girl!" There was truly no point in explaining this to Michael. He was certainly conducting this liaison on purpose to ruin her and vex me.

"Catch what? What exactly am I going to do to her?" His

question was filled with venom, rather than the sarcasm I was accustomed to.

I shot up, my seat no longer able to contain me. "You know damn well what you're going to do to her! Even being seen with you is enough in some circles." The heat was rising in my chest with every attempt at deflection, curses flying freely now.

Rather than share in my fury, Michael was cool, loose-limbed. The disinterest was infuriating, fueling my own fire. *That* was matched only in his eyes.

"Let's not be coy here, Hugh. Say it," he pressed, striding toward the desk between us.

"You're a bastard! Everyone knows it. All of London! You're a dishonorable bastard whose own living comes at the expense of the gullibility and dishonor of others."

And with those words, the fire rushed out, leaving behind nothing but an ashen taste in my mouth. Still, I had to make him see, make him understand. "She is not for you," I added, desperately willing him to comprehend the stakes of the game he was playing with her. He was wagering with her life.

Instead of delivering the punch I expected—deserved—Michael collapsed into the chair across from me. He looked up at me, his eyes sorrowful now.

"Sit," he said softly, nodding toward my empty chair. I followed his gaze and realized I was still standing, fists clenched and braced for a blow. "I'm not going to hit you," he added.

"What just happened?" I asked wearily.

"You won. You can wipe the befuddled look off your face now."

"I... do not know what I've won."

"You're right. I'm spending too much time with her. Unchaperoned. I just.... I can't stay away from her, Hugh."

Realization crashed over me, muggy and frozen at the same time. "Oh, lord."

"You have the right of it."

"Michael, I had no idea. I thought you were toying with her. Perhaps to get at her father."

"That's flattering," he replied, sharp and brittle.

"I did not mean…"

"No, you did mean it," he corrected. "And why would you think otherwise? After all, I am a dishonorable bastard."

"I did not mean that." I tried to explain, tried to clarify. Every sentence, every word, I etched the lines of hurt deeper into my brother's brow.

"Seven years. I was viscount in all but title for seven years. In seven years, the *ton* never once forgot. And neither did you, so don't try to deny it."

"I did not know you wished to be thought of as such."

His laugh was bitter, and so sharp I could feel it slice my skin. "Yes, who would want a title and wealth and power handed to them at birth? Who would want the chance to marry the woman he cares for? I had four years before he married your mother. Four years where no one treated me as lesser than. Four years where I thought I could do anything I dreamed. Then he married Agatha. I was banished from her sight. Worse still, she had a son, and everything that I deluded myself into thinking could have been mine was handed to you. I never, not once, complained. But don't for one second mistake my silence for lack of feeling."

Words failed me. They had never been my strong suit, but in this… the words didn't exist.

"It doesn't matter. The things I wanted were never mine to dream of in the first place. She's not mine to wish for either."

Desperate for a moment to think of anything else, I seized on Lady Juliet, still my responsibility. "Do you… Has she been compromised?"

"Not irrevocably," he replied. He baited me, again, arguing

with me over the state of the girl's purity before adding, "I'm not a seducer, Hugh. I've never touched an innocent."

"As far as I know, you never cared for a woman until now either. Are you going to offer for her?"

His brow furrowed. "What do you mean, offer for her?"

"Are you going to ask her to marry you?" I asked slowly, deliberately.

"She's already promised to Rosehill. And more besides, as you so kindly pointed out, she's not for me."

"Damn it all, Michael, I did not know you actually felt for her."

"My feelings hardly change the situation."

"You could ask her. She might say yes." It wasn't entirely out of the realm of possibility.

"She. Is. Already. Promised. To. Rosehill,"

"Has it occurred to you that she may be expecting your address?" I reminded him. A lady didn't walk out of the woods looking the way Lady Juliet had without expectations.

"Even if she wanted to, I could never ask it of her. She could not understand what a life with me would mean. She would be ruined. Never to be accepted in polite society again. I couldn't do that to her." His speech was hoarse and pitchy, too full of desolation to be contained.

I sighed. "You are determined then? Nothing I can say will convince you?"

"I won't drag her to hell with me."

"Very well then. I must ask you to refrain from engaging with her unchaperoned. No more strolls to places unknown. No more cards in the drawing room without Kate or myself present. The strictest proprieties must be followed." I could not, would not, allow that girl to be ruined. I was a poor gentleman, but in this, I was firm. No matter how much Michael loved her, if he wouldn't offer for her, then my only choice was to protect her.

"I'll leave," he replied.

"What?"

"I'll go back to London."

"That is not what I said, Michael."

"I can't stay here. I can't be this close to her and not be with her."

"Are you certain?" I asked.

"Yes."

"When?"

"Tomorrow, first light."

Alone once again, I realized that somehow, after nothing but a singular twenty-minute conversation with my brother, I had only begun to see him for the man he truly was. How many others had more beneath the surface than I knew?

Twenty-Nine

THORNTON HALL, KENT – JUNE 4, 1814

KATE

I AWOKE to Anna's quiet rustling in my dressing room. Basin filling, tray settling, I had grown used to the ambient noises of married life. It was familiar now, comforting. Today the light streaming through my curtains was muted, a gray day then. No matter, we would not be in England if those were not an occasional nuisance. I did hope the rain would stay away, at least until the afternoon. Both Michael and Jules became restless and snappy if they weren't able to sneak away for at least an hour each morning.

Jules had been frustratingly closed-lipped about where they went and what they did each morning, but her smile was infectious. It warmed my heart to know that, if I could not have the love match of my dreams, she would. There was no more deserving person in the world, and Michael seemed poised to offer her the world.

Anna's customary, brisk knock, interrupted my reverie and I bade her entry. It had become my favorite morning ritual, discussing Michael and Juliet's budding relationship and analyzing Augie's business-like letters to Michael for any hints of his feelings toward Anna.

Instead of her usual grin, Anna's expression was tight, worried.

"What is the matter?"

She hesitated, searching for the words; Anna never hesitated. Finally, she said, "Michael is gone."

"Oh, that's unfortunate. When will he return?"

"He won't."

My stomach dropped. "What do you mean?"

She bit her lip, wavering once again. "I'm given to understand that Lord Grayson spoke with Michael yesterday afternoon. And they decided it would be best if he returned to town."

"Hugh and Michael spoke?" *What have you done, Hugh?*

"Yes."

"And Michael suddenly decided to leave the country without a word or warning."

"Yes."

"And you're certain he's gone?"

"He left before first light on horseback. They're packing his trunks to follow now." That was certain then, no misunderstanding.

"Does Juliet know?"

Anna hesitated again. That meant yes and the reaction hadn't been pretty. "I believe Lady Juliet ran into Stevens while he was supervising the packing."

"Where is she?"

"She left shortly thereafter for a walk." *Oh, Jules.*

"And she has not returned?"

"No."

"Right." I rushed past Anna, heedless to my state of dress or the surely scandalized servants I passed.

HUGH

I still had one of Mother's megrims nearly a full day after my conversation with Michael. So many revelations in so short a time, it was enough to drive anyone to distraction. My brother, ever the gambler, bet his heart on Lady Juliet and lost.

I had not been hiding in my study because that would be cowardly. But I took no pains to rush to the breakfast table, to see the wreckage my brother left behind. Lady Juliet seemed a sensible young woman, surely she would see reason and—

The door flung open, banging against the wall with an impressive strike. In the doorway was Katherine, a flurry of curls and fabric. Still clad in her nightdress, with her hair unbound. I had never seen her that way outside of the bedroom. The sight would have been enticing if the fury raging in her eyes were not so apparent.

"Katherine? What the devil?"

She strode into the room, spine tall and proud, and steps purposeful, frustration barely contained. "What did you do?" Her words were low and quiet, a hiss.

"What do you mean what did I do? I haven't done anything?" I've been in my study all morning, and this was how she greeted me?

"Michael, where is he?"

"He returned to London." Now my frustration rose, my wife had no business concerning herself over the location of my brother.

"Why?"

"We discussed it and thought it was for the best. Why do you care where my brother is?" Rising, I rounded my desk to stand before her. Gaining the upper hand through height alone. She stood firm, not backing down in the slightest.

"Because he is supposed to be here! Wooing Juliet!"

"What? Lady Juliet is engaged. To Rosehill, or have you forgotten?"

"You sent him away!"

"Yes, I sent him away! Your friend is here under my protection, and I cannot have my brother seducing innocents in my home."

"He wasn't seducing her! They were falling in love!"

"They were doing a great deal more than falling in love! And she is engaged! To another man."

"She doesn't love Rosehill!"

"What has that to do with anything?"

"She was supposed to have love. No one deserves it more. And you destroyed it! You destroy everything!" The words were ripped from her throat, harsh and unyielding. She stepped forward with that attack, bringing us closer. Not near enough to touch, but her head tipped back to maintain eye contact.

"Excuse me?"

"If I couldn't have love at least she would have! And you just took it from her. Just like you took it from me." *What the devil—?*

"I took love from you? Are you referring to this marriage that you masterminded?"

"Me? You think I wanted this?"

"Of course you did!"

"Did your mother convince you of that? Because it would not be the first time she was wrong, I can assure you of that. If you were the only man in the world, I would not have chosen you! You think I wanted to marry a man who hates everything about me?"

"What?"

She affected a masculine voice, her tone mocking. "You may want a tumble, but I could not stand it. The girl is too much. Too bold and loud. With bad teeth and massive lips and eyes and her body is simply too much. Everything about her is abhorrent." Something about the speech rang as familiar, but the memory remained out of reach.

"What are you talking about?"

"You said it! You said it about me. All those gentlemen were talking about me, saying licentious things. But you, you could not consign yourself to insinuations and jives. You had to destroy everything about my appearance! About my very being! And to eligible gentlemen, no less. It wasn't enough that you didn't want me. You had to ensure no one else ever would either. I was trapped in that closet trying to get away from you! And look where that landed me. Married to a man who hates everything about me. A man who insists on ruining, not only my happiness, but that of my dearest friend. And you think I wanted this?"

"No woman in the world could possibly take one look at Lord Grayson's handsome countenance and title and find you wanting? It's no matter how you treat her? She will be happy with whatever scraps you deign to give her? Is that it? Because you, my lord, are not the catch that you think you are. You are heartless, and you are spineless. And I deserved more." She seemed to deflate with the end of her speech, curling in on herself. Eyes widening with something akin to shock as though she could not believe that she said it.

I, on the other hand, was numb.

My life was a lie. And I was a monster.

All this time... She hated me. She didn't say the words of course, but I had never been more certain of anything else in my life. My wife loathed me.

A thousand moments rushed past; memories I had read as instances of quiet contentment, grown from our inauspicious start. And she was miserable.

Now her face was flushed, a burning red, and her eyes were

impossibly wide. Beneath her nightrail, her chest heaved, panting with the effort of her exertions, lips parted slightly. In other circumstances, I would find the vision stunningly beautiful. But she was smaller now, somehow, as if her bottled rage was all that kept her upright, and that shrinking spoiled the effect.

It reminded me that I had ruined her life.

I remembered the speech now, the unkind drunken words designed to earn the approval of men no more worthy of the title of gentleman than me. All this time, she thought—. The exact words refused to return to me, but her version of it was surely accurate, or close to it.

She let me in her bed when she believed I held her in such little regard. Was she remembering those words when I... The metallic tang arrived just as my stomach gave a lurch, but I managed to swallow it back down.

It was a strange thing, having thousands, millions, months of memories rewrite themselves in an instant. Every touch now took on a sinister tint. Every abrupt subject change, every slipped smile, every unexplained uneasy moment made a horrifying sense.

My eyes had not left her form since she entered. That was how I knew before the first tear fell that they were coming. They pooled just above her bottom lashes for a few seconds before making their escape. My legs reacted before my mind, lurching a single step forward. And then, even worse than everything that came before, she broke me. Her answering flinch was instinctive. My body froze at the sight.

My wife was afraid of me. She believed I would hit her.

My step back was slow, deliberate, until I hit the edge of the desk. Leaving as much space between us as possible. This, at least, I could do.

She was the one to break the silence. "I'm sorry—I—

excuse me." She all but ran from the room. If her footsteps in the hall were any indication, she did run there. Racing away from the monster that was her husband. I certainly could not blame her.

Thirty

KATE

WHAT HAVE I DONE? Oh good lord, what have I done? I was sure to wear a hole straight through the floor with my pacing. I didn't say those things. It was a horrible dream. It had to be. I was not the kind of person who said things like that. A person who said such deliberately hurtful things. And I took pleasure in it, that look of horror as it crossed his face—almost sick. It was fuel to the bonfire.

I had to live with that man for the rest of my life. And I just—oh I couldn't even remember what I said. Did I call my husband spineless? Everything in me wanted to flee, flee this house, flee this country. I heard the journey to America was nice enough this time of year.

At some point, he would lose that sick, sorrowful expression and it would twist into anger and hatred, it was inevitable. And what will become of me then? What did the *ton* do with hateful wives? Could he throw me out? Beat me? I didn't think he would. Not truly. He had been disinterested, condescending, and prideful but never violent.

The worst part of it all was that, objectively, Hugh was right to send Michael away. Juliet was engaged. Their relationship was inappropriate. She was under his protection. Even when I was hissing hateful things at my husband, I knew he was right. It smarted all the worse for that understanding.

It was just so lovely to see her budding happiness, knowing that she could possibly still have that even if I could not. I felt her loss more keenly than I had felt my own. Her dreams were more tangible perhaps, where my dreams of a love match were amorphous, nameless, faceless. But Jules... He was right there, to be seen, to be touched. And the way Michael looked at her... The same way Sydney looks at my sister. The way Father looks at Mother. It was everything I wanted. And no one was more deserving of that look.

Their love was everything my own marriage was not. Even before their arrival in the country, Michael hung on every mention of her. Selecting books he thought she might enjoy and leaving them for her to find. He did it with no hope of acknowledgement or appreciation. And when they were in the same room, even when his eyes were not upon her, he was turned toward her, his body seeking hers even without his knowledge. It was beautiful. So unlike my own marriage.

Hugh took little if any interest in me. He hid from me in his study, day after day. His interest in me seemed to begin and end in the bedroom. And he was not overly attentive there either. Hugh's eyes did not follow me, and his body did not turn toward mine. There was nothing like love in his expression when he looked toward me. I was more likely to receive the steely gaze and stern slash of a mouth than a smile. He had never once glanced at me with his heart in his eyes.

And now he never would. Any progress I had made in inserting myself into his home and his life lay in pieces on the study floor. All because I could not hold my tongue—would not.

Dinner was stone silent, marked only by the plink of raindrops against the window. Hugh remained in his office, citing a headache. Jules was red-eyed and downturned. Tom seemed to lack the energy to deal with either of our foul moods. And, for once in her life, Agatha timed her megrim well.

Neither Jules nor I had much of an appetite. Tom too, ate little, instead preferring to drink his supper. Had he spoken to Hugh? Did he know what had happened? What I had said? Did he hate me now too?

With little interest in supper and even less interest in entertainment afterward, there was a mutual agreement to go to bed afterward.

It was only after—when I was in my night shift once more, that I realized I had no idea what to expect. Would he come? He had come nearly every night before, but now...

Instead of finding sleep, I curled up in the wingback chair near the window. Staring as the rain outside grew steadily stronger, heavier. First it dripped, eventually it poured in straight sheets. As the wind grew angrier, the sheets angled to the left. The thunder had begun so gradually, with nearly inaudible rumblings that reached a crescendo so slowly that I did not notice it. Not until the first flash of lightning slashed through the sky, followed by the deafening crack.

It was impossible to miss now, the rain that threatened to flood the world, the thunder that threatened to crumble the house beneath its rage, the lightning burning the very sky. Eventually my candle burned down, extinguishing itself in a brief whisper of smoke.

And still I waited. And still the storm raged.

Midnight. One. Two. Nature extracted its toll. Finally, at nearly two thirty, the time between lightning and thunder began to lengthen again. The winds cried instead of howling, and the rain once again straightened, slowed. Only when it stopped entirely did I hear the footsteps down the hall.

The flickering glow of a candle grew underneath the door. The light reached its peak, and the silhouette of two feet paused before my door. I waited, breath trapped in my chest, but a moment later they continued down the hall, the door next to mine opened and closed. The candlelight, now gone from the hall, found its way through the crack underneath the adjoining door. The padded thunk of heavy boots on carpet, the brush of cloth against skin, the sounds of undressing echoed painfully loud in the absence of the storm. The music of domesticity in the room beside mine, tonight the innocent sounds were ominous, threatening.

Instead of a knock, or worse the turning of a handle, I heard the groan of the wooden bed as it accommodated the weight of my husband. And then, accompanied by little more than a breath, the candlelight went out.

My vigil continued. I sat, unmoving. Watching as the clouds dissipated and the silver sliver of the moon made an appearance, gliding across the sky before sinking beneath the horizon. Not long after that when the black of night transitioned seamlessly to a dusky purple. I rose, slipping beneath the covers of my bed, falling into a fitful, exhausted sleep.

HUGH

My entire life was a lie. That much was clear. My marriage was a farce, my viscountcy was a joke, and I was nothing like the man I thought I was.

All this time she hated me.

The portrait of my father in the study... I used to find his smile comforting, approving. Now it was a twisted mockery. Cannot manage an estate. Cannot woo a wife. The title should have gone to Michael. He could have done this. He had done this. Without the benefits and respect the title brought with it, he lifted the estate from poverty. Hell, he managed to make a woman fall in love with him whilst engaged to another man. I could not even convince my own wife to tolerate me.

And Katherine, I had stolen her light. Every forlorn glance, every solemn mood—they were my doing. She was so bright before we wed, airy and free. I had forced her into the mold of viscountess I had in my head. And she had tried, that I knew, it was apparent. She bent and she backed down. Every time I pushed, every time Mother pushed, she sacrificed her own happiness for our convenience. And she did it without asking for anything in return.

It was impossibly late when I finally retired for the evening, well into the early morning hours. The walk to my chambers was quiet and dark, and the only light was my from my singular candle.

My stomach dropped as I approached her door, shut firmly. All was quiet within. She would be asleep, dark hair tumbling across the linens in one of her white nightdresses, innocent and seductive in equal measure.

But they were not intended to seduce. She had no interest in my attentions, they were another sacrifice, another concession my wife made without comment. That fact, more than any other, made my stomach turn. Night after night wrapped in her arms, moving within her, and she loathed me. Did her stomach make a similar protest at the thought of my touch?

Finally, I continued to my chambers, changing for the evening and crawling beneath the covers before dousing the candle. I knew sleep would not come, but the ritual was a familiar comfort.

MORNING CAME SLOWLY, inevitably. From my bed, I watched the horizon lighten to pink, then turn to orange, and finally yellow as the sun made its appearance. Nothing of my situation looked better in the daylight.

Still, I dressed long before Stevens would typically arrive to assist. Stepping into the corridor, I shut my door and turned, only to find Katherine in the same position, wide-eyed and hand frozen on the handle.

The only certainty I arrived at during the night was that we needed to speak. To forge some sort of path forward.

Unfortunately, she had not reached that conclusion, starting abruptly, returning to her chambers and closing the door firmly behind her.

Two halves of me warred, the desire to give her the privacy she craved, and the need to have some resolution, even if it was only a plan for our remaining time in the country.

I settled on knocking. "Katherine? May I come in?"

A small voice from within asked, "do you have to?"

"No, but we should make a plan at some point. Obviously, avoiding each other seems likely to be ineffective."

"Fine."

I was greeted with the sight of my wife, curled into a small ball on the settee. Her feet were up, allowing her chin to rest on her knees while she wrapped her arms around her legs. I had not known an adult could contort themselves into such a small form, but she seemed comfortable. I looked for a seat; bed too intimate, settee too close. I settled on the trunk at the end of her bed.

She eyed me warily from her curled position. Now that I was here, I had no idea what to say. I started, hoping the answer would present itself in time, "Katherine..." She flinched, as though struck by the single word. Best to begin there. "I understand you're weary of me, that is understandable. But I need you to know, I will never, ever, hit you. No matter what happens, if you take nothing else from this, take that."

She nodded, head bobbing on her knees. Her expression was unconvinced but at least I said it.

Briefly, her lips parted, as if she wished to speak, before they closed again. The silence dragged before I could take it no longer. "What is it?"

In the same, small, childlike voice from before, she asked, "are you going to throw me out?" She thought—?

"No, of course not! This is your home, and Grayson House is your home. When I married you, I swore to protect you. I would not have you on the street! Do you really? Am I truly that... awful?"

"No," she paused, a contemplative expression on her face, "no, that was an unkind worry."

The relief I felt at that answer was palpable.

"Do you wish to be established elsewhere?"

"No."

"Do you desire to return to London as planned? Or remain here?"

"My sister is nearing her confinement. Perhaps I should visit with her? Until she has the babe?"

"If that is what you want, I would not stop you."

"Very well, I shall leave from town."

"As you wish."

Thirty-One

THORNTON HALL, KENT - JULY 8, 1814

HUGH

THE FIRST THING I noticed was the music. Or lack thereof. I would not have guessed that. Day after day, night after night, the pianoforte remained silent, gathering dust far too quickly. I had not noticed the tinkling of keys as she worked out a tricky passage, the lilting melodies, the rhythmic plunking when it was there. But its absence was unmistakable.

Her scent dissipated next. The jasmine and orange blossoms lingered for several days. It disappeared first from the study then the dining room. The drawing room and music room were next. After a week, it lingered only in her bedroom. After a fortnight, I could only detect it on her bedclothes. Soon I knew it would be entirely undetectable.

After her scent, her meal choices were run through. Instead of the flavorful combinations my wife preferred, supper after supper reverted to my mother's preferences, dry and tasteless. I could not recall Mrs. Hudson's meals ever being so bland, even under my mother's direction. It was entirely possible that my taste buds had abandoned me in my sorry state.

Laughter too left the house. Gone were the days of easy smiles and jovial manners amongst the staff. Instead, their previous stiff behavior returned. I would have sworn that was my preference, but I could not say that now. Mrs. Tanner, the housekeeper who Katherine hired, appeared on the verge of turning in her notice every time she spoke to Mother. The tenants missed her as well; I heard nothing but questions of her welfare and anticipated return wherever I went.

Was it truly possible, having lived my entire life without her, that she had become so essential in a matter of months? Before her, I would have said that I was, if not happy, at least content. It should not have been so difficult to return to that state. But no, she was indispensable to my happiness now.

Night after night staring at an empty table proved that beyond a doubt. Worse was the sight of my mother in her position. The smug satisfaction with which she took her seat when she was well enough for supper made my stomach turn.

No one told me, I did not know, just how completely my wife would turn my life upside down in the best possible way. Or how I would ache when she was gone. She wrote, of course, from Lincolnshire. They were perfunctory letters with no empty promises of a swift return. And I returned with equally perfunctory letters urging her to take her time. As if her absence was not as though I had lost a vital organ.

I could not bring myself to ask for her return, to encourage her, to drag her back to where she had no wish to be. Not again. Never again. She would return to me of her own volition, or she would not return. I would never force her again. I made that vow every single night. And again, every morning after haunting dreams. Horrible dreams where I slaked my lust in her while she stared at me with nothing but contempt in her eyes. Deservedly so. Months and months she endured my attentions with nothing like a complaint, and month after month I baselessly assumed she welcomed those attentions.

What a fool. A monstrous fool.

TONIGHT, once again, Mother had taken Katherine's place at the table. Every glance from my tasteless plate was a hateful reminder of my failures as a husband. She was chattering on about something insipid, as was her wont. I was wallowing in self-pity, as was my wont.

"You know, I may need to let Mrs. Tanner go. She simply refuses to make the changes I requested. We cannot have such impertinence from the help."

Something about my mother's tone drew my attention, and it was fortunate. My wife liked Mrs. Tanner; I knew she did.

"It is not your place to dismiss staff any longer. And, it is my understanding that Kate is pleased with her performance."

"Well, Katherine is not here, is she? She abandoned her husband and ran off to whatever swamp she calls home. Which staff she is pleased with is hardly relevant. I am here to manage them, and I must be free to do so as I see fit."

It was the exact sort of argument that would have won me over. Perhaps even as recently as a month passed. "Cannot possibly have another place setting at Christmas dinner, Kit cannot attend." "She's a vicious fortune hunter who purposefully locked herself in the closet to entrap you." "Michael is determined to steal your fortune and title and left your father to die." Something about the nonchalant manner in which she said it chafed. As if there was no question that I would allow her to denigrate my wife and do as she wished.

"I am sorry, Mother. I had not thought you were incapable

of managing the household. Do not worry, I will handle arrangements with Mrs. Tanner in my wife's absence, you need not tax yourself."

"I did not say that! Of course, I am perfectly capable of managing any staff. But to tolerate such behavior, it is unseemly."

"Mrs. Tanner stays. All of the staff stay. The curtains stay. The furnishings stay. The table stays as it is. This is Kate's household to run as she sees fit. If you cannot or will not manage it in a manner that meets my satisfaction during her *brief* absence, then I will. Am I understood?"

It was, without a doubt, the most unkind speech Mother had ever heard from me. Perhaps from anyone. Her owlish eyes and gaping fish mouth announced her astonishment, plain for the world to see.

"Am I understood? Yes or no?"

Her "yes" was a quiet, petulant thing, and I had no doubt that I would pay for this in some not particularly subtle way.

"Good," I replied, declaring the discussion over whilst pushing my unappetizing plate to the side. "Now, if you'll excuse me. I believe I'm finished."

Thirty-Two

EARNSHAW FARM, LINCOLNSHIRE –
SEPTEMBER 30, 1814

KATE

Lizzie's house was crowded, stifling. How was it that the bustle and noise I longed for was now irritating, confining?

It was no smaller than it had been a year ago, and the baby, now born, took up little more room than he did in his mother's belly. But my adorable nieces and nephews found a way to be underfoot at absolutely every moment of the day. Sydney, though far too large to be underfoot, was quite skilled at ensuring his possessions more than compensated for the absence.

Fortunately, the birth was an easy one, and Lizzie was well on her way to recovery after little more than a fortnight. My mother and the parishioners had Lizzie and baby Elliot's care well in hand. I was completely superfluous, and they were taking no pains to hide it.

Worse still, my hands were unused to chores that were once as easy as breathing. They were chapped from washing powder, sore from darning, and burned from the ovens. Lizzie once again tutted at the sight when I placed Elliot back in her arms. Settling him to her breast, she fixed me with the disapproving older sister stare, years in the making. "Kate, what are you still doing here?"

"Helping you with the babe, of course."

"Mother is helping with the babe while you're making a mess of yourself." I could not hide my stricken look at that comment. She rushed to explain, "I didn't mean it like that. It's just, you have your own household to run. Should you not be working on making little lords and ladies of your own?"

"You think I'm superfluous?"

"Oh, Kate, no. I think you are married. Marriage changes people. I am not the girl I was when Sydney and I met. I would not slot any better back into Mother's household than you are here."

"But..."

"Kate, why are you really here? Do not say for the birth, for you know Mother is well capable of providing far more assistance than I know what to do with."

"I missed you. Is that so difficult to believe?"

"No, it's not difficult to believe. But it's not the entire story either."

She burped Elliot, and he made a sleepy smacking sound with his lips as he settled comfortably in her arms for a nap. I traced a gentle finger over the wrinkles on his forehead, softly not to wake him. He looked like an old man, bald on top with tufts of hair over his ears and around the back. Even in sleep, his face was scrunched in something that looked adorably like irritation. But he was a quiet boy, none of the incessant screams I remembered from his eldest sister. Every time I looked at him, really looked instead of just changing or bathing him briskly, there was a pang of longing. It was one I was not interested in examining too closely.

"I know he's the handsomest of grumpy old men, but you're evading the question," she said.

"Did you always love Sydney?"

Out of the corner of my eye, I saw her tilt her head in question, searching for an explanation on my face. She must have found whatever she was looking for because she sighed before answering. "I didn't know what love was, Katie. Not then. If you had asked me, of course, I would have said yes. But I didn't love him then as I do now. Marriage isn't easy if that's what you're asking. Even now, there are days when he leaves his muddy boots in the middle of the floor, and I swear he won't make it through the night.

"So no, I didn't love him when I married him. I liked him very much. I thought he was unbearably handsome. But, it wasn't love, that took time. All that to say, you may yet come to love your Hugh."

"How did you—?" She cut me off with a withering look. Right, Lizzie knew all.

"Do you know, I think I was married for about six, maybe seven months. Sydney and I had a huge row. I cannot even remember what it was about now. But, do you remember when I left to attend to cousin Daphne during her confinement?"

"You ran away too?"

"Oh, yes. Stayed away a full two months before she finally sent me back. A word of advice, it won't be easier to return for staying away longer. And whatever the problem, it won't get any smaller for time and distance."

"When did you become so smart?"

"I've always been smarter than you. You were just too dense to see it. Now, tell me, how is Juliet? You said you received a letter?"

"Oh, Lizzie! You will never believe it. Her father was

arrested for gaming debts. And she is to be married but not to the Duke of Rosehill. She will marry Michael, Mr. Wayland."

"I beg your pardon?"

"That is what I thought too, but it's all right here." I said, pulling the letter from my apron pocket.

LETTERS BETWEEN HUGH and I had been superficial, with a forced casualness that left far more unsaid than said. I spent nearly a full day attempting to find words to announce my return.

Far too much wasted parchment later, I settled on a cursory, "I am returning to Kent. I should arrive in a week's time, perhaps eight days."

I signed it simply, Kate, as I had all my letters. Anything else was too formal or too intimate. If there was one thing I did not want to be, it was "too."

As the carriage pulled to a stop in the round drive, I could not help but recall my first visit to Thornton Hall.

My honeymoon.

How imposing the redbrick building once was, with its stories, wings, and towers. Now though, it was familiar, welcoming. Even though my reception there was likely to be far from pleasant, I was glad to be home. Uneasy, nervous, terrified, but glad, nonetheless.

I had barely stepped from the carriage when the door flung open. Hugh skidding to a stop in the gravel before me. Out of breath and gasping for air, he stared at me. His hair was overlong and scraggly. His beard, too, was overgrown and unkempt. Wrinkles were etched into the linen of his shirt and the silk of his cravat.

Quite frankly, he looked like rubbish. Unbearably handsome rubbish.

Seeming to remember himself, he straightened slightly before saying simply, "Welcome home."

And just the smallest bit of my unease melted at his words coupled with his painfully earnest expression.

HUGH

Her letter arrived only a few hours before she did.

Forty-eight days. And, somehow, the three or so odd hours between receiving her letter and her arrival were the longest of them all.

I lived more than twenty years without her. Somehow forty-eight days had seemed an eternity. And now she was in front of me, close enough to touch, and I had no idea what to say.

I had raced out here, slipping on the gravel drive and nearly landing on my face. Surely, I looked like a schoolboy desperate for a present when his father returned from travel.

She had nothing to say in response to my daft greeting. Instead, she surveyed me, a slow perusal from the tip of my head down to my feet.

Though it lacked physicality, that look burned, low and interested in my belly. Distractedly I ran a hand through my hair. That's when I remembered just how slovenly and disordered I looked.

No wonder she was staring in astonishment, it was not interest but disgust. "Sorry. I, uh, I did not receive your note until a few hours ago. I had not yet found the time to set myself to rights."

"Don't." The response seemed more reflex than thought, and she looked as shocked to have said it as I was to hear it. "I mean, no need on my account." Her cheeks were flushed most fetchingly and her eyes downcast.

"I should have put more effort into my appearance before your arrival, it is disrespectful."

She was staring somewhere in the vicinity of my creased cravat when she answered, quiet and low, "I... maybe keep the beard?"

She wanted me to keep the beard? She liked it? Stevens could shove his lectures then. I ran a hand across the growth of several days. It would be inappropriate in town, but here, in the country...

The early autumn breeze tossed her scent my way. It was even lovelier than I remembered. *She* was even lovelier than I remembered. Unlike me, Kate was in perfect order, her deep teal gown was pristine and wrinkle free, not a curl out of place, not even a smudge to be found on her leather gloves.

How could I have thought her "too" anything, unless it was too exquisite to be beheld?

She shifted, adjusting her weight, transferring her bonnet from one hand to the other, discomfited. The movement shocked me from my inane silence. "Of course, if it pleases you. It will certainly vex Stevens, which is always amusing. He will be unhappy though, he was counting on your influence." The half joke, half statement of fact earned me a small, gapped tooth smile. I missed that gap, it was quite charming really, lending a sweetness to her countenance that matched her heart.

"Send him my way. I shall endure his wrath."

"Oh no, it is my wrath to endure. I just got you back—I could not bear for anything to send you away again."

I recognized the intimacy implied in those words only after her eyes widened slightly in response. I could not bring myself to regret them. The sentiment was certainly true.

Rather than draw further attention to my slip, I offered her an arm to escort her into the house.

Six months ago, I would have missed it, hell, forty-nine days ago I would have missed it. Were I not so attuned to her in this moment, I never would have seen the tiny flinch she made before sliding her hand in the crook of my arm. It served as the slap to the face I needed. We may have flirted about my unkempt beard and jested about servants' disapproval, but our situation was untenable, nothing was all right.

There was still work to be done.

Thirty-Three

THORNTON HALL, KENT - OCTOBER 15, 1814

KATE

THE HOUSE WAS THE SAME. Somehow, I had expected Agatha to return everything to the way it was before I existed. The only difference was the lingering scent of lilacs and death in the drawing room. It seemed that, after weeks away and a catastrophic shift in our marriage, the house should have reflected the turmoil.

My husband's appearance certainly did. Hugh was a handsome man. Even when I disliked him, there was no denying that. But now, with several days of growth on his chin, and several weeks of it on the top of his head... He was devastating.

I had little more than half an hour to refresh myself before supper. I briefly wondered how long we would retain Mrs. Hudson, now that Anna was to wed her Augie. I suspected she would retire when her first grandchild made their appearance. Mrs. Hudson's loss would be a devastating blow. I would need a new lady's maid as well. Mary was the obvious choice, and she had proven a more than adequate substitute the few times Anna had been unable to attend me. Such things were worries for tomorrow.

Agatha had made herself scarce in the brief time I had been home. It was a welcome reprieve, and I could only pray she had another megrim. I was not ready to face her tonight. Days in a carriage had left me weary, and the nerves over my reception had made me tetchy.

Hugh seemed pleased to see me, eager even. I could not think I would have received such a welcome if he were unhappy to see me.

Mary made quick work of my coiffure and selected a lovely seafoam gown. "Mary, is there anything I missed when I was away?"

Mary had looser lips than Anna, so I would need to be more careful in my confidences, but it would serve me well tonight.

"Well, at first, the dowager was quite busy, making all sorts of demands. She wanted all your changes put back and was ready to fire Mrs. Tanner for refusing, but His Lordship put a stop to that right quick. Said we weren't to change a single thing without your approval. Well, she was in such a state over it that she refused to give any sort of direction. I think that was supposed to be a punishment, but the house always runs better when she is away. His lordship took over the food orders and such, so I doubt you'll find much out of place."

"Hugh refused to let her change anything?"

"Oh yes, it was an entire ordeal at supper one night. Timothy saw the whole thing. His Lordship said it was your household to run as you see fit."

"He missed you something fierce. Stevens was quite ready to turn in his notice when we got your letter this afternoon. He said that he refuses to have his good name associated with a gentleman running around so unkempt like His Lordship. But, between you and me, some of the maids and I were thinking you wouldn't mind it so much. We certainly didn't." I couldn't restrict a pointed cough at that—that was too much, even for my purposes. They may be right, but they ought not to be ogling my husband. "Sorry ma'am."

"No, I asked. Perhaps you might discourage speculation on my opinions of various aspects of my husband's person though?"

"Yes, ma'am." She glances down, properly chastened.

Studying my coiffure, looking for wayward strands, she deemed it acceptable. Turning her attention toward the bouquet at the window, she grabbed a single jasmine blossom, and slipped it in my curls, pinning it in place. The effect was lovely.

MY TENTATIVE OPTIMISM was shattered when I stepped into the drawing room and was immediately beset by the overdrawn scent of lilacs.

Agatha.

Hugh was there too, clothing less rumpled but the beginnings of a beard and his scraggly locks were still present. Stevens may have been disappointed, but I was not. He startled to his feet at my appearance, his gray eyes flitted over my person, not steely but... warm? Interested perhaps?

I could not explain exactly the reason, but I felt as though he was looking, not for fault, but simply because it gave him pleasure. I enjoyed a single moment of revelry before Agatha interrupted with a pointed hoot-cough.

Reluctantly, I turned toward her, offering a nod of acknowledgement. I expected she would like some sort of appreciation for managing the estate in my absence. Fortunately, I was armed with the knowledge that the credit was not due to her.

She was still petite, pretty even, but I could swear her slightly hooked nose had gotten more birdlike in my absence. It was likely the combination of feathers in her hair and the perpetual squawks for attention that made it so in my mind. Why on earth was she wearing feathers for a family supper?

One of the servants directed us to the table—still sized for no more than six. I thought that would be one of the first things she would have changed. Agatha made her usual dash for her former place.

Certainly, she had adopted it for her own once more. With a resigned sigh, I moved toward the open seat, unwilling to take up the fight after so long a journey.

Hugh glanced across the table and stared at the sight. "Mother, Kate has returned. You are in her place."

I imagined the expression of shock on Agatha's face was mirrored on my own. She offered a slow blink but no comment before stepping away from the chair and forfeiting my rightful place to me. Hugh noticed where we were seated? Hugh cared where we were seated? And when did he start calling me Kate? I had always preferred it over Katherine. It was even more delightful in his voice, deeper for his warning.

I couldn't hide the small smile as I took my seat. It would read as smug to Agatha. There *was* a hint of smugness there but warmth too, affection for my husband.

I was delighted to find my favorite of Mrs. Hudson's soups set before me, the earliest of fall squash and comforting spices was a far better homecoming than I could have expected, especially with so little notice.

Glancing up, Hugh was watching me with an interest that my dining did not usually warrant. It was slightly unnerving.

I seemed to have broken my husband in my absence. Gone was the disinterest and obliviousness, in its place I seemed to find evaluating looks and captivated expressions. I thought it might be an improvement. At the moment, it was warming something high in my chest, near my heart. The newfound interest may suffer from brevity, but there was only one way to know.

Seeming to realize the staring was disquieting and a silent dinner was dull, Hugh asked, "How did you leave your sister? She is recovering well from the birth?"

"Yes, quite well. She was ready to have me out from underfoot. It seems I've become quite redundant in my absence."

"I'm certain no one could ever find you expendable," he said.

"She is not one to mince words. I think, should you ever meet, she would be more than willing to list the ways in which I am superfluous."

"I would like that. Not the discussion of your superfluousness, of course. I meant meeting your sister... Is the babe quite well?" Hugh spoke quickly, correcting himself almost before he had finished the sentence.

"Oh yes! Elliot, the grumpy old man, is perfect. Ten fingers and toes all accounted for."

"Grumpy old man?"

"He's, uh, not the cutest babe I've ever seen," I said, sheepish for insulting an infant.

Hugh covered his snort behind a napkin, feigning a cough. "Oh dear, I hope you did not tell your sister that."

"She is the one responsible for the moniker. She is not overly sentimental. That is why she was so comfortable labeling me as underfoot and sending me on my way."

Agatha chose that moment to cut in, reminding us of her presence. "I sympathize with her desire for you to be elsewhere. It is a family trait, I presume. Ugly offspring." Unable to resist twisting the knife, she continued, "I do hope any children from your marriage take after my son."

I was at something of a loss, floundering for redress for the sheer number of insults inherent in that speech. That was when Hugh surprised me, catching my gaze before replying simply, "I don't."

"What?" she asked, startled.

"I don't. I hope they look like Kate. With big, blue-green eyes, and her pretty curls."

Oh. Oh my.

That was a worry I hadn't even recognized in myself. I studiously avoided thoughts of our future children in all but the most abstract sense. The flicker of warmth in my chest burned hotter, affection blooming for this man. His eyes never left mine; his expression one of perfect sincerity. He hadn't been considering our children in the abstract. He had been picturing them. And he had been imagining them with my features. Best of all, instead of finding them wanting, he wanted them.

Abruptly, my vision blurred, tears filling my eyes. I swallowed back the lump in my throat. Hugh began to rise but I shook my head, urging him to stay seated. If he reached my side the tears would be unstoppable, of that I was certain.

My revelation was interrupted by the arrival of the roasted duck, another of my favorites. It, too, was perfectly seasoned and tender. Agatha had made her dislike of duck plain; it was a wonder Mrs. Hudson was able to prepare it so quickly.

Hugh, again, shocked me with his interest. "Your parents, I hope you left them in good health?" The question wasn't perfunctory, there was nothing but sincerity in his countenance.

"Oh yes, they're both thrilled to have another grandchild to dote upon. I do not think any of the elder children went without a sweet for more than a quarter of an hour between the two of them."

"I know the weather will turn soon, so perhaps next summer they will be able to visit. After the planting?"

"Be careful what you offer, my lord. You may never get my father out of the library."

"If that becomes an issue, we may send him over to see Michael and Juliet. Their library will certainly surpass ours by the summer. Particularly if what I have seen of their efforts is any indication."

"You've been to see them?"

"Yes, the renovations on Revello House are coming along nicely. They're deliriously happy as well. I am glad they were able to find a path through their difficulties." His gaze was significant, willing me to understand.

Agatha interrupted before I could reply, "A path through their difficulties? Honestly, Hugh, what is going on in your head? That chit has ruined herself and is forever saddled with a no-good, swindling, bastard. She has doomed not only herself, but her children, and her children's children. Honestly, I am ashamed to have had her in my home."

"That is unfortunate because I invited them to dine with us on Wednesday, in my home. Mine and Kate's. I suppose you will have to dine elsewhere."

"Excuse me?"

"I have invited my brother and his wife to dine with us. I am not sure where the confusion is in that statement."

I broke in. "Hugh..." My voice was too thick with emotions. Nothing but his name would break free. Gratitude, astonishment, feeling, it was all too much to bear. Somehow, in my absence, my husband became the kind of man I could love. It was an overwhelming realization. It would be all the more crushing if it were temporary. *Please let this be true. Please.*

Once again, we were interrupted by the arrival of almond cakes. Argument temporarily suspended until the servants left, I couldn't resist a fortifying bite of a favorite treat. The hint of orange flower and citrus offset the nutty earthiness of the almonds in a perfect balance.

I caught Hugh's eyes from across the table and I knew. He planned the menu. He selected my favorites. Whether he had learned them without my notice or whether he had asked Mrs. Hudson, he arranged this welcome supper for me. Who was this man? Where did he come from? How did I make him stay?

Thirty-Four

HUGH

THE FIRST NOTES washed over me from where I braced against the doorframe. Dark and rich like the finest drink, with the same warmth that built in my chest. She was playing again, deft hands dancing over ivory keys with an unstudied air. She was unbearably talented, my wife. The melody was unfamiliar to me but watching her play... I thought I understood how much I missed her. But, having her here, it was as though a limb had regrown. The tightness in my chest that had become so familiar that I no longer noticed its existence was now gone. I could breathe again.

The piano bench seemed to sooth her, too. Her back straightened, her motions became more fluid, confident, elegant. Why did I not spend every evening watching her play? Instead, I had spent the evenings shrouded away in the study, only leaving the door cracked so some of her notes might find their way to me. I could have spent night after night with this vision before me. My wife in her favored sanctuary, waltzing with fingers and keys.

Faced only with her back, I was treated to the sight of a jasmine blossom tucked in her dark hair, the crisp white contrast of the petals against mahogany tresses drew the gaze. A curl escaped her coiffure and now called the base of her neck home. The desire to brush it away warred with the need to hear her, undisturbed.

Mother had, most fortunately, decided to take to her bed with a megrim. I was free to my own, uninterrupted, musings. Had she been particularly awful tonight? Or was I oblivious the entire time? Nearly every comment had been a purposeful slight against my wife in some subtle or less subtle manner.

That could not stand. Frankly, I felt a twist of shame low in my gut for allowing it to go on for as long as I had. I was a poor excuse for a husband. No longer.

Never again would this woman be made to feel unwanted or unappreciated. I was the luckiest man alive, and I would be ungrateful no longer. I would endeavor to deserve her.

The piece ended softly, each note decreasing in volume until there was nothing more than the suggestion of a note, a whisper. She startled at my applause, turning to me with hopeful eyes.

"You do not usually join me," she breathed.

"A travesty I plan to rectify."

"I thought you didn't care for music."

"I do not play myself, but I have always appreciated the skill and passion you demonstrate."

"I didn't realize."

"No, you would not have, I suppose. I did leave my study door open so I could hear you though."

"Why did you never join me?" she asked.

Because I was busy sorting out years of financial neglect. Because I was determined to dislike you. Because I was afraid you would be ashamed of me when you discovered what a fraud I am. This was the part I dreaded. Much as I missed her, much as I prayed for her return, I wished to avoid this for as long as possible.

"We have some things to discuss. Or—that is—I need to tell you some things. Are you overtired from your journey? Or is now acceptable."

Her gaze narrowed warily, and, without moving a single muscle, she closed herself off from me. Perhaps it was the stiffness in her posture, I could not be certain how, but the reality was plain before me.

"I would prefer now."

"Very well," I answered with a weary sigh.

Shoving myself off the frame and closing the door behind me, I made my way to the settee. Her improvements had not been implemented here. The room still bore the markings of my mother, down to the ostentatious brocade on the furnishings. But Kate's orange blossom and floral scent had already begun to overtake the lilac my mother preferred.

I gestured toward the chair across from me and she took it as indicated. Much as I wished her close, I must face her judgment head on. My heart was making a valiant attempt to escape my chest. I was not entirely certain why. She already hated me, how much worse could it possibly get?

"Hugh?"

"Sorry, I am not entirely certain where to start."

"The beginning seems as good a place as any."

"That's quite a long way..." I warned.

"I've got time."

"Very well. For the record, this story does not paint me in the very best of lights."

She chuckled at that. "I could hardly think worse of you than I did on the eve of our engagement."

"There is that, I suppose. I have nowhere to go in your esteem but up." With a fortifying breath, I began. "For my entire life, I have been... wary of Michael. I suppose it was my mother's doing, some imagined battle where she pitted us against one another. As far as I can recall, my father never had any designs for legitimizing Michael. He certainly had none after I was born. There was never any question of the lands and title falling to me. But that did not stop her. Michael lived in this in-between realm, half-son, half-servant."

"But he was better than me at everything, studies, sport, everything. Some of it was age, certainly seven years will ensure superiority in most things when you're young. but I could not see it that way. It is difficult to see injustice when it is the only thing you have ever known. Michael had always lived like that so why should I consider it strange, or wrong?"

"Do you know, when Father died, I actually convinced myself that Michael had, not necessarily killed him, but allowed him to die. I was certain that if I had been there, I could have saved him. Eleven years old and miles away and I thought myself a hero."

"Hugh—"

"I know, I saw him that day at the lake. Michael was far more a hero than I would have been, or at least he tried. Nearly killed himself trying to save me when I wasn't even drowning." I broke off with a bitter chuckle. "I cannot imagine what he did attempting to save Father. It was winter too, the lake must have been near freezing. It is lucky he did not perish in the attempt."

"I was too young. And my mother was too—well my mother. Michael took over managing the estate. He did it for seven years. Then he handed it over to me without a word of complaint. What I did not know then, what I did not know until quite recently, in fact, was that the estate was all but bankrupt when Father died. A fact that has me questioning the timing of his death."

I cracked there. I had not voiced my thoughts before, not about that. But to suggest such a thing... And about my own father... My throat was thick and tight with unbidden sentiment, and it was a real question whether I would be able to finish this sorry tale.

Without a word, Kate rose from her seat across from me, moving to my side, slotting her small form near mine. She took my hand in both of hers, rubbing her thumb along the back of my own. It was that gesture, more than anything, that broke me. A few tears escaped without my permission.

Swallowing harshly, I continued. "I have not been able to bring myself to ask Michael, but the timing is too convenient to be coincidence. Tom and I have been sorting through back ledgers. It seems that Michael somehow managed to gamble our way out of debt. Not only out of debt but into prosperity. Then had enough remaining to open his club. And I accused him of skimming from the estate to open it."

"In my infinite wisdom as new acting viscount, I released the solicitor he hired. I would have terminated the steward as well but there were no others qualified. I was convinced that I needed someone loyal to me and not Michael. Some months ago, I discovered that the funds the solicitor told me were sent to the estate and the funds the steward reported receiving did not match. Had not matched for some time. It is a discrepancy to the tune of some £15,000. I did not want to believe it at first. Then, of course, I was convinced that the culprit was Michael's steward. But it was the solicitor of course. I have determined that now. I will pursue legal action, of course, but it is unlikely that much if anything will be recovered.

"So you see, in addition to being such an arrogant ass that I made the sweetest woman in the world loathe me, I am an utter failure at the role I was born to as well."

"Oh, Hugh..." She freed one hand from mine, brushing my overgrown hair behind an ear. "I do not loath you. Find you irksome and astonishingly disinterested on a frequent basis, yes, but loath no."

"Oh, well, that is good then," I tossed back to her with my most sarcastic tone.

"Well, the astonishing disinterest at least has a cause now, given enough groveling I may even be able to forgive that."

"Kate, I did not mean to make you feel unimportant."

"I never thought you were doing it intentionally. Also, I can thoroughly disabuse you of the notion that I am the sweetest woman in the world. I did call you spineless and heartless I believe."

"You were not precisely wrong in your assessment. In fact, you were right, I do not deserve you. Michael took an estate on the brink of bankruptcy and made it more than prosperous in less than seven years without the weight of a title to throw around. I managed to take the same estate back to the edge of bankruptcy in four years. You deserve so much better than that."

"Hugh, I did not marry you for your lands or your title."

"You did not wish to marry me at all."

"Fair, but if I had, it would not have been for lands or titles. That is never what I wanted out of a marriage. I wanted someone who looks at me the way Michael looks at Juliet, the way Father looks at Mother, the way Sydney looks at Lizzie. I know we cannot have that. But I hope we may be able to have a marriage of mutual respect."

I tried to recall how, exactly, my brother looked at his wife. The expression on his face when he was courting her surreptitiously, scandalously, but there was nothing. Even in that I had been distracted and unobservant.

Still, the ache in my chest when Kate was away, the rising hope now, those did not feel like respect. At least not entirely. Was my punishment for my marital failings to fall in love with my wife, a woman who would try her best to respect me? It was no less than I deserved. I owed her that. "I would like that."

"Very well. Allow me to help. When I married you, this became my home too, these are my tenants to care for just as they are yours. Let me help."

"I cannot allow you to—"

"Respect, Hugh." The scold hung in the air between us. Her eyes were wide, shocked that it had escaped. She was right though, as usual.

"Very well. It is quite late tonight and you have been traveling for the best part of a week. I should allow you to retire."

"I suppose so," she agreed.

I rose, assisting her up. I trailed after her up the quiet steps, down the hall, and to her bedroom where I left her to get ready for bed.

Somehow I was both pleased and disappointed in the outcome of the evening.

Thirty-Five

KATE

"February 10, 1807, modiste bill for £27. Same day, £5 at the cobbler. February 11, 1807, Flowers for £56." Hugh read off the banking documents before him while I checked them against the solicitor's documents.

"What on earth was going on that she needed to spend quite so much on flowers?"

"My mother was hosting a ball, I believe."

"Did she purchase the entire florist shop?"

"Perhaps they had to grow the lilac trees specially." He glanced up at me from beneath dark lowered lashes. The corner of his mouth turned up just slightly.

"Was that a joke, Hugh Grayson?"

"Only if you found it funny, Kate Grayson."

"I did, more of those please," I demanded.

"That is a great deal of pressure."

"You can manage, I have faith."

That statement earned me something even closer to a smile. His lips were fuller when he wasn't frowning. He was beautiful, my husband. It was a masculine kind of beauty, but full pink lips, long black lashes, and silver-blue eyes could never be anything but *beautiful*. It was a good thing he never smiled at me, or I would be in great danger of falling in love with him.

We continued on, comparing the years that all matched to perfection. Michael had been meticulous, down to shillings and pence. With every ledger closer to the time that Hugh took over, he grew more and more tense.

"What do you say we break for luncheon?" I asked.

"All right."

"What do you say we eat outside then continue out there? The day is too fine to be cooped up in here."

"But... It is work. Work is done in a study."

"So says who?"

"Well... everyone," he blustered.

"Just try it? Please? If it's a mess, no harm done."

He nodded his assent, and I went to find Mrs. Hudson to alert her to the change. She agreed with only a little tutting.

He found me in the rose garden, in the last crimson blooms of fall. Timothy had brought out a blanket and some finger sandwiches. Hugh joined me on the blanket with the ledgers, setting them off to one side.

I settled on my hip, knees bent with my feet tucked against my side, leaning toward him with the picnic basket between us. He settled with his legs in front of him, unaccountably stiff.

"Hugh?"

"Yes?"

"Is this your first picnic?"

He tucked a loose, overlong strand of hair behind his ear, shifting into a looser position. "... yes. Am I doing it wrong?"

"I don't think there is a wrong way to picnic. You've really never done so?"

"No. I believe Michael and a few of the servants would occasionally. Obviously, my mother would never allow me to join."

"And she never took you on one of your own? With Tom?"

A gentle breeze began, flipping one the ledgers open and flipping pages. He grabbed at the ledgers, answering me distractedly. "It is improper to eat with rodents and insects." He lifted the basket to slip the ledgers underneath. Turning back to me, he froze. "I did not mean... That is what she always said."

"But not what you think?"

"I do not know what I think, as I have not tried it yet."

"Well, let's gather the necessary data then." I said, handing him a plate. "Sandwich?"

"Yes, please." He took it from me, taking a hearty bite.

I turned to grab my own, and joined him in quiet munching. The breeze was pleasant, and the sun was warm. These days would be fewer and farther between as the days grew shorter.

"Do you remember that day in the park?" I asked.

"With your brother?"

"Yes."

"I do," he said.

"This feels like one of those days. The last truly pleasant weather before winter. I love these days."

"Yes." He considered his last bite of sandwich thoughtfully. "I am sorry about that day."

"What for?"

"My mother was horribly rude. And I did not check her."

"Ah... Yes. Do not be sorry. Lady Rycliffe had the most amusing things to say about her once you were out of earshot."

That earned me a chuckle and a "fair."

The breeze kicked up a bit, pulling a few of my curls from their pins and brushing them across my face. I tucked them back and away.

"I did have a thought I was wondering if we might consider," I said.

"What was that?"

"Kit is a solicitor now. He and his partner, William Hart, own offices in town. One of them may be able to assist us in this endeavor."

"No." Hugh brokered no room for argument.

"All right then," I said, tone hollow.

He looked up from his sandwich, brow furrowed. "Oh, Kate. I did not mean... I am rubbish at this." He trailed off, pinching his brow between thumb and forefinger.

"What did you mean?"

"I... Your brother already loathes me. I cannot admit what a mess I have made. Particularly after the way I have treated him."

"Yes, he had quite a lot to say on the subject of you before we wed. But that hardly matters. He is Kit. He will always help if I ask."

He considered me for a moment, head tilted, and eyes narrowed. "You say that with such conviction."

"What do you mean?"

"He will help if you ask. There is not a doubt in your mind that he will, is there?"

"Of course not. That is what brothers do."

"Not all brothers." There was an edge to his tone, like broken glass, harmless but cutting with the wrong move.

I considered my response. "Michael and Tom would do anything for you, Hugh."

"We do not have that kind of relationship. Especially not after what I did, sending Michael away."

"He almost drowned you whilst trying to save you from

drowning. Which, while ironic, was touching if you were not the one inhaling half the lake."

"And then I nearly ruined his every hope of happiness."

"Almost. But you didn't. And you weren't entirely wrong, what you said. He should not have been courting her."

"You..." His jaw hung slightly slack as he trailed off.

"You were right, and I'm sorry. I should not have encouraged their relationship. I am glad that I did, and I am thrilled with how it ended. But it was wrong, and it could have ended much worse."

"I... I did not know he loved her. It never occurred to me until he said as much. Because I do not know my brother at all. All this time, he has been the villain in my story."

"Perhaps there are no heroes and villains. Just people making choices, good and bad. Except your solicitor. I suspect he is merely a villain." I teased, pulling the ledgers free from their basket binding and handing one to him. Hoping to draw out one of the quarter smiles of his. If I were truly lucky, I could achieve half of a smile.

"Where did we leave off?" He asked.

"Farming equipment from spring of 1811. Speaking of, Sydney, my sister's husband, was making some adjustments to his plows. He tested the changes to one last year and found great success, so he was applying them to all of his equipment. I could write to him, if you would like. For the plans, I mean."

Hugh had his full lower lip trapped between his teeth as he stared at me in an entirely new manner. The breeze caught a curl again. Before I could brush it away, his hand came forward to tuck it behind my ear for me. His touch, first cool but leaving a brand of fire in its wake, startled me. He ripped his hand away, settling it in his lap. His gaze dropped too.

"I would appreciate that very much," he murmured.

"They have implemented a four-crop rotation as well.

Unfortunately, I was distracted by Elliot and did not listen to the reasoning. I can ask about that as well?"

"Yes, thank you."

I considered him for a moment. "Why is Sydney different from Kit?"

"I was an arrogant ass to Kit during the settlement discussions. I have not directly slighted your sister's husband."

"Kit would still help us. I know he would. And I think we need it if there is any hope of getting the funds back."

He sighed, tipping his head back with the effort. "I will write to Kit, will that satisfy?"

"I can do it."

"Kate, I owe the man an apology. Let me do the gentlemanly thing, if for the first time."

"Fine. But I am adding a postscript."

"If you insist," he said, the corner of his lip tipping up in a third of a smile. I counted it a success.

"I do. Now, March, 1811."

"£17..."

Thirty-Six

THORNTON HALL, KENT - OCTOBER 20, 1814

KATE

THERE WAS no knock on my door last night, or the night before. Even now, I wasn't certain if I wanted there to be a knock or not. At some point the nightly visits had to resume, right? Hugh needed an heir, tenuous marriage or not.

Was it even an unhappy marriage any longer? The days since my return had been... Pleasant? Astonishing? Confusing?

Hugh spoke to me in a way he never had. He asked my opinions, considered them thoughtfully, and implemented my suggestions. More than once, he sought me out. I was fairly certain, if I met *this* man in that ballroom all those months ago, I would have been desperate to marry him.

But the change was so abrupt. How could I trust him to remain like this? I had no idea he was even capable of it in the first place. Was this man my husband? Or was it the man I spent all those taciturn months with? Something in between? Someone else entirely? I liked this man very much, so I wanted this to be the man he truly was.

I could think of that later, for it was all I did when I was not buried in ledgers. Tonight, Mr. and Mrs. Wayland were due to dine with us. *How nice that sounded.* I'd had no time to visit Jules between my return and tonight's supper. But I cried when I read her letter in Lincolnshire. The lengths she undertook to be able to wed the man she so loved... It was too much. And now, to be settled so near... I could not be happier for her, it simply wasn't possible.

Agatha had kindly feigned another megrim. It was most gracious of her. That left Hugh and I alone in the drawing room when our guests arrived. And oh, what a change in her. When I had left her in London, Juliet had been withdrawn. Now she sparkled. We exchanged giddy smiles. Michael, on the other hand, looked exactly as he had when I met him, and nothing at all like that man too. Somehow, he'd managed another blackened eye. But instead of being surly and taciturn when he greeted Hugh, he was warm and affectionate. It was everything I had hoped for.

Michael, one spoonful of soup into dinner, commented, "if I thought we would have her for any length of time, I would steal Mrs. Hudson away from you."

"I would fight you. It was miserable enough the week she was away for the wedding. And that was when she was stifled with my mother's preferences. Now that Kate has returned, she will stay here for as long as we can keep her," Hugh answered.

"I suspect it will not be long if Augie has his way. He's had names picked out since we were fifteen."

"And pray tell, what names does a fifteen-year-old boy select for his future offspring?"

"I believe the girls were named for their mothers and the boys for their fathers. It was tragically sweet and not at all worthy of mocking, which was a sore disappointment to me."

"Most inconvenient. Is Anna aware she's birthing at least four children?"

"She agreed to wed him, so I suspect not," Michael answered with a crooked grin.

"And, Michael, may I inquire as to the cause of today's injury? Was it caused when you informed Anna of her husband's plans for the birthing bed?" I asked.

"Certainly not, Anna knows to direct her fists where they belong. No, my darling wife was overly enthusiastic during her morning constitutional."

"Michael! Ignore him, he walked into a worker carrying a rather large beam."

His grin weakened only slightly when a rather indelicate thunk sounded from beneath the table. The bruising in his eye may not be from her, but there would be a dark spot on his shin with her name on it.

"Duchess, darling, you're ruining the roguish reputation I've managed to build for Kate. She'll begin to suspect all of my other blackened eyes have perfectly innocuous causes as well."

"And then where will you be?" Juliet asked.

"Quite right. She finds me amusing and charming now, but if she realizes that I'm actually quite a suitable choice, she may drag some other rake out to the country to woo you."

"I would never," I replied in an attempt to clear my name from such obvious slander.

"Oh yes, your matchmaking machinations had nothing to do with why you begged me to join you in the country," Michael teased.

"My machinations were responsible for perhaps as much as thirty-six percent of the *polite requests* that *may* have occurred."

"You brought him out here for me? I assumed it was a coincidence." Juliet was far too good for the rest of us.

"Oh no, my darling," Michael corrected. "She found my courtship via surreptitious book selection to be charming."

"I found it to be somewhere between endearing and pathetic. But they made her happy. I did wonder though, when did you meet? Surely you were not leaving novels for a mystery woman."

"I should not say, for you will be far too smug," Michael answered, taking a healthy sip of wine.

"Oh, now I must know," Hugh added.

"She will be insufferable. Women always are when they're right." Michael directed at Hugh before turning to me. "If you must know, it was at your ball. You were quite determined to find me a wife, if you'll recall."

"I was, but not that wife! And then you were late. And you left early, I might add. When did you even find the time to meet? I know it was not on the dance floor."

"In your library."

"You were in the library? During a ball? I should have known. Certainly, my original choice for you would have been a poor match. I don't know what I was thinking. She adores dancing."

"And who would you have chosen for me?"

"Lady Rycliffe, she is the marchioness—" I began. Before I finished the title, he choked on his wine. Juliet burst into a fit of giggles at the sight. "What have I missed?"

"Nothing," Michael answered far too quickly.

"Tell me."

"It's not fit for the dinner table," he said.

"Well, now you must tell me."

Hugh sighed, pinching the bridge of his nose between two fingers. "I believe my brother and Lady Rycliffe had an agreement of sorts..."

"What sort of... oh."

"Precisely."

"Well, why did she not tell me that? "

"It's not entirely appropriate, Kate," Juliet replied.

"Well then, perhaps my matchmaking skills are not so dismal after all." I replied cheerfully. "Who else is in need of a bride? What sort of ladies does Tom fancy?"

"I don't actually know," Michael answered, brow furrowed.

Hugh added, "Tom is just nineteen. He is far too young to think of marriage."

"Perhaps I should focus on Cee after all. At least now that I know I was not so far off. Jules, who do we know?"

"I do not know anyone. I had less than half of a season."

"Surely there is someone?"

"Kit."

"Oh dear, no. Kit is far too studious."

"Ladies, perhaps we should leave the matchmaking to the fates. After all, I would never have expected that Hugh would have chosen you, yet here we are." Michael's comment, delivered jovially, stung.

Hugh straightened. "Why should I not have chosen her? There is no better choice in all of London."

It was the first time all evening that Hugh had been anything but easy, pleasant. His tone was sharp, and his gaze narrowed at Michael. My heart skipped for a moment. There was no lie in his countenance; he believed that, really truly, at least for this moment. And my heart believed him, too.

"I agree completely. With the one exception of course." Michael said, tipping his head toward his wife. "I only meant that she is far too good for you. I had not thought your taste was that refined."

Hugh held his brother's gaze for a moment, staring him down. Michael's explanation tracked through; he was far more likely to tease his brother than insult me outright. Hugh, apparently arrived at the same conclusion, easing back in his chair, warning gaze still hovering over Michael before shifting to me. His eyes flitted over my person, settling on my face. Finding whatever he was looking for, he took a calming swig of wine.

Juliet, ever skilled at managing tempers, suggested that we separate so the ladies could have our gossip time. We had been managing perfectly well with the gentlemen present, but she seemed to be communicating something with her husband with widened eyes and brow raises alone.

Thirty-Seven

HUGH

THIS CONVERSATION WAS GOING to be costly. In order to lure Michael into the study, I had to bribe him with the good port. Unfortunately, once he was seated, I lost my nerve somewhat. It had taken two subsequent glasses to return the words to the tip of my tongue where they now hovered.

"Out with it," he demanded.

Apparently, my unease was more obvious than I realized. "Out with what?"

"Whatever you're trying to gather the fortitude to ask. You don't share the expensive stuff lightly."

With a sigh, I forced myself to begin. "You and Juliet, you seem to have an... affectionate marriage."

He chuckled and took another sip. "That's one word for it." He was far too pleased with himself, and it was an irritating look on him.

"How does one... that is... how should I go about—"

"Increasing the *affection* in your marriage? I'm not certain how much assistance I can provide. Juliet's... enthusiasm was somewhat of a surprise to both of us. A welcome one of course." He paused with a significant brow raise and another sip, finishing the glass. He reached for the bottle between us and poured another glass with a heavy hand. "I think she was starved for affection—actual affection, not the euphemism—and I was the first lucky bastard to show her any." He examined the contents of his glass with a furrowed brow, contemplating the condensation.

I was forced to abandon metaphors in favor of transparency. "Kate flinches at my touch." I swallowed back the rest of my port, desperate to dull that memory.

When I finally risked a glance at him, his furrowed brow had turned in my direction. "Did you hurt her?"

"What? No, of course not."

He relaxed somewhat, a more thoughtful expression blooming. "She flinches when you're trying to be *affectionate*? Or at all touch? Is it just with you?"

"I suppose it is not so much a flinch. It is a pause. She has to think about it. It is just with me, you have seen her and Juliet embrace. And it is not all my touches but most."

"Does she react that way with any other men?"

My hackles were raised at that thought. "When would my wife be touching other men?"

"I didn't mean to imply anything untoward, just trying to clarify. So, she hesitates even when you're just trying to be near her? Not trying to initiate anything more?"

"Yes?" The word was more hesitation than answer. His question had me desperate to recall the last time I touched my wife without expectation. A sick feeling was building as I struggled to bring forth a memory.

"You are affectionate with your wife without further expectations, aren't you?" My silence spoke more than my words ever could and the shame was all encompassing.

"Right, well I'd start there. Gentle touches with no intentions of further intimacy. What about the rest of it? Is she... enthusiastic generally?"

"She always allows my attentions."

"She allows them? What does she say when you ask what she'd like to try or whether a touch is pleasurable?"

"I don't ask."

"You don't ask?"

"You do? She's my wife. Until I saw you and Juliet kissing around every corner, I thought my relations with Kate were what was expected between married couples."

His face landed in his palm, and I was regretting this entire conversation more than any I have ever had before. Why did I think the man would be helpful for the first time in my life when he could be obtuse and smug? When he finally surfaced, he threw back his glass and did not refill it this time.

"All right, clearly I've failed you as an elder brother. I'm sorry for that. I'm going to speak plainly, no more euphemisms."

"Do not touch her again until you ask if she's amenable and she agrees. Nothing beyond the barest touches necessary to maintain propriety. I mean it. Once she's agreeable to the most basic of touches and learns that they're not only offered as a prelude to something more you may press on. Ask her about more affectionate touches, gentle kisses to her hand or her cheek, that sort of thing. If she initiates casual touch, be appreciative of it but don't treat it as an invitation to press further." He paused there, waiting for acknowledgement.

I was frozen into stunned silence. I had rarely heard him string so many words together. Only once had he spoken so passionately in my presence. That disaster of a day when I realized what a sham my marriage was. All I could manage was a nod.

"I want you to accustom yourself to the idea that you may not be having marital relations for some time. Kisses, amorous touches, anything further does not happen until she asks for them, until she begs for them."

Now I was concerned, as I was still responsible for providing the next viscount. "But—"

"But nothing. Trust me, there is nothing in the entire world as heady as the woman you love requesting your attentions, craving your touch. You will thank me. You'll never want her to endure your attentions again."

"How can I be certain she will? Request that is."

"Because you're going to be the most charming man in existence. She is going to find her favorite flowers on every available surface. You're not going to present them to her, they're going to appear. She loves to play piano, so new arrangements will materialize at her place setting in the morning next to her favorite drink, which you will prepare—not the servants. You're going to express your love for her quietly, without expectation, every single day. You will ask her about her day and her interests and her hopes and her dreams. You will actually listen to what she tells you and ask thoughtful questions. You are going to learn what makes your wife feel loved. You're going to do those things for her, every minute of every day. You're going to make her fall in love with you. You're going to be a man who deserves that love."

"Just like that?"

"Just like that. Falling in love with Juliet was easy, figuring out how to love her the way she needed me to was the difficult part."

"And once I've done that, once I've earned her love and made her ask, what do I do then?"

He sighed and poured himself another glass. "Have you any parchment and ink? I need to draw a diagram."

Thirty-Eight

THORNTON HALL, KENT – OCTOBER 20, 1814

KATE

Marriage agreed with my friend. She was free with her smiles and unguarded, perhaps even sitting taller. I liked Michael in his own right, but even if I did not, I would adore him for the effect he had on Juliet. This was everything I had ever wanted for her.

It was all I had ever wanted for myself, too.

Something about the tentative truce Hugh and I had found made the pain of watching Jules and Michael all the sharper. Before our fight, it was a dull ache. It was a given that I would never have the love that I wanted. But now... It was closer. Closer but forever out of reach.

I felt the first flutterings in my heart when Hugh's hand brushed mine, or when his breath kissed my cheek. My stomach gave a pleasant jolt when I caught his eyes on me in that way that could never be interpreted as critical.

But I knew he would never feel the same, and that made it worse.

I thought being in a marriage with a man who I loathed

was bad. I had not considered the circle of hell that was lower still, the one where I fell in love with Hugh, and he did not return my affections.

"—and you are not listening to a word I'm saying, are you?"

"Jules?" Something about my tone must have given her pause. Wordlessly, she left her chair to join me on the settee, pulling my hand into her own. I opened my mouth, not entirely certain what I was going to say. Instead of words, a sob escaped.

Juliet pulled my face into the crook of her shoulder, rubbing my back softly. Whispered apologies and reassurances washed over me. Eventually the time between inelegant sniffs lengthened and I pulled free from her shoulder.

"Can you tell me? Can I help?" she asked, her own eyes a bit red. I glanced toward the still open door. She rose quickly, pulling it shut and snapping the lock into place before finding her way back to my side.

"I think I've ruined my marriage."

"Lord Grayson spent the evening staring at you like a much-denied treat. I very much doubt it is ruined. Also, I am given to understand that the success or failure of a marriage is very much the responsibility of both parties."

"I told him that I hated him and I never wanted to marry him."

Her blue eyes widened, shocked. "You did not want to marry him? Why did you not tell me?"

"Aunt Sophie had just passed. I didn't want to bother you with something so trivial."

"I thought you were happy! I've spent the last year thinking you found your love match. Marrying a man you loathe is anything but trivial. What happened?"

I had not considered this part of my confession, the part that would ensure that Jules never wanted anything to do with my husband again. "You will not like it." She made a go-on gesture with her hand. "Do you recall when Michael returned to town in the spring?"

"I am not likely to forget that," she said with a wry smile.

"That was Hugh. He cornered Michael and threatened him away because he was compromising you. I... you were so happy, I just wanted you to be happy, and he was ruining it. I just kept thinking that if I couldn't have the love I wanted that you should. And he destroyed it. He had doomed us both to unhappy, loveless marriages."

"I didn't even realize I was so angry until I was shouting at him. I cannot even remember all the horrible things I said."

For what seemed an eternity, Juliet merely blinked. I forcefully reminded myself that, unlike me, she preferred to consider her answers. Finally, she broke the palpable silence. "First, I knew about the conversation that Hugh had with Michael. Frankly, Michael had one foot out the door from the moment we—well, it is no matter. He would have left regardless of what Hugh said to him."

"If I thought he required forgiveness, I would have done so, but Hugh had my well-being in mind. If you are still unhappy with him for his interference, please do not hold onto it for my sake."

"You knew?"

"I suspected and Michael confirmed. Why on earth would you marry without love, though? It's all you've ever wanted. Your parents would never force you to wed without affection, I'm certain of it. Why did you choose him?"

"I was compromised." The words escaped in a miserable whine. At her questioning look, I continued. "It was so ridiculous that I can hardly believe it myself. I overheard him at Lady James's ball. He was insulting me to every gentleman in the billiards room. He told them I was too short, and too round, and too ugly, and too loud, and too—everything!"

She rose instantly, turning toward the door. "Oh, that wretch of a man, I am going to—"

"Don't, Jules. It's long since passed. After I overheard it, I went to hide away in the retiring room. Except I found a closet by mistake and the doorknob came off in my hand. No one could hear me calling out. I had resigned myself to death by starvation when Hugh stumbled in too. From what I understand, he was searching for the study and found the closet by mistake. Before I could stop him, he closed the door, and we were both stuck."

"You were not!" She laughed.

"We were. He was quite drunk, you see. Eventually, he accepted that we were trapped. There was a window, but he couldn't reach it on his own. We decided it would be best if he helped me up so I could escape and free us both.

"That was when the entire billiard room full of gentlemen found us. He already had his hands around my calves and his face pressed against my bottom."

She was laughing so hard she could barely breathe. It was the infectious, giddy kind of laughter that cures all ills and leaves you languid and sore in the stomach after. Tears formed between giggles, but it could not stop either of us.

We were interrupted by a knock and Michael's quiet, "Jules? Darling?"

She looked at me in askance, at my nod, she stood and unlocked the door. A few chuckles continued to escape while she wiped tears away with the back of her hand. She was still incapable of words when Hugh and his brother entered the room.

Each man cocked his head at a slight angle to the left with a furrowed brow. The matching quizzical expressions set both of us off into peels of laughter again.

Jules actually snorted, which might have been the least

lady-like sound she had ever made, and it caused another round of giggles.

She made a move to return to the settee, but Michael wrapped an arm around her waist, catching her from behind. He pulled her, still giggling into his chest and wrapped his free arm around her shoulders, pressing a kiss behind her ear. That gesture seemed to calm her, and she settled against him, covering his arms with her own.

He whispered something I could not hear in her ear and she shook her head in response.

Their easy comfort was lovely and envy inducing in equal measure. There was no woman on this earth more worthy of the affection and adoration plain in Michael's eyes. But it was everything I ever wanted and nothing I could see my way to.

It was Michael who broke the silence that descended in the absence of our mirth. "Just what is so amusing, ladies?"

Hugh hovered uncertainly next to me, glancing between the chair and settee indecisively.

Juliet answered for me. "Kate was telling me of a scandal that I missed at a ball when I was in mourning for Sophie."

"Hmmm, are you being petty and judgmental?" Michael asked.

"Tragically, no," I retorted before she could reply.

Hugh was having some sort of internal argument before he finally spoke. "May I sit?" he asked, gesturing to the space beside me.

"Of course," I replied. "It is your home. You may sit wherever you like." He froze in midair, turning to Michael for some incomprehensible reason. He only finished the task of sitting when his brother responded with a halfhearted shrug.

Jules met my gaze with an equally bewildered expression.

"We should return home, actually," Michael offered.

"But—" Juliet's protestations were interrupted when he

pulled her more firmly against his body. Another whisper in her ear and they evaporated entirely.

She melted into him, her body slid into place against his naturally. They fit in a way Hugh and I just... didn't. Where they were elegant in their similarities. We could not be more physically different. Hugh was tall, broad, hard in the way I was short, small, and soft.

Juliet addressed me, "I'll call on you on Wednesday?" She paired the question with a significant look, and I nodded.

Michael tugged her away and I was left alone with my husband once more.

With the departure of our guests, a poignant silence overtook the drawing room. Hugh was poised on the settee next to me, close but not quite touching. Even still, I could feel his presence nearly as strong as a physical touch. He adjusted slightly next to me, and gooseflesh rose along the side closest to him.

He cleared his throat before breaking the silence. "They seem happy. I'm glad for it." I nodded in agreement while he continued. "I was thinking I might go for a ride tomorrow morning. Would you be interested in accompanying me?"

His offer was a pleasant surprise because it seemed as though we had been staring at ledgers for days. I longed to agree because I missed riding terribly, but I knew I couldn't manage the exercise with all due propriety.

Sensing my hesitation, he added, "only if you wish. I recall you mentioning that you enjoyed the activity in the country. I would be glad of the company if it would please you." This man, whoever he was, was not my husband—such hedging.

I owed him an honest response. An explanation to soothe his apparent agitation. "I would love to join you, only... I don't know if I can manage sidesaddle on an unfamiliar mount."

Relief overtook his countenance. "I promise not to alert the scandal sheets."

"A joke again?" I asked. His brow raised and his lip quirked again. "Then yes."

"I must ask, how do you ride astride in a gown?" His tone was light with no hint of judgment.

It fortified me to answer with a cheeky, "I don't."

His owlish blink was all the answer I received for a moment. His astonishment was comical, a chuckle broke free. At the sound he remembered himself. "You don't?"

"I wear breeches."

"Oh, that's..." I feared the worst, that I had shocked him with my uncivilized manners. But then he finished. "That's quite nice."

His expression was quite dazed. It seemed far from disapproving. He was intrigued. At least if the way he was adjusting in his seat was any indication, it was interest. "You will wear them? Tomorrow? With me?"

"If it will not shock you too terribly."

"It may give me a fit of apoplexy, but I shall die with a lovely view."

He was *flirting* with *me*. I had no doubt of that. It was a rare occurrence, but I was finding that I quite liked it.

His gray eyes held none of the ice I was used to. Instead, there was a teasing light in them that softened his entire expression. His accompanying smile brought tiny crinkles to the corners of his eyes. I was possessed with the inexplicable desire to press a kiss to them.

I managed to refrain and instead strove to continue the banter we created. "I had no idea that breeches were all it took to receive your admiration, my lord. If you had informed me earlier, I would have incorporated them into my wardrobe sooner."

His mirth evaporated. I had seemingly made some sort of

misstep. Parsing my response, I couldn't see where I brought the mood down.

He cut through the rising frustration. "Kate, you've always had my admiration." His voice was deeper than usual, softer too. His palm rose, hovering over my cheek, unsure. "Even when I had no wish to bestow it, it was yours. I am so sorry that it's taken me so long to let you know."

I had no idea what to say in response. He started to pull his hand away from the air near my cheek. Without thought, my own caught his and pulled it back toward its original destination. My stomach flipped pleasantly at his touch. His fingertips slid lower, curling around my jaw while his thumb brushed my cheekbone. The touch was so achingly tender I pressed my own hand down, ensuring he remained there.

"Is this all right?" I felt his question more than heard it, it was little more than a breath.

"Yes, of course."

"No of course, my Katie. I have taken a great deal of things as a matter of course in our marriage. No more." That whisper was forceful, a vow—a vow of what, I was not entirely certain.

"I don't understand."

His eyes dropped, and his fingers flexed on their home on my jaw. With a deep breath he explained. "For the last year, I have done everything wrong. I have taken from you. Taken things that I assumed were my right as your husband. Those were not my rights. They were gifts for you to bestow on whomever you chose. I hope to become a man worthy of those gifts, to be the one you choose."

"Hugh..." His name was the only sound I was capable of. My heart was throbbing against my ribcage. The blood ran faster through my ears. I was not prepared for the direction this evening had taken. I was completely out of my depths, and I had no idea how to answer him.

He continued, "I have not earned your trust yet. I know

that. I am going to give it everything I have though. I need a promise from you though, if you feel up to making it?" My nod bade him continue. "I need you to promise me that you will only accept my attentions if *you* want them. Do not welcome me into your bed until you wish for it, my Kate."

He was *wrecked*, pupils blown, lips parted and breath harsh. He was wrecked, and I had no notion of it. *All this time.* Oh, he had been more attentive and considerate, but I never thought... My words hadn't just affected him, they had destroyed him.

I gave him the only response I was capable of. "I swear it. Never again." My own vow was just as forceful as his. He needed this from me. His eyes fell closed again, as his breath escaped in a sound of relief.

"Thank you." His hand fell from my cheek and the absence was stark. I could sense the reluctance when it dropped but I was too shocked to place it back where it belonged. "It is late. I think I will retire for the evening. May I escort you up?" I nodded absently but it was insufficient for him. "It would be... helpful, if you could say the words. I think it would be a good habit for us both." His gray eyes met mine, beseeching.

"All right, I would like to retire now. The escort would be appreciated. What time would you like to go for a ride tomorrow?"

He offered me his arm but didn't place my hand in the crook as he would have previously. Instead, he waited for me to settle it there of my own volition. The difference was not lost on me.

"I'm available at your convenience."

The path through the hall and up the stairs was punctuated only by footsteps. Outside my sitting room, he opened the door for me. Once inside, he paused, hesitating. "I was wondering—that is—would you like me to have a lock installed on your door." He gestured with the door itself, nodding through my open bedroom door to one that adjoined his. "Would you feel safer?"

Now it was my turn to press a hand to his cheek. "I don't feel unsafe with you, Hugh. I never have. I don't need a lock."

He swallowed heavily, looking as though he might protest. "I promise," I added. Those two words seemed to appease his concern.

"Well then, I suppose I should bid you goodnight. I will see you in the morning for our ride?"

"I look forward to it."

"Goodnight, my Kate."

"Goodnight, my Hugh." He chuckled at that, before shutting the door between us.

Thirty-Nine

THORNTON HALL, KENT - OCTOBER 21, 1814

HUGH

SLEEP WAS SLOW TO COME, and when it did, it was in fits and starts. Michael's gentle reproach had taken hold thoroughly. Thoughts of Kate, uncomfortable in my arms, refused to be shaken.

I finally abandoned my effort well before dawn in favor of fussing with the ledgers in my study. I did not expect Kate to rise for some time, so I was surprised when she peeked her head into my study. The rest of her hidden behind the door frame, I could only appreciate flushed cheeks, bright eyes, and long silken curls—left unbound today.

"I await your pleasure, my lord."

I stifled a groan at the thoughts those five words conjured. Neither of us was ready to press last night's tentative intimacy further.

"Very well. Would you like to head to the stables?"

Her eyes were wide, and her teeth found her lower lip. With a heavy breath, she stepped into the doorway. I was lost.

I had wondered, more than once since our wedding, how I

could have found this woman unappealing. That was certainly no longer the case.

Though I had felt the silken skin of her hips and thighs, I had never seen them. I meant to remedy that situation as soon as she allowed it.

For now, though, the sight of her lower half, encased in breeches, may have actually given me that fit of apoplexy I teased about last night. Words escaped me, along with the air in my lungs. She was... stunning, breathtaking, all delicious curves encased in tight fabric. A men's linen shirt that surely belonged to her brother, draped loosely over her upper body. She topped the shirt with an unbuttoned spenser. Unlike the shirt, it was tight across the chest, pulling against her ample bosom. Without thought, my hand dragged along my mouth, checking against drivel.

"Is it too much? I can find something else." She offered haltingly.

In the moment it took for her words to penetrate my thoughts, my heart processed the comment, though, and cracked at the edge.

"It's not too much. You're not too much, Kate. Please don't find something else. You're beautiful."

She eyed me suspiciously before determining my sincerity with a bright smile in exchange for the compliment. My answering smile seemed to please her, and she performed an adorable little hip swish in the doorframe. I stepped around my desk and held my hand out to hers. She took it easily, allowing me to lead her out into the first rays of sunlight.

Though brisk, the morning was warmer than usual for midautumn. Her loose curls caught the light, a dark caramel color against the coffee-colored tresses beneath. I had always loved her hair, even when I found everything else about her objectionable. Today was no different, my fingers itched to run through the silky waves. In fact, now that they were free from pins and ribbons in the cool morning air, the desire increased tenfold.

Not our purpose this morning, I remind myself forcefully.

Much too quickly, we reached the stables, and I was forced to release her soft hand. The stable master was likely out exercising some of the mounts, and I hadn't the funds for more grooms. We were left quite alone. I directed her toward the back stalls to the two thoroughbreds I was hoping to ride this morning.

The blood bay stallion and rose gray mare, Perseus and Andromeda, were well suited to ride together and particularly fond of a good run.

"Have you had the opportunity to meet these two?" I asked.

"Oh yes, we're old friends. We haven't ridden together though. Have we, darlings?" While she got reacquainted with the pair, I pulled out two sets of equipment. Before I could ask, she brought over Perseus, and I saddled him. When I turned around for Andromeda, she was halfway to saddled, with Kate making familiar work of the process.

Within minutes, Andromeda was ready to go. I turned to fetch a mounting block but by the time I had returned Kate was already mounted. It was a disappointment to miss that sight. The view was surely spectacular, and I was somewhat intrigued to see such a small woman mount a horse so much taller than her.

"Did you have a destination in mind?" She asked.

"I thought Margate Lake? About seven miles east."

"That sounds perfect."

She set off at a trot, leaving me to catch up. I made quick work of it and once we reached open land Kate urged her mount to a canter.

From behind I was left to admire the fine figure she cut. She moved with Andromeda as if they had been riding together for years, anticipating the horse's gait with ease. Her hair flew behind her, caught in the wind.

Now that I have witnessed *this*, I could not imagine her riding sidesaddle. Not when the two of them move as one with such elegance and beauty, it would be a travesty.

I hovered behind, allowing myself to admire the sight, shelving thoughts of her astride me for later thought. Eventually she turned, catching my eye with a grin before slowing her mount. I pulled Perseus beside them, he had been antsy hanging behind, straining against his reigns. He was not as appreciative of the view as I was, wanting, instead, to race with them.

Kate's breath came in harsh pants and again I was forced to set that image aside for when I was alone.

"I hadn't realized how much I've missed riding. Thank you for suggesting it."

"Thank you for joining me. You are very natural on a horse. If I had known, I would have suggested it sooner. Why did you not mention it?"

She bit her lip thoughtfully. "I cannot ride sidesaddle comfortably. It spoils my enjoyment." In her words I could hear the unspoken addition—I didn't believe you would allow me to ride astride.

The worst part was that she was not wrong either. Had I not spent weeks longing for her, I would have balked at such an improper proposal. And certainly, I would have missed the enticing sight before me—pale skin and a rose flush with bright eyes and tousled curls. And a scantily clad wife, mustn't forget that. What a tragedy that would have been.

"I am sorry. I have been a right arse in our marriage." She began with a token protest. I stopped her with one hand raised. "I am trying to be better, to do better. I want to be the kind of husband you can approach with this. Who you could rely on to assist you in fulfilling your desires, rather than putting a stop to them. Can you be patient with me while I learn?"

"I shouldn't have assumed you wouldn't be amenable."

"Oh, I definitely would not have been amenable. But, I was a daft fool." She laughed gently. "I would have missed out on the sight of you in breeches."

"You don't object to them?"

"Object? No, I rather think not. Fantasize about them? Absolutely. Wish to purchase six more pairs so you can wear them every day? Definitely." Her flush increased when my gaze returned from her hips and thighs to her face.

"There was once a time you objected to my form, what has changed?"

"I always appreciated your form. I used to dream of it, and still do, in fact. As established, I was a simpleton."

"I've never asked you, why were you speaking so disdainfully of me?"

The words poured out before I gathered my thoughts. "I dreamed of you, like I said. There was one in particular, it *haunted* me. You came down a staircase in this rose-red gown. It was not a fashionable gown, far too low cut and tight. But it was made for you. Your hair was loose, like it is today. You approached me, all pale skin, kissable lips, and impossibly large, mischievous eyes."

"You were everything I never knew I wanted. I thought I preferred statuesque blondes because that is what I was told to prefer. I was taught to expect certain accomplishments from a prospective bride. My mother raised me to believe that these things were essential in order to maintain the viscountcy, carry on my family name, and make my family proud. I needed to find a bride who was all of those things. And you were none of them. And the moment I saw you, at Lady James's ball in that red gown—looking exactly as beautiful as you had in my dream, more so, even, because you were there and real—the air left the room. I did not care about duty or honor or respectability. I just wanted to be near you, but I knew you weren't for me."

"And so, I drank, I drank until I thought I was clever. And Parker was there, saying all the unbearably crass things I had been thinking. I could not stand him thinking about you that way, could not abide any of them thinking like that. And so, I said all the things that I had been telling myself over and over again. But I said them out loud."

"I did not consider what my speech would do to your reputation or your prospects. Honestly, I think discouraging your suitors may have been the point. All I knew was that I wanted you. I did not believe I could have you. And I wanted to be sure no one else could either. "

She blinked up at me, eyes an impossibly blue-green shade. Aquamarine? Her cheeks had flushed further, and her lips were parted. A pink tongue darted between them, enticing. I resisted the allure, but it was a near thing.

"You thought I was beautiful?" She breathed.

"*That* is what you took from that? Yes, of course, but there is no past tense."

"I took a great deal more than that. I just happened to like that part best," she said with a shy smile.

"I think I have always thought you were beautiful, even before the dreams started. You were beautiful even in that ill-fitting lavender gown covered in lemonade."

She laughed, a smile teasing at the corner of her lips. "Tragically that was the best of the lot. Aunt Prudence was convinced she could force the gowns to suit me by sheer deter-mination."

"I liked the color, particularly when wet."

She chuckled easily, before considering, "You will not speak of me that way again?"

"Never. It was as much of a lie then as it is now. I am, in point of fact, the luckiest man alive."

She said nothing now. Nothing beyond a thoughtful hum, dropping her eyes to the grass beneath our feet.

"You do not believe me?"

"I'm not certain. I want to believe you."

"But?"

"I have spent the last year believing my husband found me to be too loud, too vulgar, too unappealing to consider. This has been my truth and it's a difficult truth to overcome."

Every time I thought that I comprehended the hurt I had caused the woman at my side, I learned of yet another agony I was responsible for, another atrocity I had committed. I was slightly sick at the thought. No wonder she shied from my touch, it was a wonder she was still willing to be in the same county with me.

I did not have the eloquence to express the feelings in my heart. I settled instead for an empty platitude. "I wish I knew how to convince you of my truth."

"I do as well. Perhaps time."

"Anything. Everything." *Forever.*

We continued our ride in silence for some time. Since her return she seemed more content to allow the silences to linger, rather than filling them with chatter. I missed her babbling. Even when I had not been paying attention to the content, her husky voice had become a balm to the worries and self-loathing that occupied my own head. Now there was no distraction from it. I was left to sit with the consequences of my actions.

Forty

KATE

I WASN'T certain what to make of his assurances. Did his intentions even matter if the end result was the same? Could I trust the admiration he expressed now more than the disgust he was so free with?

I allowed the silence to fall between us with Andromeda carrying me steadily forward. In the last few days, my husband of few words and even fewer of those kind, had become a veritable poet.

With a sigh, I set those thoughts away for later examination, refusing to sully this outing. The horses clopped beside each other down the lane, an apple orchard at our sides. Hugh glanced around surreptitiously before grabbing an apple and tossing it to me. He took a second and chomped into it with no decorum.

"I have come to find myself quite fond of this part of the country. It's quite beautiful," I said, desperate to move on to easier topics.

"You have?" he asked, throat bobbing in that infuriatingly attractive manner.

"Yes, and your weather is quite fine here. Every fine day, I expect will be the last of the year, but it never seems to be."

"We seem to have had a stroke of luck today." His voice was thick and strained in an unfamiliar way. "Kate, I... I hope you find Kent to your liking. And Thornton. I—the countryside was bereft in your absence."

"I do not expect to leave for Lincolnshire again in the near future. You may assure the countryside of my continued presence."

I sensed more than heard the weight of his exhale. "That is good to hear."

"I discovered on my trip that my home is no longer in Lincolnshire."

"I... I know I should express my regrets, but I find I cannot. I find I much prefer... that is—damn it all! Kate, I missed you like the devil!"

Perseus started at the abrupt shift in his tone, dancing restlessly forward until Hugh pulled back on the reins. I urged Andromeda to a stop. Hugh tossed one leg over and hopped to the ground, grabbing at my mount's reins and tying them both to a nearby post. He appeared at my side, catching my hips as I dismounted before settling me onto the path. Releasing me just as quickly, Hugh began to pace to and fro in front of me, agitation clear in his countenance. It was... I had never seen him so... My mouth hung open in unladylike astonishment and I could not bring myself to care.

"I missed you." He said, finally ceasing his pacing and facing me. "And I am so damn tired of doing things properly. I was so caught up in doing what was correct that I forgot to do what was *right*. I wasn't supposed to care about Michael, and it cost me a brother. I knew how to manage the estate best and

I lost nearly everything. And you—you, Kate. You weren't what I was supposed to want and I just—I will do *anything*—do you understand—anything to keep you. But you must tell me what it is you need, frankly and in the plainest terms. Because if these past few months have proven anything, it is that I have no idea what that is."

He towered over me, chest rising and falling in rapid, heaving breaths. His hands hovered inches above my shoulders, fists clenching every so often. My own chest was heaving under my spencer in time with his. The air between us was thick and present, tangible.

"I have not been hiding my feelings without reason, my lord. I was trying to be the viscountess you wanted."

Rearing back, he strode over to the fence, dropping his head to rest against a post. "I know," he said, defeated. He turned to face me, back against the fence. "I know you were. And it was what I thought I wanted but I was wrong. I have been wrong about a great many things, Kate. But never anything as much as I was wrong about this. I cannot go back to the way things were. I cannot play act at what I was taught a husband should be. And I cannot accept a lie, not from you. I want to be married. To you. I want to be your husband in every complicated, messy, beautiful definition of the word. And I want *you* for my wife. Not a perfect viscountess, just you."

"What does that mean? For you?"

"I want to tell you when I make mistakes, so we can solve them together. I want to know about all your ridiculously ill-advised matchmaking endeavors, and your music, what it is you giggled with Lady Juliet about in the library, and whatever ridiculous gowns your aunt purchased for you. Anything, everything you wish for me to know. And I need you to tell me if you find something upsetting. Please. Preferably before you reach the point of storming into my study like an avenging angel."

"I will do my best," I said. I found my way to his side, leaning against the post as well.

A sigh left him and most of his agitation escaped with the breath. Part of me lamented upsetting him, but it was the truth, and he had asked for the truth. I had been hiding for months, so it wouldn't be an easy habit to break.

"That is all I can ask, I suppose. I... may I ask something?"

"Yes," I breathed.

"Were... was... that morning in the study. Was that everything? Or is there something else I should know?"

"It will not upset you to hear it?"

Another sigh. "It will upset me greatly to learn of yet more ways I have failed you. But I cannot rectify that which I am ignorant of."

He was determined to press on this bruise then. Safest to start with the oldest of wounds then. Time has lessened its sting. "You did not allow me to invite Kit to Christmas last year."

"I knew that was poorly done as soon as I did it. I am sorry. You have invited him this year, I presume."

"I have not."

"There is still time. You should write to him when we return to the house."

"I do not think it is a good notion."

"Tell me," he said. His voice was honey deep and rumbling beside me.

"I would not subject him to your mother's commentary." I could not allow anyone I love to be spoken to the way his mother spoke to me.

"Is it safe to assume that is another concern you underreported that day?"

Underreported? He still did not understand the extent of his mother's vitriol. "Yes," I said simply.

"I have been thinking about that. I believe it may be time to move her to the dower house. She will, perhaps, be more comfortable there."

"You would move her to the dower house?" I asked, utterly confused by this man before me.

"Well, yes. That is what it is there for, is it not? It is right in the name."

"And she would be amenable to that?"

"Oh, most certainly not. But she really has little say in the matter. Particularly if she wishes to continue overspending her pin money," he said with an easy shrug.

"Just like that?"

"Just like that." he said, considering me thoughtfully in a sidelong glance. The sun gleamed from behind him, catching in his overgrown hair and beard and lighting his lashes. His eyelashes really were unfairly long. "I really do not think you understand just how miserable I was without you."

"You missed me. And that is enough to remove your mother from your home?"

"Our home. And yes. The way she treated Michael, also. Or the way she taught me to treat him. She has fostered and encouraged all the worst parts of me for far too long. I wish to avoid a return to that way of thinking. If that means she must live in a perfectly well-situated house built specifically for the dowager viscountess... so be it." He loosened the reins beside him, handing me Andromeda's. "Shall we lead them? It is not much farther."

I was only capable of a nod, too lost in the changes my husband displayed. We continued in silence along the path. We rounded a bend, and I was met with a mirror-still lake. It was surrounded by trees, each at a different point in readying itself for winter's bite. Both horses decided that the water was there for the drinking and pulled us toward their desire.

Hugh allowed them their fill before tying them off once again at a nearby branch.

"Tell me, what other concerns do you have," he asked, half-distracted. He found a bench underneath the tree and was brushing the leaves and dust away before gesturing for me to sit.

"I am... frightened."

"Of what?" His voice is soft, thoughtful.

"You."

My husband's eyes found mine, wide and full of worry. His lips were parted with concern. A hand made to grasp my shoulder before he caught himself. Instead, it froze between us, settling into a fist in his lap after a beat.

"Have I... done something to—"

"No, or at least not specifically. But you are so altered from the man I married. The man I lived with for months... How am I to know which is the real Hugh? The prideful, taciturn one who sought to look through me? Or the man before me, promising to fulfill my every dream at a word?"

He started once more, intending to interrupt with what would surely be more passionate words and tempting promises. I raised my hand in a gesture to let me continue. "You cannot possibly maintain this change, Hugh. And if you can... What does that mean? If you were capable of this behavior all along, what should I make of that? This man was under there, all this time, just waiting for the proper motivation to reveal himself. Was I unworthy of this effort until you thought you lost me for good? Will you continue to act this way once you are certain I will stay? When I bear your children and I am even more thoroughly bound to you than I am now, what then? And those children, what if they are equally too loud, and too bold, and too much?"

Astonishingly, my eyes were dry, and my voice remained clear throughout the speech. It was only when I saw the crest-fallen expression on his face that my feelings found the truth of my words. The tidal wave of emotion settled, trapped in my throat, waiting to break.

~

HUGH

Every single time I believed I had discovered the true depths of my depravity she unfurled a new layer.

Words abandoned me early in her speech. Air followed not long after. My chest was tight and aching. Even if I could find the words, they would be nothing more than the empty plati-tudes I had offered her thus far. The words were the very things hurting her. With a surety I knew deep in my bones, there was nothing I could say that would fix the mess I had caused.

The three words that were desperately trying to escape would be of no use. I bit my tongue against the urge. They had been there since her return, perhaps before, waiting in the wings for the perfect moment. I knew now that moment would never come. Certainly not now, they would serve in no way but to be cheapened in this moment.

It was a fitting punishment I suppose. Months of saying nothing, now there was not a single word left to me. No apology would be sufficient; no words of affection believable. The irony was unbearable.

I cleared my throat in the desperate hope that whatever came out of my mouth would somehow repair this damage, knowing all the while the endeavor was fruitless.

Still, I asked for this, and I needed to offer her something in return. "Kate, I... there are no words—obviously there are no words—the damn words are the problem. I will regret the things I said in that study and all the ones I did not for the rest of my days. I do not wish to offer you banalities and trivial promises. The only thing I can offer is changed behavior and the hope that someday it will serve as proof. But I need you to know, you were always worth the effort. You were never too much. I was just not enough. I am trying to be enough. I hope someday I will be."

"Hugh, I should not have said that."

"I am glad you did. I asked you. I needed to know where I stand, so I know how far I have to climb. Now, I must ask, is there anything else I should know?" She shook her head. At least that was a relief. "All right then, are you hungry?"

"What?"

"Are you hungry? I brought sandwiches from Mrs. Hudson."

"You brought sandwiches?"

"Yes?"

"Thank you." Oh, she was surprised. My wife was surprised that I was thoughtful enough to bring food for us. That would have stung more were I less wrung out. Fortunately, I didn't seem to be capable of falling further at the moment. I retrieved the sandwiches from Perseus's saddle bag, turning back toward her, she looked as overwrought as I felt.

I could not decide if this ride was a good idea or a terrible one. I did not think she would have been as open in the house, particularly if given the opportunity to escape or the possibility of interruption. But now I needed to find a way to recover the mood somewhat. Introspective, forlorn, and raw was not precisely the emotional state I was aiming for this morning.

Sitting beside her once again, I spread the sandwiches and fruits Mrs. Hudson packed between us. She made a selection and took a delicate bite, and I did the same, chewing thoughtfully.

"Tell me about your family?"

"What?"

"I have met Kit. Hopefully he will join us for Christmas, I would like to become better acquainted. Ideally when he is not doggedly protecting every shilling of yours and glaring at me for stealing his sister. But I have not met your parents or your sister and her family."

She studied me carefully for a moment, before coming to some sort of decision. "Father is a vicar, as you know. He was the youngest son of the Earl of Leighton. Aunt Prudence is his elder sister."

"Mother and Juliet's stepmother were sisters. Father said he took one look at Mother and was determined to marry her. He was sixteen and she was fifteen. His parents were not overly pleased with the match as her family was untitled, but he was the second son and unbearably determined so they relented."

"Lizzie is my eldest sibling. Sydney, her husband, was the farmer's son and now he has taken over. The two of them have been in love for as long as I can remember. She has five children now. Kit is in the middle and just a year older than I am."

"I have never traveled to Lincolnshire, perhaps we could visit next summer when the weather turns?"

"You wish to visit?"

"If you'd like. Or, if you would prefer, they could visit us here. Or in town. But I imagine it's difficult for a farmer to leave for any great length of time while the weather still allows for travel."

"I would like to visit."

"Then we shall."

"Just like that?"

"Yes. It is all right to ask for things you want, Kate. I want to be able to give you those things, but, as we have already established, I am not the most observant of men.”

I managed to get a giggle out of her there. “Certainly not,” she commented, popping a grape in her mouth. Such a lovely mouth. She dabbed at her mouth with her napkin. “What? Is there something on my face?”

“Nothing at all. I was just trying to recall what it was I found objectionable about your mouth in my drunken stupor. I was a daft fool. What was I thinking? Her lips are too full and too lovely a color? She is too kissable?”

“I believe it was too wide.” She pinched the corners of said mouth together.

My hatred of the motion fueled me. “Ah, I remember now. I was driven to distraction by lecherous thoughts of your lips. I was still under the delusion that as a gentleman, you see, I should not be having such thoughts.”

“And I was to blame for such thoughts?”

“Certainly not, but I was an immature ass.”

“I cannot disagree with you there. What kind of lecherous thoughts?” She raised one brow with the question. It was an arch look and unfamiliar on her face. I rather liked it. Particularly juxtaposed against the pinched one.

“Kate...”

“If you will not tell me, certainly Juliet will.”

“Oh good lord, the two of you will be unstoppable.”

“Yes, I rather think we will.” She smiled at the thought, taking another bite. “Or you could just tell me.”

“Not yet. Perhaps when I have earned a bit more of your trust.”

“Fine, but I will be asking her.”

“Yes, and I will be sure to leave the study door cracked open when she arrives.”

She considered me for a moment before asking, “Do you really wish to know what she has to say about Michael?”

Ugh. "Never mind."

"I thought so."

"Should we set off for home?"

"I suppose. Can we return via the mill? I wish to see it."

"We can go whichever way you like."

Forty-One

HUGH

IT WAS a long ride back to the house. And an even longer few days after, a stretch of cold, autumn rain delayed further work on the mill and the tenants' roofs. In that time, I made use of Michael's advice, flowers, drinking chocolate, and the like. After her words at the lake, they seemed pitifully insufficient.

When Tom arrived on Tuesday, he brought with him the first fine day in the better part of a week. He also brought with him all the sheet music I requested. Of course, I had no idea if any of it would be of interest to someone as skilled as Kate, but Tom spoke to a friend about it. I had left the sheets on the stand this morning, for Kate to find. I was very much hoping I could enlist Tom to solve another one of my problems in the near future. Taking Mother to Bath for the second time in as many years was quite a large request though.

He was more than willing to join me in inspecting the dower house on Wednesday morning. It had not seen regular use in my lifetime, and I was fearful the work would be extensive and expensive. He ambled along beside me, up the muddy pathway, occasionally sparing a pitying glance at his boots, now six inches deep in mud. Mine fared no better.

The dower house sat on the other side of the creek that separated my property from the Revello property Michael had purchased. It was only accessible from my side by a stone bridge, likely once an impressive structure but was now crumbling and weak in places. Without a doubt, it would need repair before Mother could be moved in. Mother's trip to Bath was looking to be a necessity.

Tom, perhaps sensing the direction my thoughts lay, broke the silence. "Why have you finally decided to move Mother?"

"Kate is unhappy."

"That is nothing new," he said, distracted by his boots again.

"Yes, thank you for pointing that out earlier in my marriage. Where would I be without you alerting me to my follies and vices after the fact."

"I did point them out, on more than one occasion if you'll recall. And you do not pay me enough to prevent you from being an arse."

"Your portion is significant."

"Michael's fortune would be insufficient to spend my days preventing you from being an arse."

"Yes, well. My wife is unhappy. I intend to make her happy." The walk to the house was thick with mud, which would need redone as well, it would be near impassible in a carriage.

"Ah..." he said, interest in his tone.

"Ah, what?"

"You've finally discovered it." Why was Tom like this? When had he become incapable of answering a simple question?

"Discovered what?"

"You, my dear brother, are in love with your wife. Hopelessly, irrevocably, and desperately in love with your wife."

"What of it?"

"Nothing at all. It just took you longer than I expected to recognize it. What finally gave it away?"

"She left me," I muttered.

"What?"

"Well, she went to care for her sister during her confinement. But that was after a rather thorough dressing down."

"Good for her, I had not thought she was capable of it."

The outside of the dower house was in better condition than I expected from the bridge and pathways. Several windows would need repair, but, from the ground at least, the roof looked to be in passable shape. I tried not to let it give rise to too much hope. There were multiple levels to the house, and I could not see all of them from my vantage.

"Yes, well. I am hopeful that having my mother removed to another building will lessen some of the strain on my marriage," I said, making for the entry. The door was stiff and swollen with disuse, but it eventually gave way under the pressure of my shoulder.

The inside was... less promising. Underneath the sheets of cobwebs and dust, I imagine the house was once rather fine. My great grandmother clearly cared deeply for it if the wall paperings and sconces were any indication. The furnishings had all been draped with fabric coverings. There was no telling the state of them underneath. The floor was warped and possibly molding in some places. And that was only the entryway.

I sent a silent prayer in hopes that might be the worst of it. We stepped farther inside and heard something skitter away. *Mouse not rat, mouse not rat please.*

"Your marriage is saved!" Tom cheered in a cynical tone. "She can move in today. The rat can act as a butler."

"You are unbelievably helpful, has anyone ever told you that? And it is a mouse, not a rat."

"I tell myself that every day. And that was definitely a rat, a large one by the sound of it. You know Mother will not be pleased to move out here. If you manage to repair it enough."

"Mother is rarely pleased about anything," I said, creeping into the drawing room with a wary eye out for the mouse.

"Still, she will not make it easy. And it will likely be costly, aside from repairs, she will want to redecorate to her taste."

"Yes, and the entirety of her taste is 'expensive.'"

"The estate cannot afford this, Hugh."

"My marriage cannot afford for her to remain where she is," I explained. There was a pitter patter of tiny rodent feet somewhere just out of sight.

"I know you said that you did not want to ask Michael for money, but—"

"No, he has done enough."

"I know, but, honestly, it will be years before you can move Mother into this place without his assistance. And you know he would give his entire fortune to never have to sit across from her at dinner again. If not the estate, consider just asking about this place." Tom wandered down the hall ahead of me, unphased by the potential residents we would disturb.

"Then he will ask why the estate could not support the upgrades."

"I would eat my left boot, mud and all, if he did not at least suspect the estate was in trouble, Hugh. He was here for weeks. And tenants talk to him, servants talk to him. I know he would help if we just asked."

"I know he would too, but it is not his responsibility. It should never have been his responsibility to begin with." The kitchen appeared to still be a kitchen? Clearly, I was unqualified to determine whether it was functional. The skittering rat-mouse was still nowhere to be found, but I could feel its beady eyes watching me from somewhere. He was the first to go, and any friends or family he may have stashed about.

"But perhaps he wants it to be? Family helps one another, or at least they should. Mother always ensured he never felt like part of the family, and that we never treated him as though he was. But, Hugh, he is. He did more for us than anyone could have expected. And he did it all without a word. Because we were his family even if we did not treat him as such."

"Tom..."

"No, Hugh. Listen, he moved here for a reason. He has more than enough money to settle anywhere, but he chose the estate next to ours. He did that for a reason."

"If I agree to consider it, will you stop talking about it?"

"For the best part of a week at least," he promised.

"Perfect, I will consider it. Now, do you think these stairs are sound enough to use?"

"I think they're sound enough for you to use."

"Not you?"

"Perhaps after you use them."

"I weigh more than you," I said.

"I know, that is why I will feel perfectly secure using them after you determine they're sound with your girth."

"It's muscle, you ought to try getting some."

"I have a lean frame, my muscles are very wiry."

"Oh, of course. I assume that is how you woo the women at the theater you are always with. Using your wiry muscles?"

"Something like that. Watch that step, there, it looks rotten," he warned. It creaked and gave way under my foot, I managed to catch myself on the banister, which shockingly held.

"Thank you ever so much for the advanced warning."

"Of course. I think we should abandon the upstairs for today."

"I suppose, I would rather not test the fortitude of the banister any further."

"You just wish to escape before you meet the rat."

"Yes, fine. I hate rats. Let us be off. Michael and Juliet are arriving early in the afternoon. Kate and Juliet wanted some time to discuss whatever it is ladies discuss."

"You," he said.

"What?"

"They will be discussing you. And Michael. And your performance during certain amorous activities."

"Why are you telling me this?"

"You wished to know what ladies discuss. As you pointed out, I spend a great deal of time around women. If they wish for privacy, they're discussing you," he explained.

"You cannot know that."

"Oh, Hugh. Have you learned nothing? I know everything."

Yanking the door closed behind me, it eventually slotted back into place. If I heard increased skittering from behind the door, it was certainly imagined. Unfortunately, the smug expression on my brother's face was anything but imagined.

KATE

Hugh and Tom returned from wherever they went this morning covered from head to foot in dust and mud. Mrs. Tanner nearly had a fit, and I could not blame her at all. Michael and Juliet arrived shortly after luncheon and, when the men came down, they were dressed for fencing. My husband did not often actually dress in his fencing... costume? Outfit? Whatever it was called, it was nice, but perhaps less enjoyable than when he practiced in his shirtsleeves.

Michael, having just arrived, quickly stripped down to his

waistcoat, and Hugh handed him a spare foil before they wandered out to the back of the house to play at stabbing each other.

Jules looked as appreciative as I felt. Mary, who had been dropping off the tea service stared longingly after them, adding, "It has been so long since they all practiced together."

"They used to practice together?" Jules managed to express my shock as well.

"Oh yes, they were still quite young though, Michael was the only one worth watching then."

"Where do they practice?" My friend asked, still peering around the corner, as if they would return immediately for her viewing pleasure.

"Back behind the house. The best view is in the kitchens. Perhaps you ladies would like to take tea in the music room today?"

"The music room that overlooks the back of the house?"

"The very same."

I jumped in. "Yes, I think that is an excellent idea. Do you not agree, Jules?"

"Oh yes, I should like the music room very much."

And so it was, that tea was served in the music room this afternoon. If that was an unusual occurrence, no one said anything and the footmen's smirks were kept to a minimum. And neither Juliet nor myself commented if Mary lingered with the tea tray or checked on it rather more often than was her usual habit.

"HUGH IS VERY GOOD," Juliet commented between sips of tea, peering out the window with interest.

"He practices frequently. I think it helps relieve stress."

"He must be very stressed then. Michael is quite out of practice."

"Yes, but I don't think Tom has quite grown into his limbs yet. He may prove a challenger for Hugh in a year or so."

"I look forward to it. Perhaps Michael can get some practice in now that he is closer."

"And perhaps we can supervise the practice while it occurs?"

"Well, yes. They're quite sweaty, aren't they?"

"They certainly are. I think I prefer it when Hugh does not wear the fencing costume."

"The lamé?"

"Is that what it's called?"

"I believe so."

"Whatever it is called, I prefer the shirtsleeves."

"I agree. But I came here to be supportive after our conversation last week."

"And you were distracted by the magnificent sight of your husband losing horribly to mine?"

"Yes, he is going to get another blackened eye if he is not careful," she commented with rather less concern than a black eye should garner. Perhaps, not Michael's though.

"At least he will be quite handsome while he does it. I wonder what the excuse will be this time?"

"You know he thinks them up in advance to amuse you."

"I suspected. I did have a question. Hugh said something the other day, that he was thinking lecherous thoughts about my mouth?" Juliet giggled a bit at that, turning away from the play-fighting briefly. "I take it you understand his meaning?"

"Well, I cannot say for certain. But I would suspect he means he was thinking about your mouth on his..." She flushed with her explanation.

"That is done?"

"Well, I do not know what is *done* but..." Juliet had done that? Prim and proper Juliet had actually?

"And Michael enjoys that?"

She laughed here again. "Very much."

"And you do not find it... unpleasant?"

"No. Not at all. It was strange at first, but he finds pleasure in my pleasure. I feel the same."

"He does not find your pleasure... indecorous?"

"No, of course not. Does Hugh?" Her tone shifted to one of indignance. Brow furrowing slightly as she glanced out the window once more with a glare in my husband's direction.

"I've never discussed those feelings with him."

"But you have them? Does he not have to work for them?"

"Well, it feels nice. But to express such things is unladylike."

"Who told you that?" she asked. "Aunt Prudence?"

"Well, yes."

"Kate, when have you ever known Aunt Prudence to be right about anything?"

"Never," I replied.

"Then why should she be right about this?"

"Right, then what should I be doing?"

"Well, whatever you and Hugh discuss. But I quite like it when Michael..."

AGATHA WAS WAITING in the drawing room when Juliet and I ventured there before supper. She had been making herself scarce in recent days. Her presence on a day that Michael was dining with us was certainly deliberate. I could only pray that Hugh's newfound backbone would hold.

Jules glanced at me, similar thoughts swirling through her eyes as she squared her shoulders. This supper just became a great deal more work for her and Tom, ever the peacekeepers. It seemed that Juliet's marriage to Michael had lowered her in Agatha's esteem because her respectful greeting was returned with a hacking, "humph."

Michael was the first to arrive, having only to don his waistcoat and overcoat. His hair was damp, as though he'd run wet fingers through it, and swept it away from his face. He was certainly presentable enough for a family dinner—with anyone but Agatha. He pressed a quick kiss to his wife's forehead, slipping a hand around her waist, before noticing the third presence in the room.

"Good evening, Agatha," he said with a weary sigh.

"It *was*."

Before the conversation could devolve further, Tom and Hugh slipped in. Hugh set about pouring drinks for the gentlemen without a word. When he glanced toward where his mother was seated, he turned back to top off the glasses without comment. Michael took a hearty sip before Juliet, still pressed to his side, plucked the glass from his hand and took her own healthy swallow. Hugh, having caught that, tilted an empty glass in her direction with a raised brow. She shook her head with a small smile. In turn, Hugh made his way over to me with a glass of the sherry I like.

"Thank you."

"Of course," he whispered low and hot against my neck.

When Timothy arrived to call us to dinner, Agatha began her usual scurry to the space at the foot of the table. Hugh called after her, "Remember Mother, Kate's place is across from me at the foot of the table now."

Hugh and I were the last to enter the dining room, and we were greeted with the sight of a slack-jawed Michael and a pinched-faced Agatha. "Of course, I remember."

"Oh, then I must have dreamt the absurd sprint and dance with the chair."

"Excuse me?" she asked.

"The display with the chair, Mother. It has been going on for a year."

"It is difficult to break a habit of many years. But I would never be so indecorous and petty as to complain about my seat at a table." She tossed those words in my direction. Clearly, I was to blame for her son's sudden spine.

"Kate has never once complained, Mother. I am the one complaining. I wish to look across the table and see my wife where she belongs. In the place of honor due to her as my viscountess and as mistress of this house. If I see the ridiculous demonstration with the chair one more time, it will be the last time you dine with us."

No one dared move. No one dared breathe. We all waited silently as one for Agatha's response. Wisely, tragically, she said nothing, instead taking her correct seat across from Tom. We all sat, Michael's gaze bouncing back and forth between Hugh and Agatha with interest.

"Actually, Mother. There is something I wished to discuss with you," Hugh said. Tom's face fell into his open palm in a way I hadn't seen in months. "Tom and I inspected the dower house this morning. Michael has kindly agreed to send some of the workers from his estate to make the necessary improvements so that it can be ready for you to move in by Christmas."

Michael appeared somewhat shocked at the volunteering of his workforce, but I imagined he would be all too willing to assist in Agatha's removal.

Tom muttered something under his breath about wishing to be excluded.

Agatha's eyes, widened with astonishment, narrowed down into a rage before me. "You wish for me to move out of my own house now? The home I raised you in. Have you no gratitude?" Turning to me, she cried, "This is your doing! You have set him against me. I told him! I told him you were nothing but manipulative trouble, using your body to get what you want."

"Mother!" Hugh cut in. "Enough. Apologize to Kate. Now."

"Why should I apologize to that hussy? She seduced you, and now she is ruining you."

"Out." His voice was honed like a knife edge, deadly with that single word.

"Excuse me?"

"You are excused. I will have a tray sent up. You may join us again when you sincerely apologize to Kate. And to Michael. Not a moment sooner."

"Never," she vowed.

"Then I hope you enjoy supper in your rooms. The dower house will be ready in a few months's time. You may eat at the table there." The scrape of her chair against the floor was deafening. She strode out of the room with as much dignity as she could muster, not turning back. No one spoke for a full moment after her footsteps softened down the hall.

It was Michael who broke the silence. "So, I am lending you workers?"

"Do you mind?" Hugh asked.

"Not in the least. After that display, you can have them all."

"Not all, Michael. We really do need a dining room eventually," Juliet said. If we heard the smashing of a dining tray upstairs, everyone pretended not to notice. And dinner continued on in a much more jovial manner.

~

HUGH

Michael swirled the scotch in his glass thoughtfully.

Finally, he broke the amiable silence after several minutes. "So, that was an interesting dinner."

"It was."

"You didn't need to include me in your ultimatum."

"I did. I should have done it years ago. I need to tell you that I know, Michael. I know and I will never be able to tell you how sorry I am. For everything. And I will never be able to thank you."

"You know what?" he asked, voice higher than usual in feigned ignorance.

"Michael..."

He sighed, dragging a hand through his hair and tipping his head back to stare at the ceiling. "How did you find out?"

"I have been reviewing old ledgers."

"Whatever for?"

It was my turn to sigh. "I have to ask a favor."

"You need money." It was a statement, not a question, and he grabbed the bottle between us and topped off his glass.

"How did you know?"

"I flipped through some of the ledgers when I couldn't sleep. Also, servants talk. And tenants. The dower house is in a right state too, that won't be cheap. Your mother has expensive tastes—hideous but expensive."

"If you knew, why did you not say anything?"

"Oh yes, that would have been an enjoyable conversation."

I hated that he was right, that we both knew precisely how horrible I would have been to him if he had suggested anything of the kind. I offered him a quiet, "fair."

"What happened? I left more than enough to be successful." There was nothing accusatory in his tone, merely curiosity.

"I fired your solicitor. The one I hired is... less than ethical."

"Should have known you would," he said with a half-baked laugh. "Who?"

"Forsyth."

"Damn, he is a cheat. Tried to swindle me when I was looking to open the club. What have you done to recover it?" He leaned forward in interest, pulling one of the stacked ledgers to flip through it.

"I have written to Kate's brother, Kit. He is a solicitor."

"Kit Summers?"

"Yes, do you know him?"

"A little. He joined my solicitor's practice, William Hart. I'm certain he is quite good for Will to have agreed to take him on as partner. If anyone can get it back, Will can."

"That would be promising if Kit would agree to assist."

"Why would he not?"

"I was... less than welcoming."

"Hugh..." The exasperated sigh ripped through him with my name.

"I know, I have done poorly. Trust me, it has been made abundantly clear."

"How much do you need?"

"Anything you are willing to part with would be most appreciated. And a loan, only. We will pay you back."

"It's not necessary. And name your sum."

"Michael, I cannot—"

"You can. Hugh, like it or not, you're my brother. I want to thrash you most of the time, but you're still my brother. On the day you were born, I promised to protect you. Even if it did get me threatened with a lashing, I meant it."

"You what?" *He could not possibly mean...*

"I want to hit you a large percent of the time," he said deliberately obtuse.

"You were threatened with a lashing for looking at me?"

"Oh, that—I was threatened with a lashing quite often.

Fortunately, Agatha is too lazy to dole them out herself, and the servants she ordered to do it liked me more than her."

It was easy to ignore the slight to my mother with such horrifying intelligence surrounding it. "Why?"

"I wasn't allowed to see you. I snuck up with Augie and Anna the night you were born. Just to say hello. We got caught."

"Michael..." I wished like the devil that his words did not ring true. But they did, I had no trouble believing it.

"I assume Agatha thought I would try to smother you or some such nonsense. I promised to protect you that day. I've done a poor job of it thus far, but I have tried. If money will help... Well, that is no hardship."

"You... why do you not hate me?"

"I do, frequently in point of fact. But... You're my brother. You didn't choose this anymore than I did. Anymore than Tom did. The only people who chose this were Father and Agatha."

"I..."

"Name your sum, you can have a look at the ledgers and let me know whenever you have time."

He could not possibly have the thousands of pounds I required. "Michael, you do not understand just how much—"

"Why does no one understand just how vastly wealthy I am?" he asked, tone full of teasing irritation. "I keep having this conversation with Jules... I can afford it, Hugh."

"But it is—"

"Hugh, in my personal coffers I have more money than I could spend in a lifetime—in several lifetimes. And I seem to have found myself an incredibly frugal wife, which is, quite frankly, adorable. Take the money, all I'm going to do is gamble with it."

"But your children..."

"Will be well taken care of. And their children. And their

children's children. After which point, they may have to work or marry for wealth. But only if I lose a substantial amount before I die." The irony of my former argument that he would swindle family funds toward his club hung bitter in the air between us, unnoticed by him.

"A loan, I will only accept a loan."

"Honestly, Hugh, it's unnecessary."

"I insist."

"It will just cost more in paperwork for a loan."

"Michael..."

"Fine. If that will make you happier, a loan," he agreed.

"I... Thank you."

"If you wish to thank me, you can stop using the desk as a footstool."

That made me smile, easing the tension just the tiniest bit. "I only do it because it bothers you so."

"I know."

"What else are younger brothers for?"

"I haven't the faintest idea." He paused, hesitating with the dredges of his drink. "What do you say we find out? Try this happy family thing that Kate seems so fond of for real?"

Tears pricked behind my eyes at the vulnerability hidden behind the casual nature of his question. I considered a sincere reply, but that was not us. When Michael began to worry his lower lip, I recognized I had given him no answer. Finally, I settled on one. "Well, Kate is right about everything. We should probably listen to her."

He set his drink down, wiping his palm on a trouser leg before holding out to me. "Brothers?"

I took his hand in mine, offering a firm shake. "Brothers."

Forty-Two

HUGH

THE LITTLE GASP OF DELIGHT, the bright glance in my direction, it was more than enough of a reward for haranguing Tom into bringing the sheet music back with him from London.

Kate played a few, more familiar, pieces for us before Michael and Juliet took their leave. Tom kindly volunteered to check on Mother. He was unlikely to be successful in his efforts to get her to see sense, but if anyone could succeed, it would be him. His retreat left my wife and I alone in the music room.

She pulled the new pages from the music desk, flipping through them with interest. "Thank you, Hugh. This was entirely unnecessary," she said, a smile in her voice.

"Well in that case I shall see them returned at once," I held my hand out for the pages with a teasing grin.

"Oh no, they're mine now," she retorted. She shocked me then, wrapping her hand around my outstretched one, pulling me toward her with some force. I stumbled to her willingly, eagerly, until my knees brushed the bench. "Sit," she commanded, dropping my hand to pat the space next to her.

Following her instructions with an overly enthusiastic keenness, I settled in beside her. Her shoulder brushed my upper arm through the thin fabric of my shirtsleeves. After several glasses of scotch, it was more than warm enough to excuse the removal of my coat, and the drink convinced me it was an excellent idea. Peering down at her, she met my gaze with ease. Her expression was the slightest bit fuzzy for sherry. "Did you ever learn to play?" She asked, tipping her head in the direction of the instrument.

"Not a single note. It was my grandmother's instrument. I suspect my father feared the havoc three boys would wreak on it."

"It is a magnificent instrument. The best I've ever played on."

"I am glad of it, an incredible pianist deserves the best. Who taught you?"

"My mother. To a certain point. Eventually, I outpaced her skill and I taught myself."

"You taught yourself?"

"Well, not the basics of course. But after those are mastered it's really a matter of practice."

"I hope those pieces will be enough of a challenge. I am afraid I do not know exactly what to seek out."

"Mozart is perfect, thank you." Kate bit her lip, watching me thoughtfully. I wanted to bite it for her. "Do you wish to learn?"

"What? Now?"

"Well, yes. If you would like."

"You are to be my teacher?" She made a show of looking around the room for some imagined teacher. "A good teacher does not mock her students."

"I never claimed to be a good teacher, merely yours. If

you'll have me." She said it easily, freely, as if the mere idea of having her for my own was not everything my heart desired.

"I would have no one else."

Her eyes shone a deeper, greener tone for the candlelight as she evaluated me with a pleased sort of smile. She took my hand in hers once more, resting her fingers atop mine, her palm against the back of my hand. I could not help but marvel at the diminutiveness of her hand. How could she reach the keys with such surety and efficiency with such a small spread. Together as one, she settled my hand across the ivory keys. She pressed down on my index finger and a note sounded, clear and rich in the silent house.

"Middle C," she said, her voice hoarse. She cleared her throat gently. "Now you can no longer say that you've never played a single note." My huff of laughter against her cheek caused a curl to flutter by her ear. She directed my finger to the next key to the right, "D, right is higher." She moved my finger past middle C once again to press the key to the left, "B, left is lower." Without prompting I ran through the three keys I had been taught. "Top of the class."

"What do the black keys do?"

"Sharps and flats, that is a lesson for another night."

"And the pedals?"

"For a night even farther down the road." Her answer was low and sensual, and her lips parted slightly. There was an interest in her eyes I was unfamiliar with but was surely reflected in my own. "Hugh..."

"Yes?"

She started for a moment then seemed to think better of it. Eventually settling on, "thank you, for tonight."

"You don't have to thank me for what I should have done all along."

"Still, it must have been difficult."

"It was surprisingly easy." It was, too. A shockingly simple matter to defend Kate—even against my mother. It was unbearably easy to set down the woman who raised me.

"Hugh?"

"Yes?"

"That wasn't what I meant to say."

"What did you mean to say?" She swallowed hard, tongue darting between her lips, drawing my gaze. *Please...*

"Kiss me?" *Yes.*

My heart skipped before resuming its beating at a more rapid tempo. I disentangled our fingers with some regret. But I was able to use my, now free, hand to tip her chin back. Just the edge of my index finger was all that I needed to direct her where I wanted her. I could not resist the urge to brush my thumb across her full, perfect, lower lip, seeking welcome. Her eyes fluttered closed and dark lashes settled on her flushed cheeks. It was my turn to swallow heavily, against nerves.

Slowly, resisting the desperate pull of desire, I leaned in. Her lips slanted against my own. Home. The lock to my key, or maybe the other way around, it was no matter. The kiss was soft, sweet, a pressing of lips and nothing more. In another life, I might have given her something similar after a period of courtship, when she accepted my proposal. Instead, it came nearly a year into my marriage. It was all the more perfect for the longing.

Reluctantly, unenthusiastically, I pulled away. I had been granted a kiss and no more. I would not press my advantage, no matter how tempting. Her lashes danced open, eyes wide and hopeful.

Her hand found its way to my chest, seemingly of its own volition. Her gaze had not left mine. Eager fingers lit a flaming path up my chest before curling around my neck. It was with both astonishment and delight that I let her tug my mouth back down to hers.

This kiss was anything but sweet, she caught my lower lip

between her own, laving it with her tongue. Where did she learn that? She had no qualms about pressing her own advantage, using her grip on my neck to pull herself higher, matching her chest to mine. Curves to planes. Pounding heartbeat to pounding heartbeat.

Permission seemingly granted, I slid my hand to the divot where the back of her head met her neck. It was sized perfectly for my hand, it belonged there, now, always. The quiet moan that escaped when I tilted her where I wanted her shot straight to my groin. Her free hand fisted in my shirt, seemingly in response to my answering groan. My tongue met hers and she tasted of sherry and Kate and perfection.

This. This was what I had been missing. This singular kiss was more erotic than any single moment in our marriage bed. I was a fool. I was a prat. I had no idea I was missing out on *this*. This was what the fuss was about. This is what it was supposed to be between husband and wife.

Even more reluctantly than before, I pulled away. I needed air, I needed to clear my head before this went further than either of us intended. Beyond here lay a conversation, and perhaps less drink. This was the line I needed to draw. Her forgiveness was too precious to push further. The forgiveness that was, if I was unbearably lucky, not as far away as I had once feared.

Her breath came in soft pants against my lips, and I could not bring myself to pull farther away than to rest my forehead against her own. Any more was too far.

"Kate... We shouldn't." Her answering whine did more for my pride than I rightfully deserved and made a far greater impact in my trousers than it ought. "I do not have your trust yet. Nor your forgiveness."

"You do not want—?"

"Oh, I want. Very much. But not yet. Not until you feel for me the way I feel for you."

"I do not understand?"

"You are not ready to hear it. Not yet. But you know, Kate. You must know." She blinked slowly, the fog of drink and what I was fairly certain was lust clears slightly.

"You?" Her lips curl into a perfect pout, frozen on the last letter. I kissed it away, quickly, freely. A man could only be expected to withstand so much.

"So you do know. That is good. The words are waiting for you when you are ready for them." There was trepidation, unease, and perhaps, just the slightest bit of hopefulness in her wide, hazy eyes. Her hand loosened its grip on my shirt and the other carded through the hair at the base of my neck, resulting in an answering shiver.

"I like your hair like this, long."

"And the beard?"

"I like that too, you already know that." Her hand cupped my cheek, running a thumb across the stubbly growth. "I like it when you are dressed like this too."

"Unkempt?"

"Less put together. This is the version of you only I get to see," she explained.

"I like that as well."

"I also prefer when you do not wear the fencing costume."

"Fencing costume? You mean the ame? What has that to do with anything?"

"Whatever it is called. I like it when you practice in your shirtsleeves." A distinctly masculine feeling of pride washed over me. She should always have opinions on my appearance. Even better still, she should always feel free to express them.

"And when is it that you've studied me enough to have an opinion on such things?"

"I watch you practice. Sometimes. Just like you watch me play on occasion. Is that all right?"

"All right? If you wish, I will have the 'costume' burned."

"That is not necessary. You should practice with Michael more, he needs it."

"Ah... Did you two enjoy yourselves this afternoon?" I asked, pleased with the answer I was confident I would receive.

"We did, thank you." Her answer was pert, cheeky. I knew her well enough to detect the front for some embarrassment. I did not want her embarrassed because I liked her looking.

"Perhaps next time you can provide me with your favor. Then I can thrash my brothers even more thoroughly."

"My very own knight."

"Your very own everything." I caught her hand, and pressed a kiss to the back of it. Her eyes darkened slightly once more, somewhere between emerald and turquoise in the firelight. I had already vowed to take this no further tonight. "We should retire, certainly Mary and Stevens will be wishing us abed."

I rose to stand, her palm still grasped in mine, before tugging her to meet me. I led her along the corridors. There was a brief hint of lilac scent in the hall, but it was swiftly, easily overwhelmed by the jasmine that curled behind me, *Kate*.

With no candle to light the way, I relied on two decades of experience. Pausing outside of Kate's door, the warm glow of the fireplace illuminating a half circle on the carpet below the door, I pressed her back against it. Not harshly, a guide really. Her head tipped back and lashes met cheeks, anticipating my goodnight.

The temptation to pillage, to take was there, but I parted from her with another chaste press of lips. I was met with a wanting gaze when I pulled away. "Sweet dreams, my Katie."

"Good night, Sir Hugh." I left her with a wink she likely could not make out in the near blackness of the hall. Probably a good thing, it felt awkward as I did it, more a flinch than the intended debonair gesture.

Inside my chambers, I could hear the soft sounds of fabric rustling followed by the tap of pins hitting the glass top of her dressing table. She must have decided not to call on Mary. I was not in the particular mood for Stevens's usual brand of sarcasm this evening either.

Eventually, I slipped between the cool sheets, staring at the canopy above my bed. If my fingers trailed across my lips, seeking the phantom press of hers, who was to know?

It seemed extraordinary, after nearly a year of marriage, to be so giddy over a simple kiss. It was a strange combination, the delight over the experience, the feeling, the promise of more some day—perhaps even in the not-too-distant future—was accompanied by regret.

Tonight was not our first kiss. If she ever welcomed me back in her bed, it would not be our wedding night. Those moments were gone, leaves carried away by the wind never to be seen again. I had taken those for granted in my ignorance and selfishness. Had I but known... Had I taken a mistress or visited a brothel, I might have understood what I was missing, and known how to do better. But if I had experienced the cheap imitation I would have found in the arms of another, could that possibly have satisfied me? It seemed entirely unlikely.

It was irrelevant. All I could do was press forward, ensure the days to come were better than the days passed.

KATE

MORNING DAWNED, bright and clear for once, on the fourth day after *that* night. Kisses came freely, eagerly. As it turned out, the most effective way to convince me of the false-hood of Hugh's words that night at Lady James's ball, was his complete inability to keep his lips off mine. A few kisses were doing more to mend that ache than any words he could have provided. Now, it seemed, the dam had burst, and Hugh could think of little else. Oh, he still had not pressed for more. He continued to honor his promise to wait. But now... I wished he would push.

The feelings he evoked, the ideas Jules put in my head, I wanted to experience them all. Hugh was proving far from scandalized when I reacted with passion to his attentions. It led to a certain confidence. But it also resulted in the frustra-tion of unmet desires. Sleep had been hard-fought and easily interrupted for days.

Had my husband always been so *present*? He seemed to take all the space in whatever room he was in until all I could see, hear, and breathe was him. Across the room, next to me, touching me, kissing me, it made no difference. I was, however, absolutely certain that the little brushes of his hand, the whisper of his shoulder against mine, were completely new phenomena.

The sudden nearness made his absence today all the more stark. I had been uneasy all day, wandering from room to room searching for whatever it was I had misplaced. It was not until I found my way into his study and caught the smoke and vanilla hint of scotch I understood. I had misplaced my husband.

He had set off for the far reaches of the estate with Tom at first light. Weeks parted from this man, decades of life before him, and now I was incapable of being separated from him for mere hours.

It seemed as though his campaign to win my affections was more effective than I had anticipated. I could not bring myself to regret it. This was the feeling that I had been dreaming of in my marriage, the first tentative steps of it anyway. Perhaps not love, yet. But it had the makings of that feeling.

Early in the evening, the skies decided to share in my dissatisfaction. A light drizzle began, cold and miserable. The servants hardly needed instructions to have water ready for baths as soon as my boys returned.

I tittered anxiously at the pianoforte, plucking away at one of my new pieces with little success and even less interest. Early evening turned into late evening. Supper came and went.

Something was wrong. Even at our worst, Hugh had always been where he said he would be, when he said he would be there. I was fully fretting now. The rains had become more severe, a steady unrelenting onslaught from the sky.

Then I heard them, the rattle of carriage wheels on the gravel drive. Racing toward the front door, I nearly collided with Tom, shaking off the wet from his greatcoat. Behind him, I could see Michael's carriage. My heart skipped with relief.

"You had us worried sick!"

"Why should you be worried, I was perfectly safe at Michael's?"

"Well how were we to know that?" My reply was distracted, as the carriage pulled away, toward the stables. Had Hugh already gone upstairs to change? How had I missed him?

"Hugh did not tell you?"

Blood turned to ice inside me. My body understood before my head. "He's not with you?"

"He's not here?"

"No! He was with you!"

"He went with the workers to the dower house. I stayed at Michael's for a drink. I was there longer than I intended, waiting for the rain to die down, but I decided to take the carriage when it seemed to be a permanent fixture. Hugh was supposed to come straight here."

"So, he is at the dower house?" Relief once again tugged at my thoughts, it may be an unpleasant night, but he should be safe there. Then I caught the expression on Tom's face, eyes wide and mouth grim.

"The workers returned hours ago. They said he set off for home at the same time they had. He should have been back before supper." The dower house, that was within walking distance, on horseback it should have been a matter of a few uncomfortably cold minutes. Without a word, I grabbed my cloak, tying it tight around me.

"Kate, wait. Let me," Tom protested.

"He is missing. I have to find him."

"Kate, you will be soaked through in seconds. Do you even know the way to the dower house?"

"But—"

"I will go. He would never forgive me if I allowed you out

in this. Especially in that gown." I glanced down distractedly, only to realize the thin satin of my gown and slippers would offer no protection from the elements. "I am sure he is just at the dower house waiting out the storm. Do not worry too much."

He sounded so confident, in that moment I truly believed him, all would be well. That evaporated almost the very second he set back out into the storm in the direction of the stables.

For nearly two hours, I was left to do nothing more than wear a hole in the floor of the entry. Oh, I directed the servants to keep the water hot, to have blankets at the ready, to keep the kettle boiling. It was entirely unneeded, but it was kind of them to allow me to feel useful.

It was after one if the clock in the hall could be believed when I heard hoofbeats. Rushing to the window, I peered out desperately but the rain was too thick and the night too dark to see. I managed to wrestle a door open just as a singular rider returned, with two horses.

Tom, with Perseus. And no Hugh. My lungs seized in terror, refusing to cooperate with even the simplest of commands. Tom grabbed me by the shoulders with sodden freezing gloves, "breathe," he commanded. His order seemed to do the trick and air came back to me, all at once and too much. I choked against it for a moment, coughing harshly. *Is this what dying feels like?*

"Tom?" My voice was small and foreign to my ears, but my lips made the motion, it must have been mine.

"My best guess is that he is in the dower house. The bridge was out. I thought I could make a bit of light out from there, but it was difficult to see through the rain."

"But... Perseus?" He swallowed harshly, and I knew he was every bit as worried as I was.

The horse should not be on this side of the bridge without

his rider. An image fixed itself in my mind, Hugh broken and bleeding in the mud as rain soaked him to the bone.

"I don't know, Kate. He was near the bridge under a tree." After their momentary freeze, my lungs had made it their mission to take in as much air as rapidly as possible. My chest was rising and falling, far too fast, but I still could not breathe.

What was I supposed to do? I didn't know what to do. My vision narrowed, blackening at the edges. All I could see was my husband, cold and alone and hurt and I was just here, completely incapable of managing even the task of breathing properly.

Someone was making great rasping cries somewhere nearby, and I needed them to stop. My panic was rising with every wheeze. I couldn't form the words to tell them to stop and after several attempts I realized the cries were mine.

My entire frame shook and that seemed to break me free, just a little.

"Kate!"

It was not the first time I had heard my name. Tom. He had been calling me for some time. He was the one who shook me. I closed my eyes, pressing a hand against my chest trying to slow my breath. Eventually it worked—somewhat—and my breathing returned to something closer to normal.

Opening my eyes, Tom's worried face filled my entire field of vision. He was soaked and every few seconds his muscles gave an uncontrollable seize. His face was wet too, wet with rain, but also with tears. They mingled together into an indistinguishable mess. That was when I finally recognized the drips falling on my own hand. Pulling it away from my chest, I stared at it inanely before recognizing that the drops originated from my eyes. They followed a trail down my nose, cheeks, and chin before hitting my hand.

I was crying, too.

I brushed them away angrily. He was fine. I had no proof

that my husband was anything other than safe and slightly damp and bleeding to death inside a rat-infested hovel. No— the dower house was fine. He was fine. He had to be.

Shaking myself forcefully, I broke away from Tom. I needed to do *something*. Hugh would not be impressed with his viscountess if, at the first sign of difficulty, I fell to pieces.

I turned around, searching for the blankets that I had readied. They were grasped tightly in Mary's arms. I grabbed them, pressing them against Tom.

"Stevens, take Tom's coat. Timothy, is the bath readied in Tom's rooms?" My voice was clearer, sharper and calmer than I expected. At my direction, the household, which apparently froze at the sight of Tom—just as I had—sprang back into life. Relieved of his coat, I helped Tom adjust the blanket around his, still shivering, form. Chafing his shoulders for warmth and in a desperate attempt to feel useful.

"Go, change out of those wet things," I directed. I called after Timothy on one of his numerous trips up the stairs. "Cool water first Timothy, we need to add the hot slowly."

"What?" Tom asked.

"My mother swears by gradual warming if someone is exposed to cold for too long."

"It is not that cold, Kate. It's not even snowing."

"Humor me?"

"All right... Do not worry overmuch. You know better than anyone, Hugh has a hard head. Even if he was thrown, it took you months to penetrate that thick skull. What is a little fall from a horse compared to that?" I gave his poor attempt at a joke a brief chuckle. It was well intended. He nodded before making his way up the stairs, with Stevens hovering at his side.

And so began my vigil. The second night of my marriage spent staring out the window, watching the rain pour down. This time I chose the drawing room, it had the best view of the drive. For another hour or so, servants scurried back and forth, bringing heated water and clean linens to Tom.

Eventually Mary let me know that Tom fell asleep but appeared no worse for his hours in the cold. I dismissed her with thanks.

Knees tucked to my face, feet on the settee, I watched, and I waited.

The rain was ceaseless, unyielding, ruthless. My only source of comfort was a lack of thunder or lightning. Hour after hour passed with nothing but the ticking of the clock for company.

Mere months ago, I sat in this same position and watched the rain drown the world, desperately hoping that my husband would not appear in my doorway. Now I would give anything, everything for that very sight.

Dimly, I became aware of my aching shoulders and back. It was not enough of a bother to adjust my position. Besides, the pain kept me focused, kept me here, kept the images of my strong, capable husband battered and broken in the mire at bay.

I finally understood how Hugh had made such a complete change of character in my absence. I would forgive him anything, do anything, give anything now. If he would just be *here* to be forgiven, to receive, to accept.

This was love. I was certain of it now. More certain than I had been of anything before. It was nothing like what I expected. It came without warning or permission.

And at this very moment, it hurt more than I could bear. Because the one thought that I could not banish with will, or concentration, or distraction, was *what if*? What if I was too late? What if I never got to say it?

And that would destroy me.

~

It was some hours into my vigil that I heard the footsteps. I had no notion of how long I had been watching, waiting. The rain had given no quarter, and I stopped counting the chimes of the clock an eternity ago.

It seemed early for servants to be about, that was certain. Perhaps, though, the clouds were too thick to give an indication of dawn. I couldn't help but hope whoever they were, they would leave me in peace. I couldn't look away from the window; I might miss him.

The clink of a decanter against a glass registered as odd but I was too exhausted and too far from sleep to give it any thought. It was the cloying combination of pine needles, citrus, and lilac that finally registered. I blinked down at the glass beneath my chin. It was held out, matter-of-factly, by a creased, arthritic hand.

For the first time in hours, I turned from the window, following the hand up a boney arm to the beady gaze of Agatha. "Hugh's father preferred gin," she said.

She lifted the glass toward me again, and I took it from her in stunned silence. She carried its twin in her other hand and tilted it back for a ladylike sip. She glared at it with a sneer, before taking a heartier sip and settling on the nearby chair. Peering out the window behind me.

"Terrible drink. But the smell—it reminds me of him," she said.

"Thank you," I said without thought.

She brushed off my gratitude. "How long have you been down here?"

"What time is it?"

"Half five."

"I think Tom returned at about half one, maybe two."

"The servants say Tom believes Hugh is at the dower house?"

"That is the hope."

"You do not think so?"

"The bridge was down, and Tom found Perseus on the other side."

"Ah, they left that out," she said with a strange kind of flat-calm in her tone.

"I am sure they did not wish to worry you needlessly."

"And yet... here I sit. With my terrible drink."

I took a sip, it tasted of pine needles as well. "Hugh favors scotch."

"He does, would you prefer a glass of that?"

"It helps?" I asked.

"It does."

"Yes, thank you."

She rose, taking the gin from me and tipping it into her nearly empty glass. She poured me a glass of scotch. Warm smoke and vanilla enveloped me the second the glass hit my hand. I took an eager sip, and it burned before settling, warm in my chest. The feeling was familiar, like his kisses. A second sip and I could taste him too, hot and keen against my lips. Just the smallest bit of tension left my spine.

"My son loves you." No other sentence could have pulled my gaze away from the window, but that did. "And it seems that you love him," she added.

It felt awkward and wrong to acknowledge that feeling to anyone but Hugh, least of all Agatha. Fortunately, she was convinced without confirmation. "You are not what I would have wished for my son," she added.

"I know."

"I love him."

"I know that, too," I replied.

"Not yet, perhaps some day. You are not yet a mother."

"Of course," I agreed.

"That being said, regardless of my wishes and for better or worse, you are his wife."

"Yes."

"He was miserable without you. Do not leave again," she warned.

"All right." It was a surprisingly easy concession to make.

"His display at supper the other night, and his coldness toward me since have made it clear that he will cut me out for your benefit." There was nothing to be added to that, but another sip warmed me still further. "It has not been easy, you know," she continued. "To see a woman so inferior in situation and rank to myself insinuate herself into my home and my life and systematically change things I once held dear."

"No, I would imagine not." I replied, ignoring the slight in favor of honesty. "I should have been more sensitive to that hardship."

"You should have. However, my manners were not always befitting someone of my circumstance."

"Yes."

She "humphed" at that, taking another sip of gin with a wince. "My sons are the most important things in the world to me."

"I believe it."

"I should like to remain in their lives. And any future grandchildren," she explained.

"I believe Hugh made it clear that it is up to you."

"Yes, the condition." She swallowed thickly, draining the glass in a single gulp. "I apologize for my behavior and unkind comments."

"Thank you," I replied. And because I could not help myself, I added, "that's the easy one taken care of." That comment earned me a glare. I continued, "You know he financed the estate, don't you. You must, you were not a child."

"I have no idea of what or whom you are speaking." Her

tone had grown slightly colder, but I couldn't help but press this advantage.

"He loves your sons too. It seems to be a trait you find admirable in me. Perhaps you would find it so in Michael."

"Yes, well. Something to consider. I believe I feel a megrim coming on. Please be sure I am alerted when Hugh returns."

"Of course. Agatha?" She paused in her retreat toward the door, not turning to face me.

"Yes?"

"What was Hugh's father's name?"

"Henry, why do you ask?"

"I just thought it might make a good name for a grandson some day." That earned me a turn, her eyes were just slightly less beady with something like sentimentality.

"That would be lovely."

"I hope your megrim improves quickly," I offered.

She left me to return to my staring. And so I did, throughout morning, and afternoon, and into evening, when the rain began to slow, and finally clear.

And then, one minute the drive was clear, and the next, at the very end, almost too small to be believed, a dot appeared on the horizon. I blinked a few times, certain that exhaustion and desperation had willed an apparition into existence. But the dot grew. Eventually it formed a man.

And then I tossed open the doors, racing to the end of the drive because I knew. And when I threw myself into my husband's arms, I felt that familiar warmth in my chest, just for him.

Forty-Four

THORNTON HALL, KENT – NOVEMBER 24, 1814

HUGH

THE WELCOME almost made the rats worth it. She was a little ball of fire against my chest; a soft, floral scented flame. And she felt *so good* in my arms.

"Hello?"

"Hello," she replied, voice muffled into my chest. She squeezed me just a bit tighter.

"I missed you too."

"You're all right." I could not resist pressing a kiss to the top of her head at that comment.

"I am all right. I am sorry to have worried you."

"Tom found Perseus and the bridge was out."

"I tied his reins poorly, so he abandoned me. I spent the night in the dower house. But I am well."

She released me and I felt the cold more acutely because of it. Kate did a visual inspection of me, searching for injuries I expected. Seemingly satisfied with her efforts, she pulled me down to meet her in a kiss. It was more passion than skill, teeth nipping at lips, tongues dancing.

She tasted of... scotch? That was new and not unpleasant. I chased a further taste.

Kate did not hesitate to position me where she liked, using a hand on my jaw to tilt my head to an angle that pleased her. I swept an arm low on her back, pulling her toward me, up on her toes. She remained there for a moment before dragging me back down with her. That was fine, for I would follow where she led.

A pointed cough sounded from somewhere behind her. I could not bring myself to care overly much but it was followed up by another, even more direct. Her grip loosened enough that I pulled free, the intent was to glare at my brother and return to more pleasurable activities. I glanced up and was met with, not only Tom, but my mother as well. That sight was enough to force me to release my wife.

"I see you are not dead somewhere and buried so deep in mud we will never find you again," Tom said.

"I was in the dower house."

"Made friends with the mice, did you?"

"They were rats, you were right. Apparently, it is also home to a family of bats," I added.

"Good, that is almost enough punishment for being safe and warm while I searched for you in the pouring rain for hours."

"I would not say safe and warm... The bats called the chimney home and were less than pleased when I tried to light a fire. Sorry to have worried you."

"You should be." He looked me up and down in askance before tentatively wrapping an arm around me, keeping as much of his body away from mine as possible. I thought it strange until I glanced down with a wince. My clothing was more mud than fabric at this point. Kate—one look at her confirmed that fear; her gown faired almost as poorly as my waistcoat.

Another pointed cough came from behind Tom, my mother. "It is good you are home."

"Thank you, Mother."

"See that you do not do it again," she ordered.

"Yes, Mother."

She offered something akin to an approving nod before returning to the house. The sight of the house reminded me of my gnawing hunger and thirst, the bone deep exhaustion, and the stabbing cold. Tom clapped me on the back, before releasing me fully, gesturing toward the house. I kept my arm banded low on Kate's waist and continued up the walkway.

"That was strange, was it not? Mother's behavior?" Tom asked.

"Very," I answered.

"We may have reached an understanding last night," Kate said.

"You reached an understanding?" I asked.

"Yes."

"What kind of understanding?"

"That is between us," she explained.

"She apologized?"

"More or less." Tom and I shared a confused look over Kate's head. He settled on a shrug and held the door for us. "Oh, and we will be naming our first boy Henry. I think Harry, for everyday," she added, slipping into the house before us.

Tom mouthed "what?" at me behind her back. I was still caught on *first*. If she wished for more than one, I could provide her with more than one. I could do that very well.

Also distracting was the sight of the soot, dirt, mud brand of my arm along her waist. That was rather fetching.

Inside the house, I was immediately set upon by a fussing Mrs. Hudson. She sat me on a blanket in the dining room with a hearty bowl of stew and Kate beside me. It may have been the best thing I have ever tasted. Another bowl and a half later, I was finally sated.

I was summarily dumped into a bath by Stevens. He said nothing but his expression said more than words ever could about the likelihood I would ever see these clothes or boots again.

I fully intended to dress and return downstairs after I left the bath. I even got so far as putting on my breeches. Unfortunately, I made the mistake of sitting down. The prospect of rising again was somewhat overwhelming, and the bed was so comfortable... The five minutes I allowed myself before I would rise and finish dressing came and went, and I was none the wiser in my near comatose state.

It could have been minutes or hours before I woke to the feeling of the bed dipping under the weight of another.

"Wha?"

"Go back to sleep," Kate whispered, tucking herself against my side, struggling to join me beneath the blanket. Where did the blanket come from? I commanded my arm to lift the blanket slightly so she could press herself closer and with some effort it complied. She settled, and I let the fabric drop. Her hand found a place atop my heart, warming it from the outside as she warmed the inside with her very presence. She rose up on an elbow, pressing a kiss there before collapsing back against me with a sigh.

"What was that for?"

"Go back to sleep."

"Kiss?" She popped back up, tilting her head up. It was probably uncomfortable. The angle I had to bend my neck to reach certainly was, but it was more than worth it. It was a simple press this time, and I licked my lip after she retreated. "Why do you taste of scotch?"

She chuckled, "it is a long story. I will tell you some other time."

"Hold you to that." She nuzzled closer to my side. I was too tired, and she felt too good to press the point further. And, for the first time in my marriage, I drifted off to sleep with my wife in my arms.

~

I AWOKE some hours later to the tinkling of piano keys and a cold emptiness where my wife used to be. I had no idea what time it was, but certainly before dawn.

The tune was not one I recognized; slower, softer, sweeter than she usually favored. The notes shifted to something wistful, calling to me.

The aching exhaustion I had felt now temporarily sated, I could no more have stopped myself from lighting a candle and padding down the stairs toward the notes than I could stop my heart beating.

The sight that greeted me would be etched in my memory until the day my breath left my body. My wife in front of the pianoforte was always a sight to behold but this was something different. Her back swayed gently in time with her motions. Her dark curls ran free down her shapely back. She was still in her silky nightdress. Had she been wearing that in bed? I must have been half dead to have missed that. It was a delicate lacy thing, intended to tempt.

Not wishing to interrupt the vision before me, I leaned as silently as possible against the doorway, watching her tiny, delicate hands work their way across the ivory keys.

Though it was unfamiliar to me, I recognized when she reached the melody, more confident for the familiarity. She turned the page so quickly I would never have noticed the interruption had I not seen it with my eyes. Watching her work, I wished desperately that we had progressed further in our lessons, that I knew more of reading music, of playing.

Anything so that I might be of assistance, I could turn the pages for her, involve myself somehow in the magic she wove in the night air. The piece was winding down now, reaching its soft conclusion.

When her fingers hovered over the final keys, she surprised me. Without turning she whispered, "you should still be asleep."

"I heard you." With that she turned to face me. Eyes wide and unreadable in the candlelight.

"I'm sorry. I thought I was far enough from the bedrooms that no one would hear."

"Do not be sorry. I love to watch you play." She hummed thoughtfully in answer.

I stepped into the room, my candlestick joining the several she already had lit. She shifted to one end of the bench, sliding more to one side, creating a space for me. I could only hope my eagerness was more charming than off-putting; masking it was no longer an option.

"Hugh," she whispered, tucking an overlong strand of hair behind my ear, before letting her hand fall to my, still bare, chest. "I thought..."

"I know, I am so sorry."

"It is not your fault. I just—I kept seeing this image of you, hurt, bleeding, in the elements, maybe even dying and you were alone. I thought I lost you."

"You didn't."

"But I could have. And you would never have known. I would never have told you..." She broke off.

My heart gave an eager lurch at what sentiments might lie at the end of that sentence. "Told me what?"

"I understand now. How you brought about such a change in your manner."

"Kate—"

"No, I know. You thought you had lost me. For months. I

fell to pieces in a single night. And you had that for months! I left you to feel that way for so long. And last night, I would have given anything for you to be all right. Because if something happened to you, if you had left me, I would never have been all right again." Her voice was thick with emotion and the tears were flowing down her cheeks faster than my thumbs could brush them away.

"Katie—" The word broke past the knot in my throat.

"I love you, Hugh. I could not be accused of loving you too quickly or too easily. But my love is deeper for it, I swear it."

My tears threatened to join hers. "Oh, Kate." I abandoned my efforts with her tears to cup her jaw, directing her gaze to mine. It was a fruitless effort anyway. They were far too numerous to slow. "It should never have taken nearly losing you to realize you were the love of my life. I will happily spend every day of the rest of that life winning your love. It is an effort well worth undertaking. I love you with everything that I am and everything I hope to be.

"You have already won me, Hugh." Before I could reply, she pulled me to her, lips slotting together in perfect synchrony. The kiss began as a promise, a vow.

Then she pressed her silk-clad form into my bare chest, and it shifted into something sensual without warning.

I ripped my lips away from her, desperate for air, but then I was presented with miles of tempting neck, shoulder, décolleté and air was the furthest thing from my mind.

"Kate?" The word came in a harsh pants, inches from her lips, as I dragged my gaze from the delicate curves of truly magnificent breasts and creamy flesh to meet her eyes. I was awestruck to find the same burning desire in her expression as my own.

"You want me?" She asked.

"More than anything."

"Tell me." The order was delivered half an octave lower than her usual register, landing heavily between us.

The "*yes*" that followed was more groan than word. "I want to kiss your lips until your fingers fist in my hair—pulling me closer, putting me where you want me." I brushed two fingers, feather light, across the full lower lip. "Then I want to taste my fill of them, I won't be done until they're nearly bruised from my attentions. I wish to slide my own lips down the column of your neck, biting at your shoulder until you arch into me." Here I trailed my middle finger lightly down the pearly column, addressing it directly. My finger caught in the hollow of her collarbone, and I followed that line to the dip at the base of her throat. Her breath caught, her breasts rising enticingly with the snag. I had to swallow against the tightness forming in my own throat at the thought. "I would run my tongue along this path. Your body has already laid it out, just for me."

"Hugh..."

"Yes?"

"Do it."

I could only hope the whimper that escaped me at her direction sounded more masculine to her ears than it did to mine. Regardless, I was hanging by a thread before her command, after... It was all I could do to gentle my approach, to resist the urge to maul her. I used two fingertips on the hinge of her jaw to tilt her full mouth where I wanted it, tugging her lips tenderly to mine.

This was home, nothing had ever felt as right as being in her arms, pressed against her, touching her. I pulled away slightly, swallowing hard against the swell of sentiment. I almost lost this, lost her. I might never have felt her in my arms again. I could have spent the rest of my days longing for her honeyed jasmine scent.

Just as I had said, her hand slid over my shoulders,

catching the back of my neck, pulling me back to her. I grabbed her waist with my free hand, appreciating the curve of her hip. This time our lips clashed again, sliding between one another. I tasted her lower lip with my tongue, seeking the entrance I desired.

She granted it willingly, enthusiastically, meeting my intrusion with hers. Desperate groans filled the air, a different music than the tune she played earlier. Her other hand found my shoulder, pulling me closer. She was systematically erasing all space between us until there was nothing but skin and fabric that I wanted to rip off her. The fingers on her jaw slid into the silky waves, wrapping around the back of her neck, gathering her tighter to me still. It was not enough, it would never be enough. Not until we were so close that the months of distance vanished from my memory.

We parted only for the quickest of breaths, only to prevent the further separation that a swoon would cause. My lips were back on hers, bruising in their intensity, the hand in my hair in a fist, pulling me impossibly closer to her.

In the brief moments of sentience between thoughts of her lips and tongue and teeth I couldn't help but wonder how I could have lived with anything but this desperation. How I could have mistaken acceptance of my attentions for desire. The thought threatened to sour this moment, but I refused to allow it. Not when her luscious breasts were pressed against my chest, pebbled nipples dragging against me with nothing but her scrap of silk between us.

She gave a gentle tug in my hair, away instead of toward. White hot panic shot through me, and for a second, I feared I had ruined everything, pressed her too far, pushed too fast.

Then she pulled her forehead to mine, breath coming in harsh pants mixed with my name. Air, she just needed air. I could allow her that. If I must. It gave me the opportunity to follow the rest of my outlined path, her lips were full and red from my attentions at present anyway. Her jaw was the first temptation I met, and I attacked with precision; pressing open mouthed kisses along the delicate line, tasting the essence of her. And what essence it was, sweet and sensuous like the finest mulled wine. Presented with the curve of her ear, I couldn't help the gentle, teasing nip on the lobe. She tried to draw me back to her mouth with an accompanying whimper, but I wouldn't be deterred. I told her my plan, and now I must charge forth.

Pressing first lips then tongue to the hammering pulse just below her jaw was no hardship. Nor were the licks and nips that followed. I had to be careful not to mark this flesh, tender as it was. When I met the dimple of her collarbone, I dipped my tongue in there.

Her fingers were clutching desperately now, holding my head in place while trying to pull my body closer. It wasn't possible given our height difference, but her efforts were equal parts stirring, amusing, and so, so sweet. Eventually, I reached the delicate swell of her breasts, as promised. It took all of my will to resist her tugging hands, and heaving chest, but this was all that we had discussed. I would go no further without permission.

"Kate…" Her eyelids flitted open, drugged gaze meeting mine. That we had been married nearly a year and I had never seen her like this was a travesty. "What do you want Katie?"

She blinked a few times, trying to clear her thoughts. She swallowed, throat bobbing with the effort, before sitting up a little straighter on her bench. She took one of my hands in her own, bringing my fingers up to the cleft I just abandoned. "I want your lips here." She directed my fingertips delicately between her velvety breasts, dragging the satin of her nightgown out of the way as she did. "Then you'll move them here, and you'll take your time." I couldn't hold back a groan as she moved my fingertips to the tight little bud on her breast, dragging them to first one, then the other.

Without her direction, I slid her nipple between my first two fingers, tightening it between them. Her answering whimper was everything—at least until I caught the sight of her thighs rubbing together, attempting to ease her arousal. I bit my lip with the effort of holding back, of waiting for further instruction.

"As long as you want. Forever." It was a vow. I would happily spend every moment until my dying day lavishing affection on her chest.

"You're not done." The command was husky with want.

"Yes madam." She cracked a smile with that, but she was still pressing her breast into my grasp, panting as I switched between the two.

There was a soft whine when she pulled my hand away, I was not certain who it belonged to. But then, she dragged my hand along the outside of her thigh, her calf, until, together, we reached the edge of her nightgown, her ankle.

I could feel the harshness of my breath rasping against her cheek as my forehead fell against her temple. I was desperate to watch as she slipped our joined hands under her hem and along the inside of her leg, repeating her path in reverse. My fingers caught in the bend of her knee, smoothing over a satin thigh.

"While you're kissing my chest, your hand is going to follow this path," she explained. I nodded, eagerly, anything she desired, it was hers. Especially this.

Her direction ended with my hand cupping her sex, hot and damp against my eager fingers. She didn't adjust my hand and neither did I, merely holding position as she pressed against me seemingly without thought. The fabric of her gown was bunched near to her waist, but I still could not see.

"You want my hands here?" I needed to confirm it, that

she wanted my touch on this, most private, part of her. I would not take this from her, not again. She would have to offer it willingly.

She did, with an enthusiastic nod, tucking shyly into the crook of my neck. With my free hand, I cupped the back of her head, pressing her there—the place she belongs.

Lech that I was, my mind was flooded with another image, one that once planted there had taken root. Much as I loathed the thought of Michael at this particular moment, I had been able to dream of little else since he mentioned it. Nightly, I dreamed of planting my lips where my palm currently resided. Images, thoughts of providing her pleasure in such a way—

"I could," I had to pause to swallow, the thought nearly too much. "I could use my mouth here too. If you think that might be pleasing." *Please, please, say yes.*

Her response was nearly inaudible, buried in my throat as she was. "You would do that?"

"*Yes.*" Something in my tone must have intrigued her because she pulled her head free from the hideaway of my chest.

"You want to do that?"

More than anything. "Lord, yes."

"Then yes, please."

I had the most perfect wife in the entire world. That much was absolutely certain.

Forty-Five

KATE

OUR CONVERSATION HAD COOLED my ardor somewhat and left me an inextricable mess of nerves and lust. I could not have attributed one emotion or the other to the tumultuous fluttering of my heart to save my life.

Hugh appeared more certain. His interested gaze flitted up and down my body. He stood abruptly. Then, without warning, my husband slipped one hand beneath my knees and the other around my back, lifting me into his arms.

In my startled state, my arms flew around his neck to steady myself. I needn't have worried because he had never lacked for strength. He answered my flailing with an amused chuckle, it was warm, and I could feel the vibrations of it deep in his chest. Down to that place between my legs, the one he's going to—I couldn't think of it.

"Grab that candle?" It took a moment to understand his meaning, distracted as I was with what was to happen. I grasped it in the hand that wasn't clinging desperately to his neck. He'd given no indication that he might drop me, but I couldn't convince my body to trust that. "Try not to set us on fire, yes?"

"Where are we going?" He blew the rest of the candles out—we were not to remain here. I hadn't thought this far ahead during our conversation that my piano bench might not be the best location for our activities. It was probably a good thing, because I would never be able to look at it the same way as it was.

"Bedroom. Need room to maneuver and you need to be comfortable." I could feel the flush building once more, stronger than before. He shifted me slightly in his arms, and I clutched him tighter still. "Much as I appreciate your grip on me, I'm not in danger of dropping you."

"Promise?" His answering grin was a little crooked, but he tightened his grip on me, grasping just a bit more firmly.

"Promise." I bit back a smile of my own, consciously loosening my death grip around his neck. His hold was steady, even on the stairs, movements confident and gentle—careful not to jostle me.

He nudged the door to his room open with a foot, still refusing to set me on my feet. Finally, he laid me on his bed. He occupied himself with lighting some of the candles scattered around the room. The fire in the hearth was high and warm against the autumn night's chill. Task complete, he turned toward me. "Kate?"

"Yes?"

"You must tell me at once if I do anything you do not like. I do not ever want you to merely tolerate my attentions again."

"I will." With my promise given, he nodded thoughtfully. His heated gaze dragged up and down my form, before meeting mine. Whatever he found there seemed to please him. He stalked toward the bed, caging me between his arms when he reached his mark. He hovered above me, surrounding me but not touching me. "Hugh?"

"Yes?"

"Kiss me." In lieu of a response, his lips crashed onto mine. It seemed he was waiting only for the invitation. The kiss was a crash of lips and tongue and teeth. What it lacked in finesse it made up for in passion. The embers that had been smoldering beneath rushed back to life, a bonfire.

I wanted this man desperately.

His hands were everywhere, one tangled deep in my hair—surely a nest that I would never untangle. The other glided from jaw to hip to waist and back down to a thigh. My hands were no better behaved, tugging him impossibly closer, sliding down his shoulders and hips to cup his backside. It was every bit as firm and shapely as I had imagined.

At my squeeze he groaned and shifted me further onto the bed, half on top of me. I didn't feel trapped; I felt powerful. Even from below, I could draw desperate moans and whimpers from this powerful man. The potential was exhilarating, I needed more: more kisses, more caresses, more groans and sighs.

At length I was forced to pull away, taking desperate gasps of air. He used the opportunity to follow his previous path down my neck, on the opposite side this time. Mouthing my jaw, tonguing my clavicle. I needed to feel him, more of him. It was my opportunity to explore the ridges and divots of his chest with eager hands. Far from disapproving, he whispered words of encouragement between kisses.

After a few moments of exploration, I turned my attention to his nipples, giving them the same treatment he offered mine before. He tolerated this for only a minute before catching my hands in his with a groan, pushing me back to the bed and pinning my wrists in one of his hands above my head. And heaven above, *that* caused a delightful feeling I didn't fully understand.

It was immediately followed by more comprehensible feelings from his lips traveling down my chest. He tugged my nightdress to the side with his free hand, making his way to my breast, as promised.

His lips found my nipple and thought was gone. I was arching into him. My hands and hips pinned to the bed by his hand and hips and were the only things keeping me in this plane. His pleased chuckle rumbled through me, dragging me still higher. I couldn't think, I couldn't speak, and he seemed pleased with the result.

Hugh had involved his tongue and his teeth in driving me insane, slipping between one breast and the other. "You may have the single most magnificent pair of breasts in the world, and they are all for me to worship."

His name escaped out in a strangled gasp which he answered with a shushing sound. Finally, *finally*, he released my hands, bracing himself with one while his mouth worked on my chest. The other slid down my waist, my hip, my thigh. Down, down, down, until he reached the hem of my nightdress.

I could do little more than fist one hand in his hair, the other dragging down his back, clinging to him. His mischievous hand was reversing course now, dragging the dress up.

It caught at my waist, and he pulled away, staring expectantly. Dimly I realized he was waiting for my thoughts to return, for me to confirm I still wanted it removed. *Oh, I do.* At my nod, he helped me free from the fabric prison.

Bare before him for the first time in our marriage, I forced myself to meet his gaze, rejecting the urge to cover myself. He hovered above me, taking in miles of skin. I fidgeted under the scrutiny, refusing to meet his gaze. It was a long moment while he studied me.

"Kate," he breathed, cupping my cheek, "my Katie, you are without a doubt the most beautiful thing I've ever seen." The compliment drew my eyes to his. He continued, "For nearly a year I've been married to the most exquisite creature on earth, and I have not told you nearly as often as I ought, how unbearably beautiful you are." He tangled one hand in my hair, "rich as mahogany and softer than silk." His hand then drew down to my face, catching on my lower lip, "sweet and full and delicate as a flower petal." Then his lips brushed my eyelid, "so wide and kind and full of love. I do not deserve it, but I'll take it anyway. You married a selfish man, Viscountess."

"You do deserve it. And nothing about this feels selfish, Hugh."

"I assure you it is, as I am taking unbelievable pleasure in exploring every delectable inch of you."

Words escaped me, I was left to whimper instead.

"Shall I continue on the prescribed path?" At my nod he stood abruptly, prowling at the end of the bed. He lifted me gently to rest my legs on the floor beside him. Then he shocked me further still, kneeling before me.

I was exposed before him in a way I had never been before. As if sensing the rising tension, he rubbed comforting hands up and down my outer thighs. "Remember your promise?"

"Yes," I nodded.

"Good." That word was all the warning I received before he dragged both thighs over his impossibly broad shoulders. *Oh, good lord.*

Our plan was all well and good in theory but now he had me spread before him. I dropped my head to the bed, covering my eyes with the back of an arm. I could feel myself tensing against my will, nerves warring with embarrassment fighting for space amongst the unendurable vulnerability.

"Kate, look at me." His voice sounded the way the scotch felt, sensual, warm, intoxicating, and I could do nothing but obey the warmth burning in my chest.

I propped myself up on one elbow to meet his gaze. It was

even more obscene than it was in my mind. But his eyes... they were darker than I had ever seen them, just a shade up from black, molten. There was no hesitation in him. His mouth hovered just inches above my center, heated breath shifting my awareness from my nerves to something much, much more pleasant. "I love you," he whispered.

Then he lowered his mouth, pressing a kiss low on my belly. Without so much as a warning, he parted my folds with one hand and dropped lower, licking a strip from bottom to top in one smooth motion.

It was... odd, not bad, but nothing like the ecstasy Jules described. Then he settled near the top. *And, oh—that is nice.*

He worked me gently, slowly, sensually. It took us a few moments to find the rhythm that worked best. It quickly eclipsed anything that had come before. There was a sense of something building, deep within. He dipped a finger inside me, joining the effort and there it was—the edge.

It was a precipice, and I was going to fall off it. It was inevitable at this point. My breath was ragged on the edges of my consciousness. The sounds Hugh was making were obscene and I could not possibly care less.

But that release was just out of reach, I couldn't quite reach it. I grasped with the hand that wasn't fisted in his hair, clutching his unoccupied hand in mine. I needed him with me when I fell, to catch me. He slotted our fingers together, sucked hard and crooked his fingers in just the right way and that was it. I was lost, falling from the impossible height he had dragged me to.

I was dimly aware of him moving me farther up the bed, arranging pillows around me, beneath me. He was saying something in a honey warm tone that was soothing and thick. Words of love, words of adoration, words of desire. He slid up the bed alongside me, wrapping an arm around my waist. I kept waiting for the embarrassment to return but I was too wrung out to care.

Finally opening my eyes, I was met with the sight of my husband, propped on one elbow, an unbearably smug quality to his smile. Even though he absolutely deserved to wear it, I could not allow it.

I tugged his lips down to mine, intending to kiss it off him. There was an unusual tang to his lips, and it took a moment to understand its origin, me. There was something unbearably erotic of the evidence of our activities spread across his lips and stubbled chin.

Moments ago, I would have sworn that I could not move for the rest of the night, possibly well into tomorrow. Now my tongue was chasing his, claiming him. "Kate..." Hugh pulled away, cupping my cheek in his hand where he was propped above me. "I adore you."

Emboldened by the honesty, the love, in his gaze, I pushed him back to seated. His back and shoulders rested against pillows propped up by the headboard. He went willingly; he was too strong, too broad for me to move without his compliance.

"What are you doing, Kate?"

"Exploring. It's my turn now."

HUGH

I could hardly be blamed for the groan that escaped me at the idea of her turn. That groan morphed into an exceptionally manly whimper when my *naked* wife threw a leg over my lap, and made herself comfortable astride me.

"What are you going to do with your turn?" I breathed.

She leaned forward, tucking a strand of hair behind my ear, trailing a delicate finger along my jaw during her retreat.

"Do you know what I thought the first time I saw you?" I shook my head. "I thought you were the most beautiful man I'd ever seen."

"You did not. I was an arse."

She hummed thoughtfully. "I did. In spite of the stern scowl." She drew a thumb over my lips, there was no scowl there now, I was certain of it. "And the angry eyes." She leaned forward, pressing her lips to my closed lids, first one, then the other.

"And now?" I was fishing, I knew, but her free appreciation was nice.

She pressed her lips together, scanning me thoughtfully. "Even more handsome. Your attractions are far more affecting when you're not being an arse."

A full belly laugh burst from me. Still grinning, I brought her mouth back toward mine, "I am glad to hear it," I murmured in the breath between us before catching her lips in a kiss.

"Now, take your breeches off," she demanded when we broke apart. Well, that was the single most erotic sentence in the English language, likely every other language as well. Particularly when coming from her full, kiss-swollen lips.

I helped her to her knees before following instructions. I could only hope she missed my fumbling eagerness. Once the offending breeches had been kicked to the end of the bed, she settled herself against that part of me I had been valiantly trying to ignore. The part of me that was desperate and aching for her. All of me was, but my manhood is particularly enthusiastic.

"Kate..." She was staring at me thoughtfully again, but it was less scheming and more nervous. I wanted her out of her head again, confident and wanton. "What is your plan for me?"

"I thought, perhaps, like this?" She gestured to our current positions.

"Anything, everything."

"Stay still," she replied, as if that was not a herculean task. She pressed up with one hand branding my chest. Her firm hot grasp on my member, aligning me as she liked. The sensations almost distracted me from the moment my goddess sank down on me.

"Kate." That seemed to be the only word I was capable of at the moment.

I pressed myself farther upright, chest to chest while she rocked, once, twice, into a rhythm that suited her.

She was unbearably beautiful, with her eyes darkened and so unbelievably captivating. Every night before this moment was a pale imitation of intimacy. Never before had I felt so connected, so cherished. Her hands were restless on my person, dragging pleasurable trails up my back and down my chest. Eventually she broke eye contact in favor of drugging kisses, to my lips, to my jaw, to my neck, my chest. I responded in kind.

She was tightening around me, her rhythm faltering. And she was making those damn sounds again. Sweet, silky whimpers and husky moans against my chest and lips. I knew now what to expect from her crest, and I found her hips, helping to facilitate the rhythm.

I was hanging by a thread, pleasure overtaking thought, leaving nothing but instinct and desperate, drugging desire. Wracking half-moans ripped from my chest with every breath.

My wife, taking her pleasure from me, lost in it, was magnificent unlike any I had ever beheld. She was close now, tight and slick around me. When she peaked moments later, I fell not far behind.

I thought I understood what the fuss was about, but this, *this* was what everyone spent their days trying to find. And I had found it—her—by accident. If I had fallen through a different door that night all those months ago, I would have wasted the rest of my life searching for the perfection splayed atop my chest right now.

I was not so delusional as to believe that I would have chosen her. I would not. I would have picked some polished society darling and would never have known *this*. This woman curled in my arms contentedly drawing absent patterns on my chest. This woman who smelled of jasmine and us. This woman whose silken waves were tickling my nose. This woman who made my chest ache at the mere thought of her.

"So," she drawled, dragging the syllable out. "That was different." My laugh stayed deep in my chest, barely audible, but I knew she could feel it.

"That was incredible."

She pulled away just the smallest bit, meeting my gaze, nodding, before returning to her tracing.

"There are some other things that I want to try."

"Kate, you may do anything you like to me." I caught her hand, pulling it to my lips to press a kiss to the palm before tucking it back against my heart. "And I am more than happy to do absolutely anything that you want with you. I am at your service."

"You're very agreeable."

"After that, I would sooner die than deny you everything your heart desires." She dropped an easy kiss on my chest.

"Just you. You will do quite nicely."

"I am yours. Speaking of... It is after midnight. Happy anniversary."

She turned to glance at the clock across the room before settling back again. "I will take your word for it, it's too dark. It's been quite a year."

"Yes, the best though."

She hummed, disbelief in the note. "I believe you have forgotten a great deal of anguish in your assessment."

"No, the best. It brought me here."

"You're sentimental when you're sated."

"Who said anything about sated? I'm not finished with you."

"Good," she said. "Because I will never be finished with you."

I caught her wandering hand before it could slip lower. Her wedding band was still pristine against her skin. An idea I had been toying with for days took hold again while I pressed a kiss to warm gold resting on her knuckle.

With a fortifying breath, I began. "With this ring, I thee wed." The sentence caught her attention, and she sat up with wide eyes and parted lips. I swallowed heavily against the emotion innate in these words. "With this ring, I thee wed, with my body I thee worship, and with all my worldly goods I thee endow."

Her answering smile was warm and full of feeling. "That part comes later. You need to start at the beginning."

"Of course, let me see if I remember how it goes. Kate Grayson, I promise to love you, comfort you, honor and keep you, in sickness and in health as long as we both shall live." She kissed me then, pressing her grin against my own. "I believe it is your turn now."

"Hugh Grayson, I promise to love and honor and keep you, in sickness and health, as long as we both shall live."

"I noticed you forgot to promise to obey me."

"Hugh, of the two of us, you are clearly much more fond of following orders."

My answering laugh was full-bodied, and my head brushed the headboard when it fell back. "Yes, that is something of a surprise. One I was hoping you would not notice for several years at least."

"I promise to use my power over you only for good."

"I am in excellent hands then. I believe it is my turn once more. My Katie, with this ring I thee wed, with my body I thee worship, and with all my worldly goods I thee endow. In the name of the Father, and of the Son, and of the Holy Ghost. Amen."

"I rather prefer this ceremony to the first."

"Kate, marrying you was the best decision I have ever made." She pressed a warm kiss to my lips.

Pulling away, she seems poised to offer some equally sentimental declaration. "I agree, it absolutely was."

I could not nor did I desire to hold back my laughter. Her's joined mine and our own little melody played into the night.

Epilogue

JAMES PLACE, LONDON - JULY 1, 1815

HUGH

"WHAT, EXACTLY, ARE WE DOING HERE?" Tom grumbled, glaring at the refreshment table as though it had personally offended him. It was a rather more dismal selection than I found two years past.

"Following instructions," Michael answered. His glare was directed to the entirety of the ton, observing him with interest.

"Ah yes, the mysterious instructions. 'Go to the ball. No, we will not join you. Do not ask questions.'"

"The instructions were not directed to you, Tom." I tossed in his direction. I had a suspicion I knew what was to happen and his whinging was dampening my anticipation.

"Yes, but quite honestly, I was hoping to watch at least one of you get tossed out by a footman. How did you even manage to receive an invitation from Lady James?"

"He is titled, and I am vastly wealthy. And I think it is Lady Chanterelle," Michael answered.

"Charlotte, chanterelle is a mushroom," Tom corrected.

"And yes, but your wife did ruin her last ball. And the year before, Hugh was caught fondling his wife in the closet."

"Tom..." I warned.

"Well, you were."

"She was not my wife yet. And take care how you speak of my viscountess." I ignored the eye roll in favor of watching the entry. There was something like magic in the air tonight, humming through my veins.

Michael returned to my side, glass of lemonade in his grasp, as he propped himself next to me against the wall. The first thing I noticed was his stiffening, straightening. The woman alone in the archway at the top of the stairs was not my wife, so she held little interest to me.

On second glance, I recognized Juliet. He shoved his lemonade into Tom's hand, clapping him on the back distractedly. "Gentlemen, I believe that is my cue."

He dipped easily through the crowd, eyes never leaving his wife's. She was draped in a periwinkle dress and could not hide the smile that brightened her face when my brother whispered something in her ear.

He escorted her easily down the stairs onto the dance floor. It was a quadrille this set, nothing like a waltz. Nonetheless he pulled her into his arms, moving in perfect formation to the entirely wrong music. Juliet just laughed at his antics.

That was enough distraction. I was now even more certain that I would enjoy Kate's surprise.

"Oh, lord. This is some sort of romantic couple liaison isn't it," Tom muttered into his drink.

"Most likely, yes."

"Enjoy. I am off in search of something stronger than Michael's half-drunk lemonade."

"Study is through there and to the left." I nodded my head

in the direction of the back door, my eyes still fixed on the main entry. "If this is what I think it is, I will join you shortly."

He finished Michael's lemonade with a grumble before following my instructions, muttering about besotted brothers under his breath all the while.

The doors opened once again, and my breath caught with anticipation. I was not disappointed.

Framed in the archway was my wife. And her eyes were on mine. She was clad in that same red silk gown, the one of my dreams. The two years since I had seen it last had dimmed my memory. She was even more magnificent than I recalled. Or perhaps that was the change wrought by the barely visible bump low on her stomach. She insisted it was my imagination. She maintained it was entirely possible that she was not—but the evidence in this gown was too strong. Glowing skin, even shinier silky curls, an increase in the already generous curves I called home...

The ballroom had gone quiet once again. Or I thought it had, it may have been the blood rushing past my ears. Two years ago, the room had fallen silent before insults had floated through the hall. Somehow, tonight, the entirety of the ton seemed disinterested. Or less interested.

While I was appreciative that I did not have a list of gentlemen to meet at dawn, I was baffled. How could anyone see this vision before them and still retain the power of speech, the ability to feign disinterest?

Of their own accord, my feet dragged me toward her. She needed only to send me a look, and I followed her unspoken orders. I met her at the foot of the staircase, pink cheeked and bright eyed with the success of her plan.

"May I have the next set?" I asked.

"That is not the plan. But I suppose you may."

I pulled Kate into my arms on the dance floor. It was actually the waltz now, but my brother and his wife were nowhere to be seen. Or at least nowhere to be seen with the amount of effort I was willing to exert.

Kate felt so good in my arms. We moved together so naturally now. She pressed herself indecently close to me without my needing to guide her there. That was where she belonged. "Just one set, you know. Then you must go to the study."

"I know. Let me enjoy my dance though. I did not get one that night."

"Very well," she answered, relaxing into the movements.

All too soon the set finished, and she pulled away, with a look that told me to stop ruining the plan. I was reluctant to leave her though, to abandon her to the *ton* and the petty women and lecherous men. But she was a viscountess now, and my title ought to offer her enough protection in a ballroom. Except, perhaps, Lady James's...

Over Kate's shoulder, I caught a glimpse of one of Kate's friends, Lady Rycliffe. That was a relief, and I was able to, reluctantly, follow my script.

The James's study was unchanged in two years. The gentlemen inside may have varied slightly but not in any significant way. I had not missed the society events since Kate and I began to spend the majority of our time in Kent.

Michael's loan had restored the estate to its former glory. Kate's improvements had brought it to new heights. Now that my mother was situated in the dower house, she and Kate had formed a tentative truce. There was no need to keep the two of them separated by an entire county. My mother's arrangement with Michael was less a truce and more a temporary cease fire, but we were making headway there as well.

Ellsworth greeted me with the conviviality that came with far too much drink, handing me a scotch from somewhere. Tom leaned against the wall, unimpressed with the company.

"Grayson! It has been an age. I think the last time I saw you, you managed to get yourself shackled to the Summers chit," Parker said, too loud for the study. Out of the corner of my eye, I caught a flash of red silk. A brief inhale was all that's needed to confirm the jasmine and citrus scent of my wife.

"Watch it..."

"Right, right. Sorry. I just remember you declaring you wouldn't even tumble with her, the next thing anyone knew she was your fiancée."

"Oh, I was more than eager to take a tumble with her. I just did not want any of you lecherous lot gawking at her."

I tossed back the scotch before slipping back into the hall, leaving the gentlemen to their bawdy jokes. I had places to be. It was not a lie, my speech. I was just less self-aware at the time.

I sauntered down the hall, displaying less eagerness than I felt, lest I be spotted. Just outside the second door, I paused for a moment. The little closet beyond this door and the incredible woman inside it changed the entire trajectory of my life two years ago. I could not help but wonder what surprises it would bring this time.

With a quick glance in both directions to confirm our privacy, I turned the handle and slipped inside, shoving the door closed behind me quickly. Without warning, I was pressed against the wooden frame. My wife rose to her toes, dragging my head down to press her lips to mine, eager and affectionate. When she pulled away, she was tousled and her lips swollen.

Pointedly, she reached down to the knob of the door beside me, pulling it off in her hand. "Oh no, the handle just came off. Whatever will we do?"

The End

~

The Most Imprudent Matches series will continue with a prequel novella, featuring Celine and Gabriel:
Devil of Mine

Check in with Hugh and Kate in a bonus epilogue: https://www.allyhudson.com/bonus-scenes.

Support the author, leave a review on Amazon!

Acknowledgments

Thank you to *all* my friends and family for your support in this and all my projects.

Thank you to my mother, for everything, always.

Thank you to Martha your undying support.

Thank you, as always, to Bryton for keeping me sane.

Thank you to Mariah for your cheerleading

Thank you Holly Perret at The Swoonies Romance Art for my stunning cover.

About the Author

Ally Hudson was raised in Hudson, Ohio. Currently, she resides in Fort Wayne, Indiana, with a very sassy dog. *Winning My Wife* is the third book in her Most Imprudent Matches series. She writes of cinnamon-bun heroes, snarky friendships, and true love. Her other hobbies include reading, embroidery, and re-watching television shows she has seen ten times already.